WaterColor Wishes

A Steamy Enemies-to-Lovers Romance

Melissa Chambers

PERRY
EVANS
PRESS

Perry Evans Press
978-1732415638

Edited by Trish Milburn
Cover image from depositphotos

melissachambers.com

For my friend, Victoria Austin.

Chapter One

For three weeks Dane had been trying to get the girl from the bonfire out of his daydreams. Just as he was getting back to sanity, there she was, leaning against the bar with a glass of white wine and a smile that practically made his knees buckle. He'd convinced himself that he'd overblown in his own head his reaction to her that night. She was hot. So what. Plenty of girls were hot. But seeing her again now in the flesh and not a figment of his fantasies, he knew his initial reaction to her had been real.

Watching her from across the bonfire that night three weeks ago, kicked back in her beach chair talking to her friend, he'd never been so attracted to a woman. Blond hair in soft curls draping down her shoulders, big eyes that went up a little in the corners, and a sneaky smile like she knew something no one else on the planet knew.

"Damn," Ethan said, waking him up.

"What?"

"Do you know her?"

Dane's cheeks went hot. "No. I mean, we met briefly a few weeks ago."

"Hang on. Is this bonfire girl?"

Dane jerked his head around to face his brother, and then he remembered that he'd broken down after a few drinks last weekend and blabbed to Ethan about the mystery girl he'd met at the bonfire. She wasn't really a mystery. Her name was Marigold. He'd seared it into his memory when his buddy Chase had introduced them that night. He'd never known a girl with that name. He'd thought a marigold was a flower so he'd looked it up. He'd been that ridiculous.

"Definitely bonfire girl." Ethan motioned toward her. "Well, here's your chance."

"Will you stop that?" Dane said, trying to make himself smaller.

"I'm sure she doesn't bite. And she'll be interested. You're the best-looking guy in this room."

Dane gave his twin brother a look, and Ethan grinned back at him.

Ethan nudged him. "Just go say hello."

"You know I can't do that."

"Why not?" Ethan asked, and Dane just looked at him, eyebrows raised. "Oh, God. This again?" Ethan made no attempt to hide his disdain for Dane's refusal to date, which pissed Dane off because Ethan of all people knew what he'd been through the past year.

"Don't minimize it," Dane said.

"I'm not minimizing anything. I'm just trying to figure out what your game is here moving forward. Are you never going to date again?"

"I can't right now. It's too complicated."

"There's an easy solution to un-complicate it," Ethan said. Dane frowned at his brother, and Ethan tossed up his hands. "I'm just saying."

Marigold glanced at Dane, and then did a double-take. Her brows furrowed, and then a little smile spread across her lips, making his stomach flop like a fish. She held her glass up in greeting.

Ethan talked through his smile, teeth clenched. "Looks like she remembers you, huh?"

She glanced back and forth between Dane and Ethan, brow furrowed.

"Ah, bless her heart," Ethan said. "She can't tell which one of us she met that night. If you don't go in, I will."

"Oh, okay," Dane said with an eye roll at his brother. "Have at that."

Ethan cut his gaze at Dane. "I'll do it."

"You can't pull that off."

"You think I can't play straight?" Ethan asked.

"You're the worst actor. You get really loud."

"I was a theater minor in college. We are trained to project."

Dane shook his head at his brother.

Marigold stared at Dane unapologetically. She seemed to know he was the one of the two of them she'd met. They were identical, but Ethan, admittedly, was a little thinner and he dressed way better. He also made an effort with his hair. Dane usually couldn't be bothered with messing too much with his own, but he was starting to wish he'd given his appearance some thought that evening. At least he was dressed up more than usual. They'd had an important meeting with investors who wanted to build a boutique hotel, which was also the reason he and Ethan were at that bar in that particular clubhouse.

"Why do you think she's here?" Dane asked Ethan.

"Hmm, that sounds like a perfect question to ask her."

Dane glanced around. "Do people hang out here after work or something?"

Ethan let out an exhausted sigh. "God, you are wearing me out."

Dane's stomach whirled as she headed toward them.

"Now here's a woman I like. Takes matters into her own hands," Ethan said. "You go, firewoman."

Dane cringed, wishing he'd never mentioned the bonfire to his brother.

Marigold pointed between the two of them. "I've met one of you." She landed on Dane. "I'm pretty sure it's you."

"Good guess," Dane said.

"Not really. You two are obviously twins, but you're different enough."

Ethan held out his hand. "I'm Ethan. The gay one."

"Ah," she said. "Makes perfect sense. You're way better-looking." Ethan smiled in a way that told Dane he was really liking this girl. Join the club. She held out her hand to him. "Marigold."

"You know my brother Dane from…"

"A mutual friend," Marigold said. "Chase O'Neil. Do you know him?"

4

"We've met a handful of times. He's kind of hard to forget, especially with his face plastered on real estate signs all along 30A."

"True." She met Dane's gaze, and he wished he could think of something clever to say, but his tongue seemed to suddenly weigh a few hundred pounds.

She looked back at Ethan who tossed up his hands. "Well, look at my brother and me without cocktails. I'll have to do something about that. Can I get you anything?"

She viewed her drink. "I'm probably good to hold at one since I haven't had dinner yet. But thanks."

Ethan nodded and headed toward the bar, leaving Dane standing there with the girl who'd been running through his imagination for weeks. She lifted an eyebrow at him. "I thought I was seeing double for a minute there, but then I remembered I was on my first drink."

"Was I the in-focus one or the blurry one?"

She smiled and narrowed her gaze. "A little bit blurry, now that I think of it. That's a good way to put it. Your brother's sort of a sharper version of you, isn't he?"

He huffed a laugh. "I guess I'll have to concede to that. I have been at work all day though. Can I get a break?"

"Well, I guess so." She pointed at him. "But you're on notice." Her smile gave him a dangerous glimmer of hope.

A loud whistle quieted the room, and Dane's attention went to a guy standing in the doorway to a banquet room. "If you're here for the meeting about lot number Z85K613 east of Seagrove, we'll be starting in five minutes, so please come get seated."

Marigold set her drink down. "Well, this is where I leave you."

Dane blinked. "You're in this meeting?"

"Yeah. Have you heard they're allowing another boutique hotel on this plot of land?"

"Well, yeah."

"My family's in the business. We're getting that bid." She waggled her eyebrows with a smile, and then her expression turned as she studied him. "Hang on. Are you here for this meeting, too?"

Ethan sidled up beside him, clasping him on the shoulder. "I was just about to put in our drink order, too. We'll have to save it for afterward." He held out his hand to Marigold. "It was lovely to have met you. Maybe we can have a drink sometime. We can get your information from Chase?"

"Sure," she said, eyeing the two of them warily.

Ethan headed toward the door, and Dane just sort of held up a hand in a wave as he followed his brother.

"Well," Ethan said. "How did that go? Do you think you might have a shot?"

Dane considered the letter of intent in his briefcase from the client they just signed...the one they were there to represent this evening. "If we win the bid on this land, not likely."

Chapter Two

"Ready, sweetie?" Cassidy asked, waking Marigold up from her trance-like stare at the ridiculously hot guy walking away. It was the guy from the bonfire on the beach a few weeks ago—the one who'd let her know her skirt was tucked in her underwear. And she'd thought she was strutting away from him so cool-like and all.

"Sure. Is Ashe here yet?" Marigold asked.

"Present," Ashe said, stepping up to her. "Did I miss anything?"

"Just a call to get our butts in there," Marigold said.

"Speaking of butts," Ashe said, "do those two belong to the Knight brothers?" The twin brothers had gotten caught in a bottleneck at the door and were standing with their backs to them.

"You know them?" Marigold asked.

"You don't?"

"Well, I met the straight one at that bonfire a couple

of weeks ago, but only for a second. He was with this beautiful blond girl, of course. Who are they?"

"Dane and Ethan Knight. They own a property development company here. They pop up in the local rags from time to time at social events and that kind of thing. I'm surprised you haven't seen them around."

"I don't do the social scene unless it's with you knuckle-heads, and that's usually at someone's house."

"True," Ashe said. "Come on, let's scoot so we can get a seat."

They filed in behind the brothers, Dane peering over his shoulder at her. "Hola," she said with a little finger wave.

He smiled with just the left side of his mouth, creating the cutest little dimple on his chin, and then turned back around.

Cassidy lifted her eyebrows at Marigold, and she shrugged back at her, unable to rein in a smile.

When they got enough distance between them, Marigold said, "Property development, huh? Do they build hotels?"

"I know they build commercial," Ashe said. "They've put up a few condos around here."

"How do you know so much about them?"

"I may have interest in Ethan."

Marigold bumped him with her hip. "You may, huh? What's stopping you from going there?"

"He's kind of a catch, but he's also kind of a slut. I don't want to be another notch for him."

"Make him work for you then."

"Maybe I will."

Cassidy pointed. "Here's three together. This okay?" They nodded and followed her down the aisle. Cassidy put her purse on the floor in front of her. "So it looks like you've got some competition with the Knight brothers."

"Mmm hmm," Marigold said. "I guess I've been a little cocky up until now. I can't help it though. Ashe, you've stayed at one of my dad's hotels. Would it not be perfect for this area?"

Ashe fanned himself with a flyer. "It's pretty phenomenal. But it is a chain. You know this place doesn't do chains."

"My dad will go off-brand for this. He's been dying to get on 30A for years."

"So he's on board?" Cassidy asked.

"He will be," Marigold said with bravado she shouldn't have had. "I'm just waiting until after this meeting to approach him. I want to be fully loaded with info."

"Just out of curiosity," Ashe said, "do you have a backup plan if your dad doesn't get the bid?"

Marigold pointed at him. "We will get that bid. I have too much riding on this. My lease is up at the end of November, and I've already given my notice of non-renewal."

"Wasn't that a bit premature?" Cassidy asked.

"My location is terrible. Renewal would mean a three year lease. I can't commit to that."

"What about a different location?" Ashe asked.

"I can't afford the rent anywhere else. I've got so many creditors calling the shop I finally had to disconnect the phone." She swallowed hard, hating what she was getting ready to say. "If I can't make this hotel bid work, and I can't find a good-paying job by the end of November, I may have to move back home to Savannah to reset."

Ashe grasped her knee and squeezed. "Don't say that. You can find a job down here if you have to close your shop."

"You think I haven't been looking? To date, I've put in thirty-four resumes. I counted them earlier today. Not one call for an interview yet. I'm telling you, seven years of owning your own gift shop is not a resume-builder for corporate jobs."

Ashe shuttered. "You just said the C word."

"You think I want to go corporate? I'd sooner ride an alligator from here to Pensacola. But if I'm going to live on 30A, I've got to make a decent living. Minimum wage isn't gonna cut it."

"Didn't you work for one of your father's hotels in college?" Cassidy asked. "What about doing that here?"

Marigold sighed. "Oh, sweet Cassidy. You have no idea the betrayal I would be accused of if I worked for a hotel that was not an Appleton. My family would disown me." She pulled a lip gloss out of her purse and reapplied. Tossing it back in, she said, "I have no roots right now. I was literally homeless until Fiona agreed to take me in."

"I don't think sleeping in Sebastian's upstairs guest room qualifies you as homeless," Ashe said.

"I was without a home of my own, and I only have this one till Christmas. Fiona's parents are back then for the winter."

"Enjoy that beach view while you can," Cassidy said.

"I know, right? With my income, the only way I'm getting a beach view is to borrow someone else's."

"How big is the space?" Cassidy asked.

"Small. Thank God I work days and she works nights or we'd be on top of one another."

Ashe squinted one eye. "There's about a dozen straight men in this room who would love that image when they go to bed this evening."

Marigold nudged him with her shoulder. "You know what I mean."

"I do, sweetie." He patted her leg. "You can crash on my couch anytime. My spare room is currently filled with lighting and backdrops."

"Mine is empty, so you are definitely welcome there," Cassidy said. She was a good ten or fifteen years older than Marigold and about eighty times more mature, so sometimes she felt sort of like a second mom to Marigold. Or maybe just a really cool aunt. Cassidy was her friend Seanna's aunt, lucky dog.

"The two of you are very kind friends, but we all know you could both handle about three nights with me before you'd kindly boot my irritating butt out onto 30A. This is the answer. Winning the bid for this boutique hotel will give me a prime location for my shop."

A smiling man stepped up to a podium in front of the room. "Hello local residents and business owners. Wow, the rumors do get the masses out, don't they?" The guy droned on with a list of announcements while the audience tapped their heels, a low grumble permeating through the room. "And now, for what I'm sure most of you came for, I'm going to turn this over to Alan Welburn."

The man shuffled some papers and then stood up tall. "Hi there. As you just heard, I'm Alan Welburn, and I'm representing the owner of a tract of land east of Seagrove. As you all know, it's been the goal of this organization and the people of this town to keep the 30A area free of chain restaurants, shops, and hotels. 30A is all about local, artisanal, unique businesses and that is not changing anytime soon. We will never allow this area to be anything other than the special, sought-after community that it is now. That being said..."

Ashe leaned in, "This is where all he just said turns to a lie."

"We are partnering with this organization to allow a boutique hotel to be built on our lot. We will not allow any businesses or homes to be destroyed to make way for this hotel, and it will need to fit a long list of requirements including no more than three stories in height."

Marigold salivated at the idea of traffic from a hotel lobby coming in and out of her gift shop. Her current location had been cheap rent for a reason. Nobody could freaking find it. She thought the traffic coming in from the restaurant in front of it would help, but that restaurant had been closed for a year now, and her business had suffered greatly from that loss. She kept waiting for something else to come in there, but the owner was asking too much and was stubborn as a mule about it.

"Yes," the man behind the podium said, pointing to someone in the front row. "Stand up and speak clearly so the whole room can hear your question, please. In fact, why don't any of you asking questions introduce yourselves to the room."

A man stood up, and Marigold's belly got the fizzies when she realized it was Dane. "I'm Dane Knight with Knight Property Development. When and where will you have the list posted of requirements for the hotel?"

"There'll be a link on our website. Check back in the morning for full details." Marigold's hand shot up before she could stop it. "Yes," the guy said, pointing at her.

She stood. "Marigold Appleton, owner of Apples to Oranges Gifts in Seagrove. What will be the deadline for submitting a proposal?"

Two matching faces turned to look at her from the front row, sizing her up. That's right. She had skin in the game, too.

"We're accepting proposals for one month, so the deadline will be November 10. And I should mention that proposals from local 30A residents will carry the heaviest weight."

She smiled. "Fantastic. Thank you."

She sat and Ashe leaned over to her. "Isn't your dad from Savannah?"

"Yes, but I am a local resident. Have been for seven years. So this proposal will come from me."

A few more people asked questions, but all seemed to be about how the hotel would affect their businesses and the protected lands. No one else seemed to be interested in actually getting the bid. But Marigold wasn't stupid. She understood that once this got out, it would be a bidding war that she may not win. And there was still the small detail of convincing her father to come on board.

She was pretty sure that part wouldn't be too difficult. Her father had said in the past that he'd love to have a 30A presence. She imagined he'd be thrilled to get the opportunity to bid. But he needed her to win the bid. Being local gave her a huge advantage. Without her, he'd be just another bigwig from the outside trying to get in. She had negotiating power here, and her father wasn't a monster, just a shrewd businessperson. But so was she.

"We'll take a short break, allowing everyone to leave who is just here for this order of business, then we'll reconvene in five minutes to continue with the agenda."

The three of them stood, making their way outside. "You're not staying for the rest?" she asked Cassidy.

"Nah. I'm just here for moral support," Cassidy said with a smile, making Marigold's heart warm.

"I just don't want it to be tacky," Ashe said.

"It won't be. I assure you. You've seen my dad's hotels."

They moved onto the sidewalk, letting people pass by as they stood in a cluster. "Sweetie, if you get the bid, I'll rest easy," Ashe said. "It's the unknown that concerns me. Speaking of that unknown." He smiled as the twin guys approached them. "Hello, fellows." He offered a hand. "I believe we've met a time or two. I'm Ashe Bianchi, By the Seaside Photography."

Ethan offered a hand. "Ethan Knight. Yes, we've met." Was it Marigold, or were these two eyeing each other like cruise ship passengers at their first buffet table?

Cassidy extended a hand. "We've met as well. Cassidy Anderson, Seaside Sweets."

Ethan smiled like he'd just won a fifty-dollar scratch-off ticket. Cassidy had that effect on people. He took her hand. "Yes, I remember you as well."

"You're planning on bidding on the hotel contract?" Cassidy asked.

"On behalf of an investor who's interested," Ethan said.

"One from outside of 30A, I assume?" Marigold asked.

Dane piped up. "As a matter of fact, yes. Much like your father's company."

Marigold stilled. "You know my father's company?"

"I know of a chain of boutique hotels called Appleton Hotels and Spas. I assume this is your family's business?"

Marigold put her hands on her hips. "You assume correctly. You can also assume we'll be making a bid."

"I figured as much when you asked about the deadline. Good luck."

She looked him up and down, trying not to take in the hotness, because *damn*. "You're gonna need it more than I am."

"I guess we'll see."

Ethan clapped his hands together and rubbed them. "Well, who would like to take this party to that bar?" He pointed to the restaurant next to the clubhouse that Marigold could certainly not afford.

Cassidy shrugged. "I'm in."

Marigold looked at her with wide eyes. "You are?" It was a rare occasion that Cassidy braved the nightlife with mere mortals.

"I'm hungry." She lifted her eyebrows, and Marigold

realized that Cassidy might have a plan to glean intel on these guys or something.

"I'm in," Ashe said.

Marigold had to go, but she knew she couldn't get out of this night for less than thirty bucks, and that was her food budget for the next three days.

"On us," Dane said, as if reading her mind. "As a gesture between friendly rivals."

"I can pay for my own," Marigold said, like an idiot.

"That works, too," Ethan said. "Shall we?"

They walked toward the restaurant, Ashe and Ethan leading the way. Cassidy followed, typing into her phone, leaving Marigold to walk with Public Enemy Number One.

She shot him a look. "So how did you know about Appleton hotels? Have you ever stayed in one?"

"No, I've been doing my research for potential competition. Appleton was on my shortlist. I didn't know you were a part of that organization until tonight though." He ran his hand through his hair. "I mean, I didn't even really know about you at all until tonight, of course."

She eyed him, wondering if he was nervous or up to something. She couldn't tell which.

He cleared his throat. "When you introduced yourself, you said you owned a gift store?"

"That's right. Apples to Oranges."

"So you do or don't work for your family's business?

"I..." She hesitated before answering, not sure how much information she wanted to give up. Luckily, they all reached the door of the restaurant right then, so she was saved from answering as they all filed in and consulted with the hostess.

Ashe turned back to them. "They're full up for dinner, but we can take our chances in the bar?"

"Sounds good," Cassidy said and they all headed that way. Cassidy waved at a woman and then turned to Marigold. "Excuse me."

"Do you want a drink?" Marigold asked her.

"I'll get one in a minute."

Ashe and Ethan were bellied up to the bar talking like old friends, leaving Marigold with the enemy...the hot enemy, but that was beside the point.

A group of people walked away from a standing table nearby, so the two of them commandeered it. "So, what is your interest in your family's hotel?" Dane asked.

She was hoping she'd gotten out of that question, but no such luck. "You're a little nosey, aren't you?"

He held up both hands. "Sorry, I didn't mean to pry."

She pursed her lips feeling guilty. One of Marigold's many faults was that she was way too honest and upfront with people. She was candid by default, so when it was time to hold her cards to her chest, she had no clue how to play poker. "My dad's hotel would be the perfect location for my gift shop. My lease is up soon."

"Ah," he said. "Hard for me to argue with that."

"Who are you representing?"

"Sorry, that's confidential."

She looked him up and down. "You know who I'm representing."

"I doubt you'd know them anyway. It's not a chain."

"Is that a dig?"

He smiled a little, giving her heartbeat a kick. "I didn't mean it that way."

She lifted her chin in concession. "I was kidding...sort of. Do you build hotels exclusively?"

"Nope."

She ran her tongue across the back of her teeth, wishing she would have chosen to be as secretive as he was being. "So what exactly does a property developer do?"

"Companies or individual investors hire us to see out their plans. They tell us what they're looking for, and we take it from there. We work with excavation, architects, project managers, construction, codes...I'm boring you, aren't I?"

More like overwhelming her. She just wanted a new location for her shop. She didn't want to think about codes. "No, I'm interested. Go ahead."

"We build stuff for other people."

"So you don't own the stuff you build?"

"No. We just hand over the keys when we're done."

Ashe appeared at the table with a glass of white wine for Marigold and a beer for Dane. "Your brother ordered for you." Ashe winked at Marigold. "I ordered for you, sweetie." She held up her glass to him with a thank-you smile. He jabbed a thumb at Ethan. "But he paid." He fell into place back at the bar.

She frowned and met Dane's smug gaze. He shrugged. "Sorry. I know you wanted to pay for your own."

"I guess they're not coming back to the table," Marigold said, looking for a lifeline. She did not want to be alone with Dane right now. She was too irritated with him, and he was way too good-looking.

"Not a chance. Ethan's had his eye on Ashe Bianchi for months now. I doubt we'll see them the rest of the night."

"Really?" Marigold asked, sizing up Dane's twin brother. "Your brother's so straight-laced looking with his GQ outfit and hair. Ashe seems way too glam rock star for him."

Dane shrugged. "Sometimes opposites attract."

Marigold sipped her wine, glancing at Cassidy who was deep in conversation with the woman she had greeted when they walked in.

"Do you not want to be alone with me now that you know I'm your competition?" he asked.

She supported her elbow while she twisted the wine glass with her other hand. "I can be alone with you. I'm just not giving you any more information."

"I am curious about why you're not in the family business."

"I'm trying to have them build a hotel here so I can be in the business."

"But you've been here a while," he said. "I've seen that shop. Or did you just recently take it over?"

"No, I've been here for..." There she went again, giving up info.

"For how long?"

"I'm not telling you."

He chuckled. "Why?"

"Because you know way too much about me and I know nothing about you."

He set his beer down. "What do you want to know?"

"Why you're trying to take my hotel from me."

He grinned. "It's not personal."

"Quit laughing at me," she said, but she couldn't hold back her smile.

"I'm not laughing at you."

"Yes you are."

"You're funny. I can't help it."

She pointed at her chest. "I amuse you?" She couldn't help a terrible De Niro impression.

He bit his lip, staring into her eyes in a way that made her whole chest light up. "Yeah, you do."

"Well, I'm not trying to." She looked away from him and down at her drink, the tension between them starting to go from friendly competition to something she wasn't ready for. "Seven years," she blurted out and then inwardly reprimanded herself. She'd been so desperate to break what she thought might be sexual tension that she said the first thing she could think of.

"That's how long you've had your shop?"

"Yes. I'm very proud of my shop. There's no need for me to hide how long I've had it."

"Of course there isn't." He gripped the bar table and sort of pushed himself away. He had his shirtsleeve rolled up to the elbow and the muscle in his forearm worked with the movement. She couldn't take her eyes off of his bare arm. She was enjoying him a little too much.

She scratched her eyebrow, refusing to look at him. "How long have you had your property development business?"

"That's top secret."

She jerked her head up at him and he grinned back at her. "I'm kidding. We started it when we moved here around five years ago."

"And you're already building hotels?"

He shrugged. "We've had a good five years."

"You're a little annoying."

"You are, too," he said with a chuckle.

She smiled. "Stop that."

"Stop what?"

"Smiling at me."

"You make me smile. I'm sorry."

She stood there looking at this guy who had woken something in her that had been asleep for more years than she could count. She'd all but thought that feeling was dead, but here it was, tickling her hopes. She inwardly batted it down right back to where it came from. "You know, I think this was a bad idea."

He glanced around. "Yeah, you're probably right. The server's never gonna get to us in this busy crowd. Wanna go somewhere else?"

Oh God, it was getting worse. "No, I mean...I need to get home. It was nice to meet you, again." She held out her hand and he blinked, but finally took it.

"Nice to see you. Good luck on the bid."

She shook his hand, not really wanting to let go. "You don't really mean that."

"If I don't get it I hope it's you. How's that?"

She let go of his hand, her throat a little hot. "That's fair enough, I guess. See you around."

"See you," he said, leaning on the table.

She headed out, scooting past Cassidy who was in

deep conversation with the woman she'd seen when they walked in. Cassidy met Marigold's gaze, and she held her thumb and pinky up to her ear and mouth, indicating that she'd call her. Cassidy nodded, concern etched on her face, and Marigold shook her off with a smile then headed out.

Glancing back at Dane just before he got out of her line of sight, she saw a really cute server talking to him, holding a tray and grinning from ear to ear. Good. She needed to see that. Marigold was nothing special to him. She was one of a dozen or more girls he flirted with in the course of a day. If she would have stayed, they would have talked for a while, and then he would have invited her back to his apartment and she'd have said no, then he'd be done. Or worse, he would have gotten her number and then she'd have waited for a text which inevitably would not have come.

Leaving now and ending the nonsense was the way to go. She made her way to her car. Two older men were admiring it. She let out a hard breath, smacking on a smile. "Excuse me," she said, squeezing past them to get to the door.

One of the men handed her a business card. "If you ever decide to sell, call me."

She probably should take him up on it right then. She desperately needed the money. But her creditors would have to pry her convertible from her cold dead hands... not that it was worth much. She spent more money keeping it running than a car payment for a decent new car. But this car was her last real connection to her family. A relic from a time when everything was good with them. Silly as it was, she wasn't ready to let go of it. She handed it back to him. "I'm not looking to sell, now or ever."

He nodded at her hand. "Keep that card, just in case."

She got in the car and made a show of putting it in her glove compartment. "Thanks." The men watched her back out of the space, which wasn't creepy at all.

As she headed to Fiona's place, she punished herself with a little made-up movie in her head starring Dane and that server. He asked her when she was getting off, and she made a clever joke. "After work, with you."

Marigold rolled her eyes at herself. "Stop it," she said aloud. "He's just another guy who everything would go wrong with. Nothing to see here, Marigold."

She cranked up her music and headed home.

Chapter Three

Dane stood in his kitchen ready for work, wondering if he should wait for Ethan or not. On the one hand, today was a big day, and they had a lot to get to. On the other hand, if Ethan had brought Ashe Bianchi home with him last night, who was Dane to stand in the way of whatever was going on in there? At least one of them got lucky.

How had things gone so wrong with Marigold? He'd thought they had something going on. He'd felt encouraged for the first time in a year, like he might actually consider asking a girl on a date again. But she'd taken off right when things were getting good. They were at that point where casual conversation turned to flirting. He'd laid down a card, showing his interest. *You make me smile*, he'd said. She'd responded with a look like she'd drank sour milk.

He responded to a few emails from their workaholic assistant, Ginger, and was just about to text his brother that he was going in without him when the door to the condo next to his opened, closed, and then a knock sounded at his door. Dane opened it to reveal his brother looking showered, shaved, and dressed for the day. Dane peered around him looking for the other guy, but Ethan was solo. "Couldn't land the plane last night?" Dane asked.

Ethan pursed his lips. "He told me it would take a lot more than a free drink and a dapper smile to get his pants off."

"Dapper?" Dane asked, grinning at his brother whose cheeks were coloring. "Wasn't so easy this go-around, huh?"

Ethan rolled his eyes. "I'll keep trying. He's close with our competition. We could use him to our advantage."

Dane grabbed his keys and his wallet. "Never mind the fact that you've been wanting to sleep with him since we first met him months ago."

"That, too. What about you?" Ethan gave Dane a disappointed onceover. "Judging by the time she left the bar, I'm guessing you didn't get any info on her family's interest."

"They're making a bid. We've got to be better."

"Well, yeah, but it wouldn't hurt to know what we're up against exactly."

"The best. Their hotels are beautiful and have five-star reviews all over the place." Dane pushed open the door to the staircase and they trotted down.

"All right then. So, did you get her number?"

Dane kept his mouth shut.

Ethan backhanded him on the shoulder as they got to

the bottom of the stairwell. "Come, on, man. Don't tell me you blew that opportunity."

"I came on too strong or something, I don't know. Screw it. Doesn't matter anyway. It's not like it could go anywhere."

Ethan stopped him once they got through the doorway to the lobby. "Why, because she's going to hook you into a relationship with her kids that breaks your heart?"

Dane's stomach swirled every time Ethan referred to his nightmare with Erin. "I don't think Marigold has any kids."

Ethan motioned at him. "Exactly."

Dane ignored him and headed toward the door to parking lot. Pushing through it, the brisk fall morning greeted him with a breeze. Ethan held up his hand. "Give me the keys. I feel like driving."

Dane tossed them to him. "Why? You never drive."

"I want to stop somewhere to eat."

"You never eat breakfast."

"I've got a hunger that didn't get filled last night. I need carbs and possibly sugar."

Dane looked his brother up and down. "Are you okay? Do you need a doctor?"

Ethan shoved him lightly. "Just get in the car."

As they passed through Seaside, Ethan shook his head. "Damn. When is tourist season over?"

"Never."

"I just want a biscuit from that food truck but the line's backed up all the way to Destin."

"We can get one from Modica Market."

"I don't wanna mess with parking. We'll stop at Cowgirl Kitchen in Seagrove. I may need some cheese grits to go with."

Dane's brother was used to getting what and who he wanted. The elusive Ashe Bianchi was taking his toll on him.

Ethan pointed. "Look, Seaside Sweets."

"Yeah, it's been there for years."

Ethan wheeled it in. "This place belongs to that woman Cassidy from last night. I've always wanted to go in, and now I have a reason."

"What reason?" Dane asked.

Ethan shrugged. "Friendly neighbor hello."

Dane opened the car door. "You do realize Ashe Bianchi doesn't work here, right?"

"Of course I realize that. But maybe she knows if he's seeing anyone right now."

"You didn't ask him that last night?"

Ethan opened the door to the bakery for his brother. "I couldn't be obvious."

"Yeah, because you're so subtle."

The tall, thin woman from last night pushed through double half-doors. She had her unruly hair tied back in a bun so her face was exposed. Dane had been attracted to the occasional older woman, and this one was no exception. Her beauty wasn't classic, but rather unique with a nose that was a bit too big for her face but just served to make her more interesting-looking.

As she made out the two of them, a smile crossed her face that both welcomed them into her store and let them know she had their number all at the same time, making Dane feel like a caught teenager.

"The Knight Brothers. Come on in."

"Hello, hello," Ethan said, glancing around at the photographic art on the walls. He walked closer to a black-and-white picture of a little boy stuffing a cupcake in his mouth, the sweet the only part of the picture that was colored.

"Photography by Ashe Bianchi," Cassidy said with a knowing smile.

Ethan pointed. "Very nice. Goes with your retro look."

"Coffee?" Cassidy asked.

Ethan pointed at Dane. "He does coffee with cream and sugar. I do green tea."

"Coming up," Cassidy said and went to work.

The bell on the door behind him got Dane's attention, and he turned to find Marigold dressed in a black cat suit from head to toe complete with ears and a tail, her blonde hair draping over her shoulders in perfectly organized curls. He swallowed hard, hoping it was still too early in the morning for his midsection to wake up.

She stopped in her tracks. "I'm having a costume contest for kids at my shop this afternoon," she said, smoothing her hands down her hips in a self-conscious way, but the movement just elongated her body and put her boobs on display, which weren't big but plenty for his taste.

She must have caught him looking because she adjusted the top of the bodysuit, pulling it upward. Jesus, he had to get ahold of himself. Last night, all he could think about was how attracted he was to her, and now, seeing her in this bodysuit was not helping matters.

He pointed somewhere behind the counter, still unable to remove his eyes from her body. He tried desperately to focus on her face. "We're just getting coffee."

"I prefer tea," she said, setting her purse down on a table.

"Iced, black, unsweet?" Cassidy asked from behind the counter.

"Yes, please."

Ethan glanced over at Marigold. "Hello, firewoman."

Marigold blinked, and Dane thought of exactly how badly he was going to hurt Ethan later on. Dane knew better than to tell him anything, ever.

Marigold gave him a look. "Did I ignite or something?"

"You mentioned you met Dane at a bonfire."

She looked confused. "I did?"

Dane got control of himself. "I thought Southern girls liked sweet tea."

"That's a myth," Marigold said, "at least for today's Southern girl. Everything we intake in this country is full of sugar. If we drink our tea sweet that takes away from sweet food we can have. And I'm not letting anything come between me and one of Cassidy's lemon bars."

Cassidy set down a cup on the bar. "Coffee with cream and sugar."

Marigold eyed the cup, and then Dane, making him feel like he'd failed a test. She narrowed her gaze. "What are you doing in here?"

Ethan raised his hand. "It was my idea. I needed

carbs."

Marigold looked him up and down. "First ones all year?"

Ethan ran his hand over his flat stomach and leaned in toward her. "I have an un-fed hunger, thanks to your friend Ashe."

She huffed a laugh. "I'd offer to help you out with that hunger, but I don't think you'd be interested."

Clearly, this was a safe comment to make on her part, knowing Ethan's orientation, but Dane couldn't help a touch of jealousy. Ridiculous.

Ethan lifted his chin. "Is he seeing someone right now?"

She shrugged, all coy. "Maybe. Maybe not. I'd say your best bet is to be as genuine as possible. Ashe can sense B.S. for miles."

"Green tea," Cassidy called, and Ethan was off.

Dane met Marigold's gaze. The whiskers she'd painted on her face coupled with the extended eye makeup was messing with him. He'd never wanted a cat before, but *meow*.

"What?" she asked, touching her cheek. "Are my whiskers running?"

"No, I was just admiring your face...your artistic skills."

"Oh," she said, dropping her hand and sort of pursing her lips at him.

"What's the prize?" he asked.

"Excuse me?"

"For the costume contest."

"Oh, a gift card for my store. They can use it on the

spot and hopefully buy way more than the card's worth." She looked him up and down. "If you really wanted to make yourself useful, you would come by sometime before four o'clock and help me hang my big ghost. It's too high for me even on the stepladder, but you look tall enough."

"I'll be there," he said.

"Good."

"Unsweet tea and lemon bar," Cassidy called out.

Marigold walked to the counter, her tail swinging in the breeze. The coffee Dane was sipping wasn't helping to reduce his current body heat.

"What do I owe you?" Marigold asked.

Cassidy pointed at Ethan. "He just paid for it."

Marigold turned and glared at Ethan, then at Dane. "Thanks, but I'm not backing away."

"Nor should you," Ethan said.

"I don't have your cupcakes ready yet," Cassidy said. "I'll swing by with them after lunch."

"Thanks," Marigold said, taking her cup and bag. "Good luck with Ashe," she called in Ethan's direction.

"I'm gonna need it."

Marigold eyed Dane as she headed toward the door. "Good luck with your hotel proposal. You're gonna need that."

As she headed out the door, her tail got caught. She tugged it through and then met his gaze, swinging it around in a circle, just barely hinting at a smile. She tossed it behind her and then got in a convertible.

Ethan sidled up beside Dane, inspecting his face. "Damn, are we in trouble."

Chapter Four

Marigold stood on the stepladder, stretching her arm to reach the hook to hang her ghost decoration. Dane hadn't shown. But of course he hadn't. He was a man. Men never showed up for her, not when it counted. That wasn't true of her friends, actually. Chase, Bo, and Blake did anything for her anytime she asked. It was cute guys she was attracted to who never followed through with their promises.

That was fine. She had an event to run and she didn't need the distraction. She had put out flyers at every daycare, community center, playground, and coffee shop in the greater South Walton area for this costume contest, but in her heart, she knew she'd be lucky to get ten kids. Still, that was more parents than were in there on a typical day.

Rent on 30A was not cheap and neither was her merchandise. She did okay, but it took so much money to run a gift shop. Inventory, rent, summer help, insurance, and that was just for her shop. Forget the cost of running her life. That wasn't cheap either, even though she'd downsized her world as much as possible.

When people found her, they raved over her shop. They always said, "Why are you hiding behind this restaurant? I only found you by mistake," or something similar. Her shop was special with its whimsical flare and local art, and it begged for a prime location, but her wallet couldn't afford it. Part of the reason she was putting up so many Halloween decorations was to hide the fact that her store was starting to look sparse. She couldn't afford to buy more merchandise, and most of her vendors wouldn't let her order any more as it was.

The bell on the door rang, but she had her back turned so she just shouted randomly, "Hey, hey!" She reached a little higher for that hook, ready to catch herself against the wall if anything went awry.

That's why she needed to get this hotel location secured. The idea of the masses floating in and out of her shop made her heart soar. The dinging of the register. Of course, she'd have to get a register. She still used an old-fashioned receipt book to seem quaint and because she never had a line of customers waiting. But that would change just as soon as this all fell into place.

She stood on the very tips over her toes, reaching the hook with satisfying success. Placing her hands on her hips, she admired her handiwork and her ability to do it all by herself without the help of the evil man who wanted to take her shop from her.

She felt a tug on her tail. "Hey."

That low voice that'd been occupying her head all day jolted through her. She turned to find that gorgeous man to whom it belonged standing beneath her. If she were in a cheesy rom com, this was where she'd clumsily fall directly into his arms. In fact, that was the exact kind of thing she would typically do accidentally on purpose. But at thirty, she realized it was time to start thinking about growing up.

She tugged her tail away from him and whacked him across the head with it. "Hands off the merchandise."

That dimple on his chin when he smiled made her belly feel like she was jumping waves in the ocean. She had to put a stop to that. "I came to help," he said.

She stepped down the ladder carefully so as not to become a rom com cliché. "Well, as you can see, you were late to the game. Your services are no longer needed."

He checked his phone. "I said I'd be here by four. It's five till."

"I meant before four. I've got kids coming for the costume contest at four."

"Then you should have specified that."

"I will next time." She shook her head. "I mean, there won't be a next time." She folded up the ladder and headed toward the storeroom.

He followed her. "You'll get your boyfriend or husband to do it next time?"

She stopped and slid him a look. "Smooth."

He shrugged. "Just curious."

She set the ladder inside the storeroom and then closed the door behind her. "If I had a boyfriend or a husband, I wouldn't have asked you."

"Did you just get out of a relationship or something?"

"Ha!" she said, heading over to the table she'd set up for the cupcakes.

"Why's that a funny question?"

She looked him up and down. "You're nosey."

He pocketed his hands, staring back at her with blue eyes so swoony she almost lost her balance. "Just curious."

She rolled her eyes at him and opened up the cupcake box. "If you must know. I haven't done the relationship thing in a while."

"How long is a while?" He crossed his arms over his chest and rested his fine ass against the wall.

She thought about it. "Four or five years I guess."

He lowered his chin. "Hang on, you mean you weren't dating anyone the past four or five years?"

What in the heck had she been saying to this man? She really needed to learn to keep her mouth shut. "No, of course not. I've dated plenty." She eyed him. "So what if I hadn't though?"

"Nothing. I would just find it hard to believe."

She picked up a chocolate cupcake with an Oreo on top for a spider's body and chocolate legs hanging down. "And what's so hard to believe about that?"

"Girls who look like you don't stay single long."

Before she could get too giddy from the compliment her B.S. meter dinged. "Oh please."

"What?"

She pointed at him around a cupcake with a green Frankenstein marshmallow head on top of it. "You can stop with the flattery. I'm not backing out of this hotel deal."

"I didn't say that to boost your ego. I was just stating a fact. You're a very attractive woman. I'm sure this isn't news to you."

Marigold got asked out plenty because of her looks. But first of all, it was never by men whom she wanted to ask her out. She got the guys who were either cocky as hell, dick swinging from side to side, or the ones who had absolutely nothing to lose and would come forward with their fingers in their noses swearing they were on a dare and could she just nod for his friends? The guys who were just okay looking but seemed thoughtful and kind and like good, sturdy men seldom approached her.

And secondly, on the rare occasions that a unicorn of a guy who had all his teeth and was nice and funny and all those things a woman looks for in a partner presented himself, she could never hook him. Those guys would take her on a few dates and then figure out that her big personality was too much for them.

Regardless, she was alone, and she'd been alone most of her life. So for Dane to be standing there all blasé wondering why she hadn't dated in the past four or five years was just a tad annoying. She thought about shoving a cupcake right into his nose, but that would be a waste of a perfectly good Seaside Sweets cupcake. These were far too precious to be squandered.

She exhaled a deep breath, meeting his stupid, handsome blue-eyed gaze. What was wrong with her? She never got bowled over by a good-looking face. She'd dated plenty of them in her time. But no matter how many wrong things this man said to her, she couldn't help but still want to lock her mouth onto his and not come up for air until Christmas.

"Thank you for the compliment." She held up a cupcake. "Would you like one?"

He studied it and then met her gaze. "You want to shove that in my face, don't you?"

She couldn't help a grin. "Are you a psychic?"

The door to the shop opened and in came at least seven or eight kids followed by their moms, who clearly knew one another and were chatting a hundred miles an hour.

Marigold tossed up her hands. "Who all do we have here?" She pointed. "I recognize you. You're Katniss Everdeen."

The girl nodded proudly. "Yep."

She pointed at another. "Elsa."

The girl held up her hair, which was a complete wreck. "I did my own braid."

"You did a fabulous job, too." Marigold made her rounds, identifying costumes and heaping praise.

"Can I have a cupcake?" one of them asked.

"We'll have those right after the costume contest winner is announced." She had to keep their moms shopping for as long as possible.

Despite her instructions, the kids hovered around the table snatching for cupcakes. Marigold could see her profits heading right down the throats of these little misbehaved monsters.

But like her own personal prince, Dane stood in front of the display, his thick arms splayed out to the sides. "Nobody gets a cupcake until after the contest, understood?" His tone was low and serious, but his expression was soft and a smile snuck onto his lips. God how she could kiss him right now.

The kids backed up like they were a little afraid and a little intrigued all at once. Marigold searched for their moms who were, to her delight, shopping.

"Where's your costume?" one of the girls asked Dane.

"I'm not entering the contest."

"But she's dressed up," another said.

He looked at Marigold for help, but she just shrugged.

"Well, yeah, but I'm—"

"Is that your husband?" one of them asked Marigold. Heat rose through her neck, and she met his gaze, but he was the one shrugging this time.

More kids piled through the door with parents and headed to the cupcake table like it was a homing device. "Hurry," Marigold said, "let's get these back to the storeroom."

Marigold grabbed the boxes while Dane got the pedestal and they headed to the backroom. "Set it there on my desk," she said, and he found a spot for it wedged between some papers. They faced each other. "That was close," Marigold said. "I've got to stretch this out at least long enough for their moms to shop. If these kids have cupcakes they'll be done...ready for the bouncy place or something."

"What do you have planned?"

"My plan was for well-behaved children to file in neatly and sit quietly for fifteen minutes while their moms shopped."

He let his head fall to the side. "You're not around kids much, are you?"

"Not a single one."

He glanced around. "Do you have any toilet paper?"

She stilled. "Yeah."

"Grab a few rolls." She headed into the bathroom. When she came out he held up a bag of miniature marshmallows. "What are these for?"

"My hot chocolate." She liked a lot of marshmallows in her hot chocolate.

"Do you have little cups of any kind?" he asked.

She glanced around, thinking, and then spotted a cabinet. "I've got these little plastic cups leftover from this event where I served wine." She pulled the sleeve of them out and presented them to him.

"Perfect."

He reviewed their supplies. "All right. This should be enough for now. Come on."

They walked out into the store where the kids were all over the place like an infestation of mice. "Crap," she said, imagining her shop in shambles at the end of the day.

He squeezed her arm. "We got this. Just follow my lead." She nodded at him, feeling like they were headed into war. Dane held up the bag of marshmallows. "Who wants to play marshmallow toss?"

"Me!" shouted a chorus of little high voices.

He handed her the bag of cups. "Set three of these out on the table in a triangle."

She followed his instructions, watching him out of the corner of her eye.

"I want to go first!" one kid yelled.

"I got second," another said.

"Third!"

"Fourth!" and so on.

Dane held up his hands. "No one's going until all of you form a single-file line. No pushing." The kids lined up while Dane checked Marigold's work on the triangle. "Okay. Each of you gets three tries. The person who gets the most marshmallows in the cups wins..." He looked at Marigold for help.

She glanced around and then grabbed a witch figurine off a shelf. "This witch." The kids all gazed longingly at the witch.

Dane handed a marshmallow to the first kid in line. "All right, you're up." He bent down, pointing at the triangle, coaching the little girl. Marigold smiled for the first time since the monsters entered her personal space. And then the smile faded as it occurred to her that the reason Dane was so good with kids could be that he had his own. Maybe he had a wife, too. She'd not even looked for a ring.

She thought back to the first time she'd met him at that bonfire a few weeks back and how he'd walked up and put his arm around that very pretty woman. Yep, he was married.

So? It wasn't like she was falling for him or anything. All he'd done since he met her was irritate her and try to take her hotel away from her. Okay, so it wasn't her hotel, but still. And she couldn't trust him. He'd probably do anything to make her back away from the hotel bidding war, including saving her bacon with these kids.

Another one stepped up to the table and put the marshmallow in her mouth instead of throwing it. He gave her a look. "Only one. If you eat another one, you can't play, okay?" She nodded and he gave her the cutest wink. God, Marigold was melting. This was just more cuteness than she could handle.

One of the moms held up a piece of art. "Is this a local artist?"

"Yes, ma'am," Marigold said, heading that way. She got swept away in conversations with the women who were all local and very complimentary of her shop.

At a point where Marigold was giving her full attention to a woman who was on the board of the local art society, she heard Dane shout, "Who wants to play Mummy Wrap?" and couldn't help a little smile. So that was what the toilet paper was for.

She rang up a few of the moms who bought early Christmas presents at a discounted rate. Marigold was desperate to make the sales. She needed the cash. She'd cut off the shop phone, but the bills and notices kept rolling in.

Bags in hand, most of the women looked ready to go, so Marigold figured it was time to judge the costume contest. She laughed as she found Dane wrapped in toilet paper from head to toe being twirled by a gaggle of girls. She really wanted to believe he was doing this because he loved it, or even because he liked and wanted to impress her, but she couldn't let her guard down with this guy. Too much was at stake.

She made her way to him. "Should we judge the contest now?"

He smiled at her, making her heart swell like a balloon. "Sure."

He broke free of the toilet paper hulk-style, cracking all the kids up. "Okay, everyone line up. It's time to judge the costume contest."

"What's the prize?" one of them asked.

"A twenty-five dollar gift card to the shop," Marigold said proudly. The kids glanced around a little helplessly, and Marigold realized she had designed this to draw in their parents, not them. Then she got an idea. She held up a finger. "Hang on."

She went to the back and grabbed the box of cupcakes. Looking at Dane, toilet paper hanging off of him, she couldn't resist. "Whoever wins gets to smash one of these cupcakes into Mr. Dane's face." The kids exploded in cheers, jumping up and down like they'd already won the lottery. She met his gaze, biting her lip. "Sorry, I had to come up with something fast."

He shrugged. "That's okay. I'm game." He addressed the kids. "And the runner up gets to smash one in Miss Marigold's face."

Equally loud cheers erupted, and maybe even a little smack talk from Katniss. Marigold narrowed her gaze at Dane. "Oh, no you didn't." He nodded, smug satisfaction covering his handsome face.

Katniss had a gleam in her eye that couldn't be

denied, so Marigold wanted her for Dane, but a little girl dressed as Cruella de Vil was the clear standout.

Dane leaned in. "I'm thinking Katniss for the runner-up."

Marigold pointed at him. "Don't you dare. Give me Wonder Woman. She seems halfway sweet."

"I'll give you Wonder Woman, if you'll give me the unicorn."

She studied the group, all of whom where shamelessly vogue-ing for them. "We can't deny Cruella."

"All right. I'll take Cruella," Dane said.

"Are you sure?"

"She's clearly the winner, and I think she has a little crush on me."

Marigold pursed her lips. "Please, you know they all have a crush on you."

He shrugged innocently, the bastard.

Marigold clapped her hands together. "Okay, I think we have a winner."

"And a runner-up," Dane said, waggling his eyebrows.

She glared at him. "And a runner-up." She surveyed the kids, all with hopeful smiles on their faces, and she wished she didn't have to pick just two. She could let them all attack the two of them with the cupcakes, but this was a place of business. She'd be cleaning icing out of merchandise for weeks.

Dane held a cupcake in his hand. "And the runner-up is..."

"Oh, so you're letting me get pummeled first?" Marigold asked.

"The runner-up is always announced first."

He had her there. She smiled and pointed. "Wonder Woman."

The little girl shrieked and came running over, wrapping her arms around Marigold's legs. Her heart warmed. She wasn't a kid person, but she had to admit she was having fun with these little goblins.

Dane presented the girl with the cupcake. "Go for it."

She winced. "Really?"

Marigold nodded solemnly. The little girl checked with her mother who shrugged. Marigold turned her cheek toward the little girl and pointed. Gooey icing smashed into her face as the little girl ground it in good.

The room exploded into shrieks and laughter. Even the moms, who'd been so kind to her before, turned on her. Marigold nodded, taking her humiliation with a grain of salt. She swiped some cakey icing and licked her finger. "Not bad." She headed for the cupcake box and found one with a particularly large amount of icing.

"Hang on," Dane said, undoing his button-down to reveal a plain white T-shirt underneath, the muscles in his biceps working as he undressed. *Hubba.* He nodded at her, arms folded over his puffed-out chest. "I'm ready."

"And the winner is..." Marigold pointed. "Cruella de Vil!"

The girl jumped up and down screeching along with the others. She came running over, and then jumped in place until Marigold handed her the cupcake.

Dane leaned down. "Do your worst."

Marigold's smile was so wide her face was starting to get sore. The little girl smashed the cupcake right onto his lips and smeared from left to right. She even took some icing and dotted his nose with it.

Marigold was happy to see that Dane's humiliation got as big of a laugh as hers did, maybe even bigger. The moms began gathering the kids and telling them it was time to go, so Marigold hurried over to the cupcake box.

"Take one for the road," she said, passing out cupcakes, Dane behind her with the napkins.

One of the moms gave her a big smile on her way out and pointed at Dane. "He's a keeper."

Marigold's face went hot. The woman was gone too quickly for Marigold to correct her, and she figured there was no use in it anyway. She glanced at Dane, but he was busy handing out a napkin and telling a kid his favorite Halloween candy, which was Oh Henry! bars, she noted. She narrowed her gaze on his left hand—no ring. That didn't mean anything. Some married men didn't wear a ring for whatever reason.

When they all left, Marigold locked the door and put the open sign to close. She turned to Dane. "I don't even know what just happened."

"You made a bunch of sales, I'm guessing. Did they all buy something?"

"I think so." Her core woke up as he licked some of the frosting from his lips.

"What? It's good."

"I owe you for this," she said. "Can I buy you a drink, or do you need to...get home." Here it came, the answer to the pop quiz she was giving him. Wife or no wife? That was the question.

"I'm good for a drink." Then...no wife? Or maybe he

was a cheating bastard. She'd get to the bottom of it in time. He pointed at his face. "But we probably need to get cleaned up first."

"Come on," she said, leading him to the storeroom. She pulled off some paper towels and wet them, handing a bunch to him and doing the same for herself. She wiped herself up, glancing in the bathroom mirror, noting she only had whiskers on one side of her face. She wiped the rest of her face clean, leaving just her eye makeup. Now she was all red and blotchy everywhere. Oh well. He was probably married anyway. She shook her head. It didn't matter if he wasn't. He was using her to get close and then convince her not to submit that hotel proposal. She had to keep perspective here.

She dropped the paper towels in the wastebasket and then headed back out to find him looking as handsome as ever. Was it her, or was he somehow better looking now?

"Do you like wine?" she asked.

"I love wine."

"My friend Fiona has a wine bar next door."

"I know Fiona a little."

She grabbed her purse. "Really?"

"She's friends with Ethan, mainly. But we've met a few times."

"Fiona's my roommate, temporarily."

"She's a cool girl."

"Mmm hmm," Marigold said, wondering just how cool Dane thought she was.

He headed to the table. "You want to get this put up before we go?"

"Nah, I'll mess with it tomorrow."

He lifted the end. "It looks kind of heavy. Let me get it for you while I'm here."

She narrowed her gaze. "Are you doing all of this to guilt me into not putting through that hotel proposal?"

He huffed a laugh, crossing his arms over his chest. "I'd have to be either an idiot or the cockiest guy on the planet to think I could play some games with some kids and offer to help you put a table up and that would have you backing away from a business venture that clearly means a great deal to you."

She raised her eyebrows, doubling-down.

He uncrossed his arms. "Let's just get something straight. I'm moving forward with that proposal and I assume you are, too, right?"

"Mmm hmm," she said, knowing she hadn't talked to her dad yet, but it'd been a busy day.

"Let's not insult each other's intelligence by thinking one of us could possibly be sweet-talked into backing down. Let's just go have a drink and put this day in the books, okay?"

She pursed her lips, gauging him, and then relented. "Okay."

He walked closer to her, causing a buzz to generate in her belly. He wasn't going to kiss her, was he?

He reached for a lock of her hair near her neck. "You've got a little icing in your hair." She tried to see it, but it wasn't on the end. "May I?" he asked.

She nodded, her pulse picking up speed. He held it with one hand and smoothed the icing out with his fingers. "Thanks," she said, gazing into his blue eyes that could swallow her up if she wasn't careful.

47

"No problem." He turned and picked up a napkin to wipe his fingers. They cleared the table and then he folded it up. "Storeroom?"

"Yep. Thanks."

She collected herself, breathing deep the moment he was gone. She would not fall for a handsome face—not when so much was on the line.

Chapter Five

Dane held the door to the wine bar open, letting Marigold through. She thanked him with that suspicious expression that she wore pretty much every time she looked at him. He had to wonder if she was this suspicious of all guys who showed an interest in her or if she was just like this to him due to them both wanting that bid.

They found two seats at the bar as Fiona spotted them and came over. "Hey, guys," she said, big smile on her face. "I didn't know the two of you knew each other."

"We just met last night," Marigold said, which wasn't altogether true. They'd met a couple of weeks ago at that bonfire. He'd found her interesting then, but she'd seemed uninterested in him, so he hadn't pushed his luck. Now he wished he had.

Fiona gauged Dane for a second, squinting. "It's Dane, right?"

"Yep," Dane said.

"I thought so, but I didn't want to sit here for an hour

talking to you like you were Dane if you were really Ethan with a bad hair day."

That made Marigold laugh. "In his defense, we just had a pretty rowdy time with the kids next door."

"Oh yeah, how did the costume contest go?" Fiona asked.

"Excellent, thanks to him." Marigold jerked a thumb at Dane.

He shrugged. "I just entertained the kids so she could make some sales from their moms."

"How'd you do?" Fiona asked.

"A decent afternoon. I may have just covered the cost of cupcake cleanup."

Dane turned to Marigold. "You're the one who offered a cupcake to the face for the winner."

"To whose face?" Fiona asked.

"His, and then he tossed me right under the bus and offered a cupcake to my face for the runner-up."

Fiona chuckled. "And all this time I was over here missing the whole thing. I'm guessing someone needs some wine. What's your flavor?" she asked Dane. "I know hers."

"What's your flavor?" he asked Marigold.

"Pinot Noir."

"Then make it two."

Fiona narrowed her gaze. "You trust me with the brand?"

"I'm no wine snob," Dane said.

"Then I've got a bottle I've been itching to open." Fiona headed over to a wall housing what must have been hundreds of bottles.

A group of middle-aged people came in talking loudly and smiling like assholes. Dane and Marigold met each other's gazes and said in unison, "Tourists."

She smiled, turning his body on like a light switch. Dane had dated his fair share of beautiful women, but he'd never lain eyes on anyone as breathtaking as Marigold. Each time he'd seen her, she'd had plenty of makeup on, but he'd been willing to bet she was even prettier without it. She looked damn good with it though.

She had these eyes that sort of drew up in the corners, especially today since she had exaggerated her makeup to look like she was a cat. She kind of had a cat-like quality to her as it was in that skin-tight bodysuit. Though, she wasn't quite so agile like a cat. She was a little all over the place, which he sort of loved.

Fiona appeared in front of them with two glasses and a corkscrew. She popped the cork and poured a little into each of their glasses. "See what you think about this one."

Marigold pointed to the glass without trying it. "It's fantastic. May I have some more, please?"

Fiona pursed her lips at Marigold with a little smile. "You're no fun," she said, pouring the rest. She looked at Dane? "Do you want to try yours first?"

"Fill her up," he said, so she did.

"Talk amongst yourselves. I'm going to see about this group of lovely tourists."

"God love 'em," Marigold said. Fiona nodded and headed off while Marigold and Dane both sipped their wine.

"What do you think?" he asked her.

"I think it's wine. I'll be honest, I've had a lot of wine

51

in my time, and my family always has the best at Christmas and Thanksgiving—bottles that cost hundreds of dollars. But to me, anything that's $9.99 or up works. I do draw the line with the super cheap brands."

"That sounds about right. I actually prefer beer."

"I won't turn down a bottle of beer." She held up her glass. "But this is the elixir of the gods right here."

He clinked her glass with his. "Cheers."

"To what?" she asked.

"To cupcakes in the face."

She smiled. "I guess I'm to blame for that."

"You guess?"

Her smile faded. "I have to ask, do you have a wife and kids at home?"

He huffed a laugh. "No, why would you think that?"

"You know an awful lot about kids' Halloween games not to have kids of your own."

He looked down at his glass, twisting the stem. He didn't want to get into this, not right now, but he realized his knowledge of kids did require some explanation. "I dated someone with kids, recently. I took them to a Halloween party this time last year. I just remembered a few things from that."

"What was that like? Dating someone with kids?"

He chewed on the inside of his cheek, not wanting to dredge up his mixed-up life choices just yet. "Um, okay." He had to shift focus, quickly. "You haven't ever dated anyone with kids?"

"No. God no. I can barely take care of myself. I can't imagine being responsible for another human."

"So you don't want kids?"

"Well, I'm not saying never, but not right now, for sure. I guess dating someone with them would be a good test run to see how you might be with them. But then, you wouldn't want to get serious with someone with kids unless you thought there was a real shot at long-term, because then you'd have to leave the kids and that would suck majorly." She met his gaze like she'd just remembered he was sitting there. He tried to keep his expression impassive, but by the look on her face, he'd failed. "Oh shit. I'm sorry. I sometimes work things out with words that really belong in my head."

He shook her off. "No, it's no big deal."

She studied him, making him shift in his seat. "It is a big deal. This was someone you were really serious with, wasn't it?"

He really didn't know how to answer that question without unloading a massive amount of his baggage. "It's hard to explain."

"*Complicated* is the official Facebook term."

He nodded with a contained smile. "Then it was complicated."

"Was?"

"Yeah, definitely in the past." That statement was partially true.

"But not too far in the past if you were taking them to Halloween parties this time last year."

He shook his head. "You don't want to hear about my mess."

She turned her body toward him. "Trust me. Nobody leaves a bigger mess behind them than me." She nudged him in the leg. "It'd be nice to know someone else is as screwed up as I am." The smile she gave him made his heart open wider than he thought it ever would again.

He winced, feeling the words coming, knowing he was an idiot to be getting ready to say them. "It was more about the kids than it was about her."

Marigold's eyebrows went up.

"I kind of fell for them. She introduced me to them after we'd just been out a couple of times. I'd never dated anyone with kids, so I didn't know the protocol. But I realize now, that was a huge mistake. I should have seen that was a red flag at the time. I learned."

"How many kids?"

"Two. Boys. They're six and eight now." He smiled, thinking about them. "Crazy and full of energy. A lot of fun."

"How did that go with their dad? Was he in their life?"

"No. She told me he'd left them several years back and moved to Arizona."

Marigold narrowed her gaze, probably reading his expression. "But you don't believe her?"

He let out a huff of air. "Toward the end I wasn't sure what to believe anymore. Lots of stuff didn't add up."

"Wow. That sounds intense."

He just nodded.

"So I take it you're in between girlfriends," she asked.

"That's a way to put it."

"When did that last relationship end?"

He thought about it. "Last November. Before Thanksgiving. I couldn't bear to spend that holiday with

54

the boys like a happy family knowing it wasn't going to last."

"And you haven't dated anyone since?"

"Not seriously. Not really interested in that right now."

She narrowed her gaze. "But you were with someone the night of the bonfire."

He frowned, no idea what she was talking about. "Hmm?"

"I saw you, when I was getting another drink at Sebastian's cabana." She cleared her throat. "When you told me my skirt was tucked in my underwear?"

He remembered how cute she'd looked, walking down the beach, sliding him a flirtatious smile. He had to keep thinking though. He hadn't been with any girl that night. He'd been with... "Oh, okay. That was our cousin, Celia. She was in town for the weekend."

Unmistakable relief flooded her face. Damn, had he missed his opportunity that night because Marigold thought he was hooked up with someone else? That sucked.

"So you've been too interested in building hotels to date?" she asked.

He was just about to say that this would be their first hotel, but he caught himself, remembering he was talking to the competition. "Yep."

She nodded, gauging him in that way that made him feel like he had no secrets.

He cleared his throat. "So tell me about the gift shop you want in this hotel. Same as what you have now?"

"Not exactly. I know I'll need to carry toothbrushes

and headache medicine, but I want this shop to be fabulous. It'll have its own separate outside entrance, and inside entrance, of course, wide open to the bar area. The thought of having that kind of traffic after being tucked back behind this restaurant over here..." She trailed off, shaking her head like the idea had a life of its own.

"Have you had any more traffic since this wine bar opened?"

She waved him off. "Drunk people don't want to go shopping. They want to go drink some more or go home and pass out. I did try keeping it open later when Fiona first opened, but it wasn't helping and I couldn't keep up with the hours."

"So you don't have any employees?"

"I hire help in the summer when I can, but in the off-season, it's just me."

"You must spend a lot of time there."

"Oh yeah. Six days a week. I have no life."

"I thought Ethan and I worked a lot."

"Don't get me wrong. It's not a bad workplace, but it's like a prison sometimes. I can't leave without locking up. I'll have days during the slow time of the year where nobody comes in for hours, then when someone does, I'm so happy for human contact that I come on too strong and they back away slowly like I'm Jack Nicholson in *The Shining*."

He smiled. "I love that movie."

"Really?" she asked.

"Oh yeah." Against his own better judgement he pulled out his Jack Nicholson imitation quoting the famous line about bashing Wendy's brains in.

She raised her eyebrows. "That actually wasn't half bad."

"Thank you," he said, feeling way prouder than he should.

"No, I'm serious. Everyone thinks they can do Jack, but few actually can."

"Well, I've only seen that movie a few hundred times."

"Me, too. So do you just like Jack, or is it all horror movies?"

He hesitated, not wanting her to think he was a freak. "It's actually all horror movies."

She studied him. "Do you prefer kitschy or serious?"

He scrunched up his face. "Both?"

"Good answer," she said with a smile. "Do you think that makes us both psychos?"

"Possibly."

"Well, as long as I'm not the only one." She grinned at him, making his heart swell.

He could feel the connection between them strengthening by the minute which was starting to freak him out a bit. "So why didn't you go into the family business?"

She let out a big sigh as if the question had been inevitable. "I actually planned on it. I majored in hotel management back in college."

"Really?"

"Yep. I seriously thought I was going to go to work for my dad. I actually don't know if I realized I had a choice back then. It was always so assumed that my sister and I would work in the business."

"She likes working there?"

"She's my dad's favorite. She's always done everything he said to do and never given him an ounce of trouble. She's like a Stepford wife, except that's weird, because it's her dad, but you get the idea." She studied him. "What about you? Does your dad have a favorite?"

His heart cinched. No matter how many times he had to explain his situation, he never got comfortable with it. "Actually, my dad isn't really in the picture." The look of surprise followed by her reddened cheeks made him wince. The last thing he wanted was for her to feel uncomfortable around him.

"I'm sorry," she said.

He touched her knee. "Please don't be. I hate having to tell people that. It's fine. I'm an adult. I'm over it by now." His words rang as hollow as they felt in his head.

"Do you mind me asking what happened there?"

He exhaled. "They were both pretty young when they had us. My dad hung around for a few years, and then when we were four and a half, he just headed out. He moved to Hawaii of all places." He smiled at her, but sludge was circulating in his stomach.

She stared at him with those big, beautiful cat eyes of hers, and then reached for his hand and squeezed it, taking his whole body off guard. "I'm really sorry that happened to you."

He couldn't remember a time a person had seemed more sincere than she did in that moment. He squeezed her hand in return. "Thanks," he said, and then let go.

"Where does your mom live?" she asked.

"She moved to St. Louis a few years back. She's remarried."

"Do you like the guy?"

He shrugged. "He's okay. I'm glad she's happy. I think he takes pretty good care of her, and she does the same for him."

"Are you close with her?"

He let out a sigh because he never liked answering that question. "I'm glad she's taken care of right now, and if that situation ever changed I'd move to St. Louis or wherever she was to help her or do whatever I needed to do. But it's tough being around her." He shifted in his seat. "Her husband makes comments about *homosexuals* like it's a dirty word in front of Ethan."

"What does your mom say when he does that?"

He shook his head as that dull pain infiltrated his heart like it always did when there was talk of his mom. "She doesn't say anything."

"He knows Ethan's gay?"

"I'm sure he does. Ethan doesn't hide anything. I'm sure she's told him. Honestly, we don't discuss it."

"So has he ever come out to her?"

"Not in any kind of official way, but she knows. He's brought a guy or two around for a dinner or special occasion."

"How does she react?"

He huffed a humorless laugh. "Fidgety, nervous. So damn ridiculous."

She frowned. "That's got to be tough on Ethan. Was she always like that?"

"Pretty much, but it's worse now that she's with this guy."

She backhanded him lightly in the arm with her

wrist. "How did you turn out so okay with Ethan's orientation?"

He shrugged. "He's my brother and my best friend. I knew he was gay before he did. Even though my mom made it clear when we were little that homosexuality was wrong, I never thought anything about Ethan was wrong."

She smiled. "That's true brotherly love."

Heat rose in his neck, and he huffed a laugh trying to cover up the fact that he'd said too much. "Probably my own damn vanity since we look just alike."

"You don't look just alike, by the way."

"Yeah, I know. He's better-looking."

She gauged him. "I don't know. You're...bigger, or something."

"Are you calling me fat?"

She pinched at his stomach. "Hardly."

He loved how touchy she was. He hadn't been touched by a woman since Erin, and at the end of that relationship her touch had given him the willies. "Ethan's thinner than me. I'll give him that. And better-dressed."

She looked him up and down. "You do okay."

That heat from his neck reached up to his ears. How could this woman be so good at making him feel like a kid again? He cleared his throat, looking for a subject change. "So is it just scary movies you like or other scary stuff?"

"Oh, I'd have turned my gift shop into a full-on haunted house tonight if I hadn't been focused on selling to the moms. I didn't want to detract from the merchandise once I had them all in there."

"You like haunted houses?" he asked.

"Oh yeah, but I can't get any of my duddy friends to go with me."

He considered her, knowing he really shouldn't go there but somehow physically incapable of stopping himself. "Have you been to the Haunted Woods?"

She straightened. "You don't mean the one north of here with the hayride, do you?"

He couldn't help a grin. "Yeah, have you been?"

"No, I've been dying to go though."

His heartbeat revved up. He really needed to get that under control. "Wanna go sometime?"

"Uh, does a cat have a tail?"

He peered around her backside. "It appears that way."

She pulled it out and swatted him with it.

Chapter Six

Marigold fixed herself a cup of green tea and headed out to the back deck. She couldn't believe this ocean view was her life for the next couple of months. With Fiona's parents staying in Lexington till January, she had the whole next two months to live like she was on vacation. But it wasn't like she could relax and enjoy it. She'd chosen not to renew her lease on the shop, and she had to be out by the end of November, so her days were filled with a low level anxiety about her uncertain future.

She had to figure out her life one way or another. Even if her family got the bid on the land to build the hotel, it wasn't like it'd be ready for her to go to work there on December 1. She had some hard decisions ahead of her. If she knew the hotel was a for-sure, she could limp along working retail somewhere until it was built. But if the hotel wasn't going to happen, she'd have to face the abysmal possibility of going where the money was.

And the only sure option she had for that was back home in Savannah with her family.

She didn't hate her family. She actually got along with them fine...just as long as they were in separate states. Marigold took a moment to imagine herself working there at the flagship hotel in Savannah, Camellia walking into the room to let her know in her gentle but yet oh-so-condescending way that she had screwed up some process or procedure. She gave a physical shudder at the thought.

The sliding glass door opened and Marigold pulled herself back to earth, smiling a silent good morning to Fiona. "We're not alone," Fiona whispered as she took a seat.

Marigold glanced back at the condo. "Beauty still asleep?"

"Yep."

"Anyone I know?"

Fiona shook her head and then sipped her coffee.

"Anyone I'll be getting to know soon?" Marigold asked.

"Possibly. It's early. What about you? Dane Knight, huh? That's a catch."

"I haven't caught anything yet. Besides, I don't think he's into me for my body."

"Uh, the grin he had on his face all night would tell a very different story."

Marigold waved her off. "He's trying to charm me into backing off of the hotel bidding. He and his brother already have a client in place."

"Oh, yeah. They do property development. So he

thinks he's going to use his charms to talk you out of it? Is that why he happened upon your shop right as you needed help with the kids?"

"I actually asked him to stop by to help me hang my big ghost."

"And then you all just stumbled into my bar afterward?"

"He earned a drink, trust me." She swirled her tea in her mug. "He actually asked me out, I think."

"You think?"

"Do haunted hayrides count as dates?"

"Are you kidding me? How can you get more intimate than voluntarily going somewhere that you'll need to grab onto each other in delightful fear?"

Marigold giggled at Fiona's turn of phrase. "How well do you know him?"

"Not as well as I'd like to." Fiona waggled her eyebrows. "But I think you've beat me to the punch."

Marigold jerked a thumb in the direction of Fiona's bedroom. "Greedy much?"

Fiona smiled. "I guess I'll stand down. He doesn't have eyes for me anyway. But he definitely has them for you."

"I've got to watch my back. He and I are out for the same thing and only one of us can get it. For all I know, he's planning on getting to know me and lower my defenses so he can get information from me to sabotage this deal or something. I probably need to cancel this date."

"You know, if that's what he's doing, that can work both ways."

Marigold considered it—using Dane and then dumping him. She winced. "I know I have my moments, but I don't think I could do that."

"It doesn't have to be all mustache-twirling evil. Just be smart. Listen and learn."

"I can do that, I think."

Fiona drew her thighs up to her chest, resting her coffee cup on her knee. "I may have some information on him, completely unrelated to the hotel business."

Marigold lifted an eyebrow. "What kind of information?"

"He went through a bad breakup a while back. Like seriously bad."

"He mentioned his ex had two boys."

Fiona pointed. "That's her. They had this really erratic relationship. She was all over the place. Took him on the ride of his life. Think roller coaster to hell."

Marigold's chest went cold. "How do you know all this?"

"Ethan and I went for a drink after one of those local business owner things. I asked where Dane was and the floodgates opened. Ethan was at the end of his rope with it all."

Marigold shook her head. "That couldn't have been good for those little boys."

"That was the key to it all. Those kids. He felt responsible for them. They'd gotten really attached to him. I hate to say it, but from what Ethan told me it sounded like she used those kids to manipulate Dane."

"Geez," Marigold said, suddenly relishing her

freedom and feeling the need to protect herself all at the same time.

The sliding glass door opened, revealing a tall, lean woman with tousled, auburn hair, a T-shirt that bared her midriff, and just her underwear down below. "Morning," she said.

Marigold held up her cup with a smile. "Hello. I'm Marigold."

"Bobbie."

Of course a girl as beautiful as this one had a sexy, gender-neutral name. Marigold indicated the kitchen. "There's a single-serve machine in there. Coffee or tea pouches beside it. Take your pick."

The girl stepped out onto the deck and rubbed Fiona's shoulders. "I'm not quite ready to get up yet."

Fiona cut her eyes at Marigold with a little smile. "I think I need a little more sleep, too."

"Mmm hmm," Marigold said, trying to hide her smile with her mug.

"You're welcome to join us if you like," Bobbie said, sizing up Marigold.

Though she had given it a fleeting thought not too long ago, she'd decided fairly quickly she wasn't exactly through exhausting her possibilities with men, as dismal as they were. She held up her mug. "I'm good, but thanks for the offer."

"If you change your mind..." Bobbie trailed off, letting Fiona pass by her, lingering for a moment to sufficiently make Marigold's face a thousand degrees.

"Leave her alone," Fiona said from inside the condo, and a moment later the sliding glass door shut.

Marigold envied Fiona, her comfort in her own sexuality. Marigold had not had sex in more years than she wished to count for reasons she didn't like to think about. But Dane was waking up sexual thoughts her body hadn't entertained in years.

Marigold had been on an emotional ride since the incident back in college. It was so silly that ten years after it had happened, she was still experiencing emotional trauma from it. *It wasn't that big of a deal*, she'd told herself so many times. She got away. That was what mattered.

And she'd had sex since then, plenty of times. But not in recent years. There came a point somewhere along the way that she just needed out of the whole business of it. Right about the time she'd closed herself off to the possibility of sex, Sebastian had brought her into his new group of handsome, straight, wonderful guy friends. Being platonic with Blake, Bo, and Chase had been just what she'd needed to help heal. Three straight men who liked and respected her and wanted nothing sexual from her had been the most refreshing blessing she'd ever been given.

Now that they were all hooked up and crazy in love, Marigold was left to figure out a way forward without them. It was time. It was so far past time. But was she ready?

She shook off the idea. Picking up her phone, she let out the sigh of the century. She'd put it off long enough. It was time to contact her dad.

"Hey there, honey," he said by way of greeting.

"Hey, Daddy. Are you busy?"

"Never too much for you. What's up?"

"Well, I've got some news that might excite you," she said, and then winced. That sounded like she was getting ready to break out an engagement story or something. "I mean, business-wise."

"Oh yeah? About the shop?"

"No, actually, it's about the hotel...or the possibility of one here on 30A, I should say. There's some land that's up for bidding on, and they're allowing a boutique hotel."

"You don't say."

She grinned at the sound of his interest. "I do. They're giving preferential treatment to locals, so my years living here may finally pay off for you."

"That's great. Are you interested in working for us there in South Walton?"

"Actually, I was thinking more of a partnership. I assume this hotel would have a gift shop, right?"

"All of ours do," he said.

"I was thinking a more elaborate gift shop with plenty of whimsy and color and a strong focus on local art."

"Like the one you have now?"

She smiled again. "Exactly. It'd have an outside entrance, and it'd be wide open to the bar area."

"And it'd be yours," he said, getting to the point, which she had to appreciate.

"With a percentage of all profits going to the hotel, of course." They'd talk numbers later.

"I don't know, sweetie. We have a few standard designs we follow."

Her heart took a hit, but she rebounded. "Just think about it, okay? I'm going to email you a link to the details for the bidding and you can see if this hotel is something you even want to pursue. We'll take it from there, okay?"

"I'll take a look," he said, but his tone was void of any sort of excitement or sense of urgency.

"Okay," she said, trying to remain hopeful. If he said he'd take a look he would. Whether or not he'd take her seriously was the question. "I'll put together a business plan, how's that?" She crossed her fingers, hoping she was speaking his language.

"Okay," he said with just enough of an uptick in his tone to give her hope.

"Awesome. I'll let you get back to work. Tell Mom hello."

"You could tell her yourself." There was that hint of disappointment in his voice, the one that said she wasn't engaging enough with them. How could they not see that this was the only way she could keep her sanity?

"I will. I'll call her when I get to the shop, okay?"

"Bye, honey."

"Bye."

She hung up, exhaling. That wasn't so bad. It was conversations like that one that made her think going back home to work wasn't the worst idea on the planet. But she had to keep reminding herself why she left. She was the baby of the family, and her parents and sister never let her forget that. Sure, they didn't specifically refer to her that way, but it was the condescending looks and tones that did her in. Subtle but deadly.

She thought about Dane and how different his family life was—no father and a mother who wouldn't defend her own son who Dane clearly cared more for than anyone on the planet. By comparison, her family life seemed like a dream.

She let out a sigh, rubbing her forehead. She'd made the initial contact and set the groundwork. Now she just had to come up with a kickass business plan to impress. She knew just the person for that. She picked her phone back up.

"Hello, beautiful," Sebastian answered.

Chapter Seven

Marigold did a 360 for her friend Shayla who was sitting up on her bed. "Are the leggings too much?" She really hoped Shayla would say no, because she'd been dying to wear her Day of the Dead leggings somewhere fitting besides the shop.

Shayla looked her up and down with that serious, discerning look of hers. "I love 'em," she said, deadpan.

Marigold grinned. She didn't have to ask Shayla twice. She was no-nonsense. You could take her at her word a hundred percent of the time, which was one of the things Marigold loved about her. "Thanks for coming over. You didn't have to do that."

"I didn't give you a choice. I just said I was coming. So tell me about this guy you're going out with tonight. I just met him that one time at the bonfire a few weeks back."

Marigold collapsed onto the bed next to Shayla. "You don't know who he is?"

"No, I'm pretty clueless though. Remember, I was gone for a few years."

Marigold nodded. "He and his twin brother have a property development company."

"Ah, that must be how Chase knows him." She lifted a dark eyebrow. "Twins, huh?"

"Yep." Marigold pulled up their website on her phone and showed Shayla the picture of the two of them together.

She smiled. "They're cute."

"I know, right?"

"Which one's yours?"

"Ha! That one, but he's not mine."

"He's the better looking of the two," Shayla said.

"He always jokes that his brother is better looking."

"His brother is cleaner cut...more put together or something."

"He's gay."

"There you have it." Shayla handed Marigold back her phone. "It's almost time for him to be here. I better go."

Marigold jumped up. "You're sure this is okay? I was trying to stay away from sexy...you know, so I don't encourage him to jump me or anything." She made sure her facial expression conveyed her sarcasm.

Shayla eyed her. "What's going on with you?"

"Nothing," Marigold said with a squeak.

"Something's going on. You don't want to have sex with this guy?"

"Well, wanting to do something and needing to, or not to, are two completely different things."

"What would be wrong with having sex with him?" Shayla asked, not in a challenging way, but like they were working through a problem. Marigold loved this girl.

She wanted to share with Shayla, but she hadn't talked with anyone about her lack of sex, not even Sebastian. She checked herself in the mirror on the back of the door, rethinking the braid she'd woven just above her forehead and pinned to the side of her head.

"Has it been a while?" Shayla asked in that easy, nonjudgmental tone of hers that Marigold really appreciated right about now.

"Mmm," Marigold muttered, inspecting her hair.

Shayla got up off the bed and came over to her. "Hey." She met Marigold's gaze in the mirror. "What are you worried about?"

Marigold turned to Shayla, running her hand down the braid. "I'm sort of...out of practice."

Shayla nodded like this was no big deal. "Okay, well, it's super easy. And you can absolutely let him do all the work. He'll be totally okay with that, trust me."

Marigold stared at Shayla, her heartbeat racing. "Can I tell you something?"

"Sure."

"I've never had real, good sex. Like, I've had plenty of college sex—hookups, friends with benefits stuff, sex with boyfriends who were shitty, but once I got in my mid-twenties, I sort of gave it up. It's been a while."

"But you think you're ready now, with Dane?"

Marigold turned back to the mirror. "I don't even know him. But I think that's kind of the attraction. I mean, I decided I was not going to have any more meaningless hookups, and that I was going to wait until I was in love. But look at me now. Still no love for me. I think I need to have an adult, guilt-free hookup to sort of get me back in the game."

"Then do that."

Marigold rubbed her face. "It's just...I'm not sure I'll want to walk away from this one, or have him walk away from me."

Shayla just studied Marigold, letting her work through it.

"God, I just want to be a normal, sexually active thirty-year-old-woman."

Shayla lifted an eyebrow. "Define normal."

"Well, look at you. You're like this healthy, sexy woman with relationships with men who's like probably had normal consistent sex since you were in your twenties or before. Am I right?"

Shayla let out an exhaustive breath and sat down on the bed, Marigold following suit. "It's true I'm in a healthy relationship now with Chase, but my last relationship was anything but healthy. I think you may have talked yourself into some idealistic relationship or person that just doesn't exist. The idea of this typical, sexual person, man or woman, with no hang-ups or baggage from their past just isn't realistic. Not that I've ever seen."

Marigold tossed up her hands. "I just don't understand what's wrong with me. I've kind of got this all-or-nothing personality. I guess part of me is afraid I'm going to have sex with this guy, and I'm going to love it, and I'm going to want to have so much more of it, then I'm going to come on too strong like I always do, then he's going to scurry away, then I'm going to be back to square one. It's just not worth it. I think I'm going to cancel."

Shayla chuckled. "Girl, slow down."

Marigold leaned into Shayla, resting her forehead on Shayla's shoulder. "Are you re-thinking your friendship with such a screwed-up girl?"

Shayla rubbed her back. "The only thing I'm re-thinking is that burrito I had for lunch."

Marigold pulled away adjusting her seat on the bed. "For a long time, I didn't have to think about guys. I had Blake, Bo, and Chase. None of them wanted to date either, so it was like, this perfect safe haven with three of the hottest guys on the planet. We flirted and had fun, and texted and talked, and hung out, but it was all so safe. I had no expectations." She smiled to herself, feeling the need to be totally transparent. "I had a little crush on Blake, but that was only because of the three of them, I knew he was the least likely nut to be cracked. I was fairly convinced he was gay."

"Which was probably what made you interested."

Marigold pointed at her. "Exactly. God, I'm messed up."

"You're human, darlin'. There's a big difference."

Marigold gave her a little smile, and then looked back down at her hands. "It's like now that the three of them are taken, I'm being forced to think about it again." She looked up at Shayla for confirmation. "You know?"

Shayla nodded. "I know. You want Chase back?"

Marigold laughed. "Would you give him back?"

"We could arm wrestle for him."

Marigold held up her arm. "With these spaghetti noodles? You'd massacre me."

Shayla's expression turned serious. "Maybe don't put so much pressure on yourself about tonight. Don't psyche yourself out here. Just go on the date, have a good time, and see how you feel at the end of the night. If you want to have sex with this guy, don't think of it as the first time in years. And don't worry that you're going to fall head over heels. Just be in the moment and enjoy whatever you do tonight, okay?"

Marigold smiled at her, wishing it was as simple as all that. "Okay."

A knock sounded at the door, whipping Marigold's head around. "Crap." She rushed over to the mirror. "I shouldn't have done this braid."

Shayla, her treasured friend, smiled at her. "You look beautiful."

Marigold let out a sigh, her core heating up just at the thought of Dane on the other side of that door. "I'm not going."

"Oh, yes you are."

Marigold nudged her. "Go answer it and say you're me. We'll make him think he's crazy like in one of those old *Twilight Zone* episodes."

"Get your butt out there and answer that door."

Marigold checked herself in the mirror one more time. A knock sounded again.

"Will you go?" Shayla said. "You're making me nervous."

Marigold smiled. "*I* am making the unshakeable

Shayla Harrison nervous? Someone put this down in the book of records."

Shayla opened the bedroom door and gave her a playful shove. "Go. Damn, I think I'm more nervous than you are."

Marigold giggled, Shayla's nervousness somehow combatting her own. Marigold opened the door to find Dane standing there dressed in all black, T-shirt and casual pants. "Hey." He smiled. "This is just a few buildings down from mine."

God, he made her feel good. "You live in WaterColor?"

"Yeah." He jerked his thumb to the side. "That way."

"Beachside?" she asked with a raised eyebrow.

"Yeah, like you."

"Well, except I'm borrowing this place."

He shrugged and then looked her up and down, focusing on her legs. "I like the skulls."

She slid her hands down her skull tights, grinning. She'd hoped she hadn't gone overboard. "I like your all-black."

Shayla appeared beside Marigold and held her hand out to Dane. "Hi, I'm Shayla Harrison. Chase introduced us a few weeks ago at that bonfire."

"Yes, I remember. How are you?" Dane asked.

"I'm good." She turned to Marigold. "I'll see you later." She gave her a quick wink before turning back to Dane. "Nice to see you." She scooted around the two of them, and they watched her head out toward her car.

Dane turned back to Marigold with raised eyebrows. God, he was so freaking handsome she almost couldn't take it. She grabbed her purse from the kitchen table. "Are you ready to go?"

"Let's do this."

Dane drove them inland to the haunted hayride which got creepier and creepier the farther they drove into the dark woods. They found the place and parked, and as they walked toward the line of people, Dane pocketed his hands. "Are you getting a little scared?"

"No, of course not," Marigold said, her heartbeat starting to quicken. When he kept going past the line directly toward the hayride, she hesitated. "We have to pay first, don't we?"

He held up his phone. "I already got our *jump the line* tickets."

She smiled, giving him a point for preparedness. "Nice."

They piled onto the hayride, scooting in close as the ride filled up. Passing the staged scenes of circus freaks and axe murderers, Marigold found herself scooting in closer to Dane's side, and he didn't seem to be arguing. If she'd have known a haunted hayride could draw such quick intimacy, she'd have suggested them for dates long ago.

They came to a stop and all got off the ride in front of a myriad of stuff to do including a pumpkin patch, a big slide that dumped the rider into a tub of corn, and a station with a fortune teller.

"Wanna do the hay maze?" Dane asked.

Marigold stood there looking at this handsome man who seemed like the greatest guy on the planet, and who actually seemed to like her. He could totally be playing her for business or even just for sex. But she really didn't think that was the case...and she *really* wanted to kiss him.

She gave him a smile, turning on her flirt. "Or, we could just explore a little in the woods." She headed that way, acting like she was looking for ghosts and goblins, but with other things on her mind. The crunch of sticks and leaves behind her signaled he was following her, which made her stomach go upside down for a quick second. "I wonder if there's anyone in here we can scare," she said in a low voice.

"Somebody waiting to scare us?" he asked.

"Mmm hmm," she said, grinning to herself, because she was so setting this up for a kiss. She needed to keep her guard up, but one little kiss wouldn't hurt. It'd been so long that she'd forgotten what a man's lips felt like on hers. She just wanted a little taste.

"I think they're all on the other side. We have to settle for scaring each other," he said.

She turned around and faced him. "You don't scare me, Dane Knight."

"Oh yeah," he said, his voice getting deeper which sent a chill up her spine, regardless of the warm fall evening.

She bit her lip. "Nope."

He moved toward her. "You sure about that?"

She stepped back, her boots crunching the ground. "Oh yeah."

He came forward again. "I bet I can scare you, even right now when you're expecting it."

"I dare you to try," she said, unable to wipe away the grin. She was so not cool.

He backed her against a tree, making her feel very Bella Swan in the first *Twilight* movie. His hand rested on her hip, sending her stomach into orbit. He leaned down, his mouth hovering close to hers. "Boo," he said, his voice velvety smooth.

His lips met hers, soft and heavenly. God, just the idea of a man's lips she liked on hers had seemed like it had become an impossible feat. But here they were in the woods in this strange little town, so isolated from the rest of the world, lips attached, moving together for the sole purpose of pleasure. His hand rested on her hip, the other cradling the back of her neck, strong and capable. It felt so good she let her head relax back. It'd been so long since a man had taken care of her physical needs in even the smallest way that the idea of this subtle allowance made her impossibly vulnerable in the most wonderful way.

"Ahhh!"

The two of them jumped a mile as a little girl appeared in front of them, hands up in the air like paws trying to claw at them.

Marigold grasped her chest. "Oh my God." The girl giggled and ran off.

Dane met her gaze, running his hand through his hair. "I think she wins the contest."

"For sure," Marigold said, and they headed toward the parking lot.

"So, what's next?"

"I'm easy," she said, and then winced. "I mean, I'm

up for anything. Well, not anything. Most things. Some things. Not, like, badminton. I wouldn't be up for that."

"Oh, I'm totally up for badminton."

They stopped at his car and she stared at his beautiful face, his blue eyes and soft lips which she desperately wanted on hers for the rest of the night. "Do you want to get some food and come back to my place and watch a scary movie?" she asked. "Might as well keep the theme going."

He opened the car door for her. "Sounds like a plan."

As he walked around the outside of the car, her body started to light up. Was this the night after all these years that she would finally break her dry spell? And with that gorgeous thing? He got in and started the car, every move he made somehow interesting to her now. His hand on the gearshift as he backed out of the space, his exposed neck as he craned his head to watch behind him, the muscles in his arm working as he put the car in drive.

He smiled over at her. "What?"

Busted. "Nothing. Just, I don't have a backup camera either."

"Yeah, this car is ancient. I need a new one. Just haven't messed with it."

They drove to a strip mall with a Chinese restaurant and ordered food for an army. When they got to her place, they unloaded it all and she showed him two bottles of opened white wine, both just missing about a glass each. "Do you have a preference? Fiona brings them home from work. She can't serve them after they've been open a few days."

"Those are some decent brands."

"Yep. That's what happens. Someone orders a glass of the good stuff, then the rest of the bottle goes to waste when nobody else orders it for a couple of days."

He pointed at one of them. "Let's go with that one."

She considered the bottle. "Good choice." She poured the wine into two glasses, leaving a little in the bottle on the table, and then took her place next to him on the couch, settling in. She grabbed the remote. "All right. What's it going to be?" She scrolled through the streaming options. "Ooh, have you ever watched these old *Twilight Zone* episodes? They are so freaking weird."

"I watched the movie once as a kid with my mom. Have you seen that?"

"With that little monster on the wing of the airplane?" she asked.

He chuckled. "Yeah, that was totally creepy. Let's watch the show." She put it on, and they ate, having fun with the acting and the generation that was so different from theirs. She settled in with her wine, tucking her feet up underneath her. He gauged her. "Doesn't that hurt your knees, to sit with your feet like that?"

"No," she said with a chuckle.

He stared at her, and she could feel the kiss coming all the way in her core. His lips were sweet and tingly with the wine, and so was his tongue which she was so happy to be getting to know. They hadn't made it that far in the woods with the little girl scaring the crap out of them.

She found her hand moving to his thigh, a natural reaction that she hadn't had in more years than she could count. He kissed her chin, working his way up her jawline to the side of her eye and then her forehead. She'd had moments like this one with guys who she hadn't felt a thing for, or who she did, but she was confident the level of interest wasn't returned. But Dane kissed her in a way that said this could be something... dare she think it...real?

Steps toward the door and fumbling keys had Marigold breaking away. She gripped his knee and whispered, "She wasn't supposed to be coming home tonight." As soon as she said it, she realized she'd given herself away. She'd lured him to her home with the intentions of getting him back to her bedroom, of course, but she had been trying to at least put up the façade that this was happening organically.

The door opened and Fiona blinked as she made out Marigold and Dane on the couch. "Oh, crap. Sorry. I'll just..." She turned toward the door and hiccupped. "Fuck."

She looked rough. "No, come on in," Marigold said. "Do you want some Chinese food?"

Fiona let out a huge sigh. "No, thanks. Hey Dane. It's Dane, right?"

"Yeah, hey," he said. "Are you okay?"

"I'm fine. Just irritated," she slurred.

"Come sit down," Marigold said, patting the armrest of the chair next to the sofa.

Fiona plopped down and sat there for a second, staring off into space. Just when Marigold was about to ask her a question, Fiona pointed at her. "You know, women are always saying stuff like, 'I'm going lesbian. Men are sooo complicated.' But women are just as complicated as men. Probably even more complicated." She drug out her words like she was struggling to say them, and it was clear to Marigold that she was drunk as a skunk.

"Amen to that," Dane said under his breath.

Fiona pointed at him. "Right? Am I right?"

He glanced at Marigold and then back down at his wine glass like he was getting himself into trouble.

"You know, take Dane here," Fiona went on. "If the two of you had sex tonight, and then tomorrow he begged you for more, wouldn't you expect that he'd want to do it again tomorrow night, too?"

Marigold's face was so hot it could melt a snowman.

"Dane, would sex three times with Marigold be too much?" Fiona held up three fingers, one of them floating down.

"Uh, no," he said, and Marigold put her forehead in her hand.

"See!" Fiona shouted and then attempted to snap. "This is what I'm talking about," she slurred. "Men are easy. They like to have sex. They don't care who it's with."

Dane held up a finger. "I actually do care who it's with." Marigold couldn't help a smile.

Fiona looked exhausted with him. "What I mean is you would treasure this woman's body and soul. Not treat it like a toy you played with once and then discarded for something more fun...and taller."

Marigold could do nothing but giggle now. She met his gaze. "Would you discard me for something taller?"

"You know what I mean. I'm making a yoof...yoof..." Fiona snapped.

"Euphemism?" Dane asked.

She pointed at him. "Yes. That." Marigold was pretty sure that was not the right word here, but she didn't argue.

Fiona leaned forward and picked up the bottle of wine. "What's crazy is I hadn't even decided if I liked her yet. I mean, I liked her when we did it the first time, but then when we did it the second time, something clicked for me, and I was like, yeah, I like her. Then she comes in the bar tonight, and I'm like hell yeah, I like her. But then this Amazon woman comes in like eighteen feet tall, and Bobbie's enthralled. They left together, right in front of my face. I swear it was like..." She swatted the air like she was slapping someone, and then looked at the wine bottle in her other hand. "What is this? I don't even want this. I'm going to bed."

She tried to haul herself up out of the chair and then gave up, closing her eyes. Marigold got up and put the bottle on the table. "Come on, Princess Fiona. Let's get you to your bed."

"I'm fine right here," she said, slouching in the chair.

Dane got up and slid his arm around her back. "Come on. I'll get you back there."

"I don't want to go back there. Bobbie was back there this morning. It's gross. I haven't changed the sheets."

"We'll take her to my bed," Marigold said.

Dane slid his hand under Fiona's legs and picked her up. Fiona glanced up at him. "I love men again. I wish you were straight. You're such a good guy."

Dane followed Marigold to her room with the plastered Fiona where Marigold pulled the covers back and Dane laid Fiona in the bed. Marigold pulled Fiona's Mary Janes off her feet then covered her. It took about two seconds before she was asleep.

Marigold put her hands on her hips. "I think I better stay back here with her in case she needs to throw up."

"That's probably a good idea. I can stay, too, and help."

"No, but thanks. I'll be fine." She followed him out to the living room where he went for the empty plates on the coffee table. "Leave them. I'll clean all this up. I need to stay awake for a while to make sure she's okay. It'll give me something to do."

"Are you sure?"

"Yep," she said, giving him a closed-mouth smile, pressing down her disappointment. She opened the door for him. "Thanks for taking me to the haunted hayride. I had a lot of fun."

"I did, too, especially in the woods."

She averted her gaze, this cute boy bringing out the fifteen-year-old girl in her. "Mmm hmm."

He took her hand in his and pulled her closer to him. "I would never discard you for a taller toy."

She grinned. "That's so nice to hear."

He lifted an eyebrow. "What about you?"

"Well, if we're talking a real doll house, then I'm not so sure."

"Oh, so I see. That's the deal breaker."

"Pretty much. I always wanted one as a kid but I never got one."

"Well, you definitely deserve all the things you want."

"You don't know that. What if I'm a horrible person and deserve a big kick in the pants?"

He smiled at her, that little dimple on his chin making her knees wobbly. "Somehow I don't think that's the case." He stepped closer to her, causing her belly to flurry, and kissed her...this time sweet and soft like he meant it.

He pulled away. "Good night." Their hands broke apart and she watched him walk away, the view beating any tropical paradise.

She floated back inside and shut the door behind her, staring at it. Maybe Fiona coming home was some sort of sign for Marigold to back off. She liked Dane way more than she had at the beginning of the night. But this was what she did. She fell hard for guys, had sex with them, and then they weren't around much after that. This was the pattern she had broken by going celibate. The idea of her being able to sleep with Dane as some sort of reawakening of her sexuality and then just walk away and be cured was starting to seem ludicrous.

The distinct sound of Fiona's dinner and evening drink exiting her body through her mouth jolted Marigold back to reality. She winced as she headed into her bedroom. Definitely not the way she'd planned on spending this evening, but as far as her own choices went, it was probably for the best.

Chapter Eight

Dane couldn't swear it, but he'd be willing to bet he slept with a smile on his face last night. Marigold had brought out a side of him he hadn't seen in a long time. He hadn't had pure unadulterated fun like that since before Erin.

Marigold made him feel like a kid and a man all at once. He could be silly and stupid, but then she still looked at him with interest, like she wanted to do more than play.

Before Marigold, Dane hadn't been able to imagine an easy relationship, one where he wasn't always looking for his footing or waiting for the hammer to fall. It was still way early, but just the idea of something like that made him feel like he could breathe clean air again.

He held his phone, staring at it like it was his lifeline to her. He knew she had the day off today, but he didn't know if she had plans. They hadn't discussed it. He wanted to see her again, badly. He texted her.

How did last night go? Is Fiona okay?

He waited for the ellipsis to appear at the bottom of his phone, but it didn't, to what he realized was his extreme disappointment.

He took a shower, put a load of clothes in, and read a chapter in his book, but he couldn't focus. He checked his phone for what must have been the tenth time, and his heart lifted when he saw a text, but then it dropped when he realized it wasn't her. It was his friend Jesse.

Come eat lunch on me if you can. Testing some new foods.

Dane figured that was as good of an offer as he was going to get today, so he grabbed his keys.

JESSE WAS behind the bar when Dane got there. With its casual, laid-back Grayton vibe, Jesse's bar had come to feel like home to Dane over the years...not to mention Jesse was his closest friend besides Ethan.

Jesse wiped his forehead with the back of his arm. "There he is. Where were you last night? I texted you to come by. There was a girl here I was talking to who I thought you might like."

"If she was cool, why didn't you go for her?"

He shrugged. "I think I'm burnt out on women."

"Uh oh," Dane said.

"It's not even fun anymore. They come in here and sit, and you flirt for a while, go home if you're feeling it, then there's either bullshit to deal with or they go back to where they came from."

"What about local women?"

Jesse grunted with a shrug. "Everyone's so busy doing

their own thing. All of us who own businesses work them all the damn time. When do we have time to have a life?"

"Mmm," Dane uttered.

"You want a beer?"

"Just a Coke, please."

Jesse shot soda from his drink hose into a cup. "You know as well as I do that the local women are all either attached or busy as hell."

Dane took the drink from him. "Actually, I sort of met someone."

"A local?"

"Yeah."

"Would I know her?"

"She owns that gift shop in Seagrove called Apples to Oranges."

He squinted. "Maybe I know it. I think I've seen a sign from the street. Is it tucked behind that restaurant that's been shut down for a while?"

"That's the one."

"What's she like?"

"Fun," Dane said, his chest lighting up at the idea of her.

Jesse grinned at him, pulling his messy hair out of his face. "Oh, fuck. You're in love."

Dane almost choked on his soda. "Oh God no. Nothing like that. I've been out with her like once."

"Like once, or once?"

"Just once, but we've talked a few times."

"Ah. And you like her."

Dane shrugged and then met his friend's gaze with a smile. "She's really fun."

Jesse leaned in, waggling his eyebrows. "Oh yeah."

"Not fun like that, asshole."

"Oh. So, she's not fun in bed?"

"No, I don't know what she's like in bed."

"Oh, shit. So you're into her and you haven't even—"

"No. Jeez. Can I have five minutes to get there?"

Jesse held up both hands in surrender. "Okay. I just figured."

Dane gave him a look. "I know in your world if you haven't screwed by the end of the night you're behind. But it's a little different once you step outside of bar life."

"Understood."

Dane ran his fingers up and down the plastic cup. "I want to though, for the record."

"Is that her?" Jesse asked.

Dane looked around, ridiculously, because how would Jesse know what she looked like? "Where?"

"On your phone."

Dane grabbed his phone and read the text.

She's alive! Thanks for checking. You'll never believe who's here though. Bobbie, the girl she was broken up over last night. They're talking.

He smiled and texted back.

What are you doing?

Sitting in my car like a dork. I wanted to get out of their way, but I'm not going to the shop on a Sunday.

"Invite her over," Jesse said.

Dane met his gaze. "But we're hanging."

Jesse waved him off. "I really just needed your taste buds. We're testing out some new food I wanted you to try. Invite her here. I could use her taste buds, too."

"Really?"

"Yeah, do it." Jesse headed over to another customer.

Dane hated to be that guy who ditched his friend for a girl, but he'd left her last night with the most incredible ache in his heart and his groin. He texted her back.

Come to the Bohemian Guppy in Grayton. It's my friend's bar. I'm here now. He's testing new food. He said to invite you. That he could use your taste buds.

A moment went by before she responded, making his stomach ache. He both loved and hated the uncertainty of something new with a girl.

On my way.

A ridiculous amount of relief poured through him, and he relaxed, resting his elbows on the bar. He must have glanced up at the door twenty times since he got her text, but finally, it was her. It'd been all of five minutes, but it had felt like a half hour.

She set her purse down on the bar beside him. "My taste buds are here and ready for work."

Jesse smiled at her from across the bar. "I've seen you in here before."

"You have. You tried to talk me into a night in your pontoon boat a while back."

Dane's chest lit up.

Jesse grinned and then hung his head. "Oh, fuck." He peered at her from under his shaggy hair with those puppy dog eyes Dane supposed some women might find attractive, the asshole. "I'm sorry. Is that why you haven't been back?"

She shrugged. "That and a wine bar opened next to my shop."

"I've seen it and the girl who owns it," Jesse said with a waggle of his eyebrows.

"She's currently hashing it out with her girlfriend back at our place, so you definitely have competition."

Dane relished the disappointment on his buddy's face. "She's gay?" Jesse asked.

"Bi...or pan, maybe. I'm not altogether clear on the details," Marigold said.

"Then there's hope."

Marigold looked him up and down. "I wouldn't hold my breath. She's pretty savvy when it comes to guys like you."

Jesse pointed at his own chest. "I'm hurt."

Marigold grinned at him. "You'll get over it."

Dane was this close to asking if the two of them needed to get a room, but he bit his tongue. Jesse met Dane's gaze and cleared his throat. "I'm gonna check on the food I want you both to try. Anything you don't like?"

"Pontoon boats," Marigold said with a smile. Jesse grinned and headed back to the kitchen.

"So you turned him down, huh?" Dane asked, a glutton for more details. "I don't think he's used to that."

She nodded toward the kitchen. "I had my time with that stuff, back in college and my early twenties." She met his gaze full-on. "That's not for me."

He held her gaze, trying hard to convey understanding with his eyes. "That's not for me either."

She eyed him. "I hope not, because he's really too hot for me to compete with."

Dane rolled his eyes. "That's not—"

Leaning in, she said, "I know what you meant,"

squeezing his thigh in a way that made him feel like the only man on the planet, or at least in this bar.

Dane looked away, not sure how to deal with the way Marigold made him feel—lucky and vulnerable all mixed up in one. "So Fiona's getting back with Bobbie?"

Marigold huffed a laugh. "Looking that way. It's so funny. They just slept together for the first time the other night, and they're already fighting. I'd say this is not the way to enter into a relationship."

"That's not how you do it?"

"No fighting until at least three months in," she said.

"What happens at three months?"

"The honeymoon gets real."

"The real's okay if it's with the right person." He couldn't believe he just said that aloud.

She pointed at him. "This is true."

He stood up and walked behind the bar, needing to put some space between them. "What do you want to drink?"

"I'll take a Diet Coke, please." He filled a cup with ice and then found the button on the hose and shot liquid into it. "Were you ever a bartender?" she asked.

He smiled. "For a little while in college. That's how I met Jesse."

"Where did you all go to school?"

"Kentucky."

"UK?"

"Yep. Wildcats."

"Ah. And you moved here together?"

He handed her the drink. "Jesse came here first. He called me and told me what a goldmine this place was for development. Ethan and I came and visited and we knew as soon as we saw the place."

"Mmm," she said, nodding. "At least you knew someone. I didn't know a soul when I came here."

He walked around the bar and sat down beside her. "How'd you get to know people?"

"Sebastian Peyton. He came in the shop the first day I opened. He's sort of famous for taking in strays. Do you know him?"

"I know the name, but I'm not sure I can place him."

"You met him, actually, that night at the bonfire. He's sort of a 30A staple."

"How long have you lived here?"

"I've been here seven years now. What about you?" She held up a finger. "Wait a minute. You told me this already. Like five years ago, right? I'm surprised I haven't seen you around before now. I used to come here quite a bit."

She was probably in there during the times he was with Erin, or with Erin's boys while she worked. That happened quite a bit. "Used to?" he asked. "Did Jesse run you off?"

She smiled and looked back down at her soda. "In a way, I guess."

"In what way?" he asked, thinking he wasn't going to like the answer.

She considered him. "Because I wasn't sure I could trust myself. I wasn't in a place for a one-night stand, and I knew that was what he was after."

Dane nodded, the thought of Marigold wanting his good friend stinging him. "What place were you in?"

She let out a deep breath, meeting his gaze full-on. "One I think I'm ready to pull out of."

The twinkle in her eye made his lap twitch.

"Okay," Jesse said, sweeping into the bar area with a platter in one hand and small plates in the other. "We've got fried artichokes, trailer trash pasta, poutine, spicy ribs, boudin balls, and smoked oysters."

Dane stared at the plate in awe. "You're adding all this to the menu?"

"That depends on what my tasters think. I'm fine to add all of this or none of it. Just want to get it right. I'll leave the two of you to it. You guys need anything to go with any of this before I leave you alone?"

"A stint for my heart functionality, possibly," Marigold said.

Jesse smiled. "Enjoy."

She handed Dane her plate. "Give me some of that poutine on your side and I'll get you some of this trailer trash pasta."

They filled their plates with the food and ate, comparing notes through the meal. "Give me one more smoked oyster," he said. "Just to be sure."

She passed him one from her side of the platter. After they had cleaned their plates, Jesse came back over to them. "Well? I'm ready for the hard review."

Marigold gave Dane a look with a raised eyebrow, and he nodded at her. "Go ahead."

She wiggled in her seat. "Okay, we both loved the poutine, but we wished the gravy was just a little thicker, because after we'd sat here a while, the thinness made the fries a little soggy."

"Noted," Jesse said, grasping the bar with both hands, flexing the muscles in his arms, making Dane purse his lips in irritation.

"The spicy ribs were a little too spicy, but they made me thirsty so that might be a good thing for your beer sales," she said.

Jesse nodded, eyebrows raised.

"The boudin balls were really easy to eat and fried to perfection, but the guts of them were just a little bit bland. We would suggest kicking up the spice a tad on those. But we both loved the fried artichokes and the trailer trash pasta."

Dane's heart swelled at the unity of all her statements, like they were a team, or an old married couple who had gotten on the same page decades ago.

"What about the oysters?" Jesse asked.

Marigold gave Dane an inside joke grin. "I think the oysters were Dane's favorite. Am I wrong?"

"They were pretty damn good," Dane said.

Jesse rubbed his hands together. "All right. Looks like I've got some tweaks to make." He pointed at the platter. "You guys finished?"

"Yep," Marigold said. "Thank you for lunch."

"Thank you for your opinion."

"I'm happy to give that anytime, and you don't even have to pay me in free food." She smiled at Jesse, and Dane was not into the way Jesse smiled back at her. It was clear Jesse had already visualized himself having sex with her since he'd tried to get her to his boat a while back. And by the way, how long ago was that? Last month? Last year? He needed details. No he didn't. He needed to quit being neurotic.

"Can I get you two anything else?" Jesse asked.

"What do you have for dessert?" she asked.

Jesse looked stumped. "People don't typically ask for dessert in here. They just munch on bar food while they're drinking."

Marigold sat back in her chair. "Who's your clientele?"

Jesse thought about it. "A handful of locals, some tourists."

"Men or women?"

"Men, mostly, but I'd love to get more women in here. Women bring in more men."

"Then you need to offer a fabulous dessert. One that's easy to eat, noncommittal."

"A noncommittal dessert?" Jesse asked.

Marigold squinted at a piece of junky bar art behind Jesse. "Warm chocolate chip cookies. But none of this crumbly, dry, wimpy crap. I'm talking big, beautiful, gooey chocolate chip cookies that stand up tall and hold their shape."

"Like a skillet cookie dessert, or..."

"Keep it easy to eat. If a girl feels like it's going to be a big production with syrup and whipped cream she's committing to a major dessert. If it's just a cookie, pure and simple, she's going to be way more willing to order that. Once it arrives and she takes a bite, she'll roll her eyes back in her head and come back for another one later."

Jesse glanced at the kitchen. "I'm not sure how well the line cooks back there can bake."

She pulled her phone out of her purse. "Source it out. There's a baker in Seaside who can handle this for you. What's your number? I'll text you her info."

"Here," Dane said, pulling up Jesse's contact in his phone. He handed it to Marigold. "Use mine."

She raised her eyebrows at him, calling him out on his paranoid jealousy.

"He's already set up in mine," he said, his cheeks heating.

Marigold took his phone and typed into it. "It's Cassidy Anderson at Seaside Sweets. Do you know the shop?"

"I think so," Jesse said.

She handed the phone back to Dane and addressed Jesse. "It's right on 30A. Do you know Cassidy?" "No, I don't think so."

"She's even more fabulous than her shop. I'll give her a heads-up that you're going to call."

Jesse squinted at Marigold. "I don't know. Sounds like a hassle, bringing in cookies every day."

"You want to bring in the women?"

He nodded.

"Then let them eat cookies."

Jesse grinned at Marigold and Dane glared at Jesse. Jesse, finally cluing in to Dane's nonverbal warnings, cleared his throat. "I'll get this out of your way."

Marigold turned to Dane with a smile that told him he was busted. "So turns out you're the jealous type, huh?"

"You said he hit on you a while back. I was doing that for your benefit."

She grinned at him with a shake of her head. "You are so full of shit."

He rolled his eyes and stood. "Do you want to go walk this food off?" When she hesitated, he said, "It's pretty outside today."

She picked up her purse. "I know, and this is my only day to get any vitamin D. Look at these arms." She held one out. "I'm about to get mistaken for a Cullen."

"A who?"

"Alice Cullen? Esme Cullen?" When he shook his head, she said, "Uh, Edward Cullen?"

He pointed at her. "For some reason, I think I'm supposed to know that last one."

She put her hands on her hips. "You've never seen *Twilight*? I'm not going to even ask if you've read the books."

"Is that the movie with the teenage vampires?" He knew exactly what *Twilight* was, but he was having too much fun watching her reaction to his pretending not to know.

She rolled her eyes at him like he was the biggest disappointment on the planet. "Silly boy. You can't be a member of our generation and not know *Twilight*. That's just wrong."

"Is it good?"

She held out her hands to her sides. "It's not a matter of good or bad. It's *Twilight*. It's iconic. You've got to see it."

This is where he should admit he'd already seen it,

but he wasn't passing up this opportunity. He'd let it slip later. "Then let's go watch it."

She looked down at her purse, fooling with something inside of it. "I probably shouldn't."

"Oh," he said, wishing he wasn't so disappointed, and before he could stop himself, "Why shouldn't you?"

She gauged him, letting out an exhausted sigh. "Because quite honestly, Dane, I like you."

His heart leapt out of his chest, but before he could respond she had set a twenty down on the bar and was out the door. He followed after her.

She led them through the warm October day and toward the beach access parking lot. "What's the problem with that?" he shouted as he tried to keep up with her. She was fast.

She held up a hand, waving him off. "Trust me, it's a problem."

"Is this about the hotel? I told you we can keep business separate. We're adults."

She kept walking without words while the lights on her car flashed. He slid in front of the driver's side door, but she just stared at him and said. "I can easily just hop in the back."

"I'm serious. What's going on here?"

She ran her fingers through her hair, letting it fall around her face in a way that made him want to snatch her up and let every man in America know that this beauty was his, and they could back off or go down.

She let out a sigh. "Why couldn't I have just made up a legit excuse?"

He couldn't help a little smirk. "Because maybe you wanted me to convince you otherwise?"

She rolled her eyes, but a small smile tugged at her lips. "You're so dangerous for me."

"Dangerous?" He chuckled. "I don't think anyone's ever called me that." He pinched at her hip. "Come on. What's going on here?"

She hesitated a minute, gauging him. "What's going on is that I can tell you right now exactly how this afternoon will go if I give in. We'll go to your place and watch *Twilight*, which I love and makes me ridiculously lascivious. Then we'll start making out, then it'll lead to the horizontal, and then before the big baseball game scene, it'll all be over."

He raised an eyebrow. "How far in is the baseball scene?"

She shoved him playfully. "I'm serious, Dane. I like you. I like hanging out with you and kissing you, and thinking about kissing you, and thinking about doing more than kissing you, and if we go back to your place, it'll all be over. And I'm just not ready for it all to be over."

He frowned. "Maybe I've got it wrong, but I was thinking we'd do it this time, and then later on in the week we'd do it some more."

She grabbed two handfuls of his shirt, pulling him toward her. "See, Dane, that's the way it's supposed to be. But that's not the way it *will* be."

He peered down at her, the close proximity begging for a kiss, but the timing being way off for that. "How will it be?"

She pushed him away and then smoothed his shirt out where she'd grabbed it. "We'll do it, and then I'll say something stupid and off-putting then you'll be weirded out, and we'll part ways. Then I won't hear from you for a couple of days, so I'll have to get with one of my girl-friends to analyze the situation. Then we'll have to watch *He's Just Not That Into You* which should set me straight, but defeats the whole purpose of itself because turns out he is actually into her in the end. Then I'll be back to square one and I'll end up texting you. Then you won't respond, or worse, you'll respond with something vague that keeps me hopeful just to the point of irritation, while I secretly know all along it's never going to happen. Then the worst part comes where you win the hotel bid against me because I was too busy watching *He's Just Not That Into You* on a loop trying to make sense of it all, and then I'll figure out that I just need to ignore you and start dating someone else like she did in the movie, restarting the cycle. And frankly, I'm too damned old for this crap."

He put his hand over his mouth to hide his smile.

She grabbed his shoulders and shook him. "I'm freaking serious, Dane. I'm a hot mess. You have no idea. I'm a train wreck waiting to happen. There's a reason I'm not married yet. No man wants to put up with all this." She motioned up and down her torso, and all he could think about was what the bare skin of her belly tasted like.

"What if I want to put up with it?"

She pointed at him, glaring. "You say that right now, but we're currently pre-sex. Once we're post-sex, this all changes. And I like you too much for this to all change.

So if you don't mind, I'm asking you nicely one last time, please step aside so that I can go home and watch *Twilight* on my phone in my bedroom with my earbuds in so I can't hear Fiona and Bobbie moaning through the wall."

He ran his hand through his hair, certain he'd never wanted a woman more in his life, but defenseless to figure out a way to have her. He studied her, wishing they were six months into this friendship or relationship or whatever it was, just so they'd be to a point that she could trust him. But that wasn't fair, because he couldn't even trust himself.

He wasn't planning to settle down with Marigold or any woman. Erin had put him through the ringer, and as much as he wanted to move past that situation in his brain, he wanted to just have easy sex first. He'd not had sex since Erin, and sex with her had been anything but easy. It'd been full of manipulation, and his trying to talk himself into thinking it was good so that a life with her would make more sense...anything so that he wouldn't have to face a separation from her boys.

Marigold was uncomplicated on paper. No kids for him to fall in love with being the key. But she made him want to do things like have kids of his own. And he was definitely in no mental place for that.

But for fuck's sake, did she have to look so damn good in those shorts?

He held up both hands. "All right. I hear you loud and clear. You can go." He stepped out of the way and motioned toward her car door. "Go home and watch *Twilight* or *Moonlight*, or whatever the hell you want to on your phone with your roommate getting her mind blown next door, and I'm going to head back to my place for a marathon of the whole damn franchise on my seventy-five-inch."

She lifted her eyebrow. "You have seventy-five inches?"

"With surround sound and a subwoofer, baby."

She crossed her hands over her heart. "I love the music in that first one."

"We can crank it up as loud as you want."

"What about your neighbors?"

"I live on the end and my brother lives next door."

"Would he want to watch with us?"

"Hell no," Dane said, knowing Ethan would probably be into it, having been the one to introduce him to the books to begin with.

She let out a sigh, glowering at him. "You're making this really hard."

"That's the whole point."

Her smooth cheeks colored, but her grin was uncontainable. "Oh crap."

He smiled back. "I'll behave, unless you decide you don't want me to."

She pointed at him. "I'm not deciding that."

"Fine. Do we need candy?"

She tightened her lips in concession. "Chocolate. Are you milk or dark?"

"If it's dark, we can have more, right?"

She shoved him again. "Quit being so perfect." He grinned as he opened her car door for her.

Chapter Nine

"I like the other Victoria better," Dane said and then offered Marigold his box of peanut butter candy. She glared at him. "What?" he asked, all innocent.

"You've seen this before."

"What makes you say that?" he asked, but he was a terrible liar. She could see a smile tugging at the corners of his mouth.

"How do you know there were two Victorias?"

"I don't know. I guess I heard it somewhere," he said. She shoved him, causing his candy to spill out. "Look at you, spilling all my candy," he said through a grin, knocking back some more pieces.

"So this was all a ploy to get me back here, wasn't it?"

"It worked, didn't it?"

She tried to pinch his nipple but he blocked her, more of his candy flying out. She wondered if that secretly bothered him. His place was pretty neat for a guy's place. Or maybe that's just how guys were at this age. She wondered what age that was, remembering that she'd asked him once before, but pretty sure he hadn't told her. "How old are you?"

"How come?" he asked.

"I'm just curious why a man of your age is so into young adult drama."

He shrugged. "Like you said. It's a product of our generation. Every kid in my high school was reading those books."

She turned her body completely toward him. "Hang on. Are you telling me you've read the *Twilight* series?"

He shrugged. "I was a big reader back then. I read anything I could get my hands on. Besides, Ethan said they had vampire/human sex in them, and I had to see how that went down." He tossed a candy into his mouth. "You can imagine my disappointment when it didn't come till the last book."

"Poor Dane, had to read angsty YA and didn't even get to the good stuff for four books."

"I lived." He pointed at her. "I was always Team Werewolf though. I never liked the way the other guy creeped into her room and watched her sleep all night. I'd get arrested for that."

She covered her mouth, wondering how many more things this man could possibly do to make her fall for him. She let her hand drop. "So what are you reading now?"

"I'm re-reading a novel right now. I'm terrible about that. I'll read the same thing three or four times, because I love the characters and want to stay in the world."

"Oh, I'm so bad about that. It's like an indulgence,

right? We should be reading new novels and discovering new authors, but the ones we love are so dear to us."

"For me, it's an indulgence to read fiction at all. I feel like instead I should be reading trade articles or nonfiction books," he said.

"But if that's what you do with your free time…"

"There is no free time when you own your own business. You know that."

She shrugged. She couldn't argue with him on that. "I barely get dinner down before I'm tucked away in my bed watching something on my phone to fall asleep to. That's on nights I'm not grocery shopping or doing laundry or whatever. I make sure I get everything done during the week so I'm not spending my day off on life. I want my day off to be pure indulgence."

He smiled at her like he was proud or something. "Is that what this is? Indulgence?"

She took his hand and cozied in next to him, wrapping his arm around her shoulders. "In the most decadent way. Bar food, candy, *Twilight* for the umpteenth time, a boy I shouldn't be with." She rested her thighs against his. She used to sit with Chase like this when they watched movies at his house on Sundays, and it never felt sexual. But she was finding that no matter how hard she tried to put Dane into the friend zone, he just kept hopping right over that line. She could feel his gaze on the top of her head, but she refused to look up at him. If she did, there was no doubt a kiss was eminent. And she knew once she got started, she was toast.

"I love this part," she said, barely even able to see the giant screen in front of her with Dane's arm around her like this, his masculine scent somehow winning out over the bar smells that had no doubt attached themselves to both of them.

"I like it, too," he said softly.

Don't do it, Marigold, she told herself. *Don't look up at him you silly, senseless little girl.*

His thumb played with her arm, up and down, up and down. She closed her eyes, letting the sensation of his touch trickle through her. His body next to hers filled her with a sense of safety and warmth, but it wasn't real. He was out to take her hotel away from her. She had to remind herself of that.

She sat up as if his touch was too hot. "I've got to see your ocean view. Compare notes with my own temporary one." She hopped up and walked that way. "Do you mind?"

"No, of course not."

She pulled back the curtain and slid open the door, letting the late afternoon breeze wash over her. The days were getting shorter, and the sun was starting to make its descent over the sea. She walked over to the rail and gripped it, trying to transfer her emotions out of her head and into it.

He walked up beside her, and she turned to him. "This is a killer ocean view. Do you live out here? I live out on Fiona's deck when I'm actually home and not exhausted." She was babbling so he wouldn't kiss her. Of course, she could just walk out the front door, but for some reason, her feet wouldn't go that way.

"It's a pretty nice view," he said, smoothing a strand of her hair out of her face.

Her chest throbbed and her body turned toward him even though her head was shooting up flares of warning. *Abort! Heart in danger of breaking!*

She grabbed a handful of his T-shirt and pulled him toward her and then nudged him away.

He lifted an eyebrow. "I'm getting some mixed signals here."

"You think I don't know that? I'm the one giving them."

"We can go right back to that couch and finish the movie. We'll start *New Moon* next."

"Yeah because a pack of shirtless werewolves will so help my situation."

He slid a finger into the front pocket of her shorts, causing her core to light up like a railroad crossing. "What's your situation?"

She glared at him. "You are, buster."

"I was minding my business, watching the movie. You're the one who had to cuddle."

"Because that's what I do with my guy friends. Except for some stupid reason it's different with you."

A smile tugged at his lips. "How's it different?"

"Oh, you know good and well."

"I don't know." He slid a finger in her other front pocket. "Tell me."

Her hands went for his chest like they were summoned there. "I want more from you."

"You can have whatever you want, you know."

She slid her hands up and rounded his shoulders, allowing herself to indulge in his strong physique. "I wish you wouldn't make it so hard to walk away."

"I don't want you to walk away."

She wagged a finger at him. "You say that now."

He grabbed her finger. "I like you, and I can't imagine those feelings going away anytime soon."

She sighed, feeling herself relenting. As logical as her brain was being with her, warning her not to give in to her traitorous hormones, her body could fry an egg right now it was so hot. She ran her hands down his arms, squeezing his biceps. He wasn't solid muscle, but he took care of his body, and she could feel the work in his contours.

She wanted her mouth on his skin. She wanted to know what he tasted like. Pulling up his shirt sleeve, she leaned down and put her lips to his muscle, kissing it softly, and then running the tip of her tongue over it. She pulled away, eyes closed, drinking in the taste of his skin.

Opening her eyes, she was hit with a gleam in his that warned her she better make up her mind quickly. He rested his hands on the curves of her hips. "You make it really hard to resist you."

"Then why are you still trying to, dummy?"

He grinned and went in, his soft lips attaching to hers like they were fated to be fused. She ran her fingers through his hair as her body pressed against his. The salty air blended with the scent of his skin for a smell so delicious she wished she could bottle it and douse herself in it every morning.

His hands traveled to her ass and he gave both cheeks a squeeze that urged her to wrap her legs around him, but she instead pulled away a moment to catch her breath. Tilting her head back, she let him kiss her jawline and work his way down her neck to her collarbone. "Mmm," she moaned, the sound of her pleasure surprising herself.

He pulled away, biting his lip, his eyes droopy and hair messed up in the cutest possible way. "I don't want to pressure you, but can we—"

"Pressure away," she said.

A grin spread across his face. "Can I take you to my bed?"

She exhaled a deep breath, tossing up her hands. "Why the hell not."

He took her hand, leading her through the living room, her whole body reacting like a shaken up can of soda. She had slept with guys before. There was nothing to be freaking out about.

He stopped just before the bedroom door and looked down at their clasped hands, and then up at her. "You okay?"

"Yes, of course. Why?"

"Because you've got my hand in a vice grip."

She let go. "Sorry. I just..." She trailed off not knowing how to finish that sentence.

He turned his body toward her, taking both of her hands. "Hey, we don't have to do this."

"No, I want to...like *really* want to."

He just stared at her, his brow furrowed.

She put her hands on his hips and rested her forehead against his shoulder. "It's just...been a while."

He ran his hand over the back of her head. "I can assure you that's not a problem."

She pulled back and met his gaze. "For you, maybe. You're probably used to doing it every night of the week."

He huffed a laugh. "I definitely don't do it every night of the week."

"Okay, every other night, then."

He took a step back from her, running his hand through his hair. "Actually, it's been a while for me, too."

This was a strange turn of events. "Really? How long?"

He walked into the bedroom and collapsed onto the bed. "Oh, a while."

This might be even hotter than kissing him. "How long?" she asked again, sitting down next to him.

"You know, I told you I hadn't dated anyone seriously since my last relationship ended last November?"

"Yeah?" she asked, realization dawning. "You mean you haven't had sex since then?"

He searched her gaze like he was looking for forgiveness. "Yeah."

An uncontrollable grin spread across her lips. "Really?"

He sort of scrunched up his face, squinting one eye. "Yeah?"

She slid off her flip-flops and hiked her leg over his lap so she was straddling him. "Are you ready to break your dry spell?"

He cupped her ass with his strong hands and shifted them around, laying her down on the bed. "I've been ready all day, gorgeous." He hovered over her, leaving an irritating space between their bodies that she was desperate to eliminate. She wrapped her legs around his lower back and pulled him down onto her, making him smile. But she kissed that grin away as fast as it appeared.

He ran his hand up her torso and through the center of her chest, and then grazed over her breast and down to her waist. Every inch of body he covered made her squirm with want. She reached up, running her fingers through his hair and pressing her middle up toward him, but he was too far away to reach her. She ran her hands over his ass and pushed him down to her, desperate to feel his erection against her, if he had one yet. God, she hoped he did.

He kissed her neck, still too far away from her, his movements all slow and sensual, which she appreciated, but she wasn't in the mood for slow. She wanted him, and she'd waited years for a moment like this with a guy she really liked. She was ready to get this show on the road.

She rolled them over so that she was on top, kissing the stubbly skin on his face. She pressed against him, the satisfaction of his erection washing over her. She undid the button and zipper on his shorts, and then slid her fingers inside the waistband to pull them down.

"Hey," he said.

She met his gaze with a start.

"What's your hurry? Do you have somewhere to be?"

"No," she said, a touch of embarrassment heating her neck. "I'm just ready to get to this."

He sat up, frowning. "What do you mean? I thought we were getting to it."

She scratched her cheek, her nerves getting the better of her. "I just, was ready. I've been waiting a long time. And I like you."

He took her hand. "I like you, too. That's why I thought we'd make an afternoon of it."

She forced a smile with a nod. "Okay, sure."

"Hey," he said. "What's up?"

"Nothing," she said, realizing she was suddenly hot, like a heat that was coming from the inside. "Are you hot?"

"No, I was afraid it was kind of chilly in here."

She fanned herself with her hand. "Definitely not chilly. I think I need some air." She backed off of him with the urge to leave his apartment and run to Mexico. "I think I'm going to head out. I just remembered I need to get groceries."

"I thought you said you did that during the week so you could have Sunday to yourself."

She slid her feet into her flip-flops. "I do, normally, but I remembered I told Fiona I would make us dinner tonight." It wasn't a lie. She had mentioned that. But she had also assumed that plan went out the door as soon as Bobbie walked into the apartment.

She moved to the side of the bed, and he grabbed her hand just before she could get away. "Hey, don't go like this," he said, his shorts still unbuttoned and unzipped, taunting her.

"I'm not going like anything. I just...I'm pretty sure this isn't going to work out. But thanks for the movie and for lunch."

"You paid for your own lunch, which you didn't need to do, by the way. It was on—"

She held up both hands. "I did, actually. I don't need to owe you. And I don't need to get myself into a position where I feel like I don't have control. And I'm definitely feeling out of control right now, so I just need to leave."

She headed into the living room and grabbed her purse from the bar where she'd left it.

"You couldn't be more in control if you tried, Marigold."

She whipped around. "What's that supposed to mean?"

He tossed up both hands. "Because you've been leading me around like a puppy all day."

"Excuse me?"

"Push and pull, push and pull. Which is it? Do you like me or not, because I really need you to clue me in."

Marigold's mind spun around like that whirly ride at the county fair. Here was this great guy who she really liked, wanting to know if she liked him but slowing her down when she tried to move too fast in his bed. She was embarrassed, and maybe even a little ashamed, though she understood that was a silly reaction to have. The mature, adult thing here would be for her to quiet the ride in her head long enough to apologize for overreacting, calm herself down, and ask if they could start over. That road would get her a long, languid afternoon with a beautiful man who she was more attracted to than any other man she'd ever been into.

She turned for the door. "I've gotta go."

Chapter Ten

Marigold knocked on the door to Sebastian's lavender house in Seacrest, her fist shaky. Ashe opened the door with a sympathetic frown. "Sweetie, come on in."

Even though he didn't live there, she wasn't surprised to find him there. Sebastian and Ashe were always together. Marigold never understood why they weren't sexually compatible. They had such a close relationship otherwise. Rumor had it they'd tried it a few times and decided they were better as friends. How adult of them. At least she surrounded herself with mature people if she couldn't behave like one. "I'm interrupting. I'll come back."

Sebastian appeared with a glass of wine proffered. "You will not. Get in here."

"What were you all doing?" she asked, realizing that sounded nosy, but not sure how to take back the question without it being a thing.

"Looking at movie times, but nothing's on," Ashe

said. "We switched to wine night after Sebastian got your text."

Sebastian handed her the glass and then led her to his couch. "We were thinking of ordering takeout from Suzi's. You want the grouper with the Brussels sprouts side you like?"

Marigold leaned into him, relishing the way he spoiled her. "I love you."

"Oh, pooh bear. What is it?" he asked.

"I'm a freaking psycho is what it is."

Ashe cozied in on the other side of her and rubbed her back. "Well, we already know that, sweetie. You'll have to be more specific."

"I just walked out on a beautiful man."

"Which beautiful man?" Sebastian asked.

"Dane Knight," Ashe said, nonchalantly.

She turned to him. "How do you know that's who I walked out on?"

He waved her off. "The two of you had chemistry out the wazoo the other night. I knew that wasn't gonna be over anytime soon."

Chemistry was definitely the right word for it. Like an erupting volcano project that went bad wrong.

Sebastian nudged her in the side. "Dane Knight. Good catch."

"I haven't caught him. I've just released him back to the sea, actually." She met his gaze. "You remember him from that night at the bonfire?"

"Oh, God yes. I said he looked like Chris Hemsworth and you said Alex Pettyfer."

"Definitely Chris," Ashe said, and then put his finger

to his chin. "Although, somehow Ethan looks more like Alex."

"Aren't they twins?" Sebastian asked.

Ashe lifted an eyebrow. "Double your pleasure."

Sebastian winked at him and then put his attention back on Marigold. "So why did you walk out? What horrible thing did he do to you that we need to kick his ass for?"

Ashe snickered.

"What? I would absolutely kick some ass for Marigold."

"Of course you would, sweetie." Ashe nudged Marigold's leg. "Continue."

She relaxed on the sofa, letting her head fall back. She couldn't tell both of these guys about her sexual hang-ups. She'd tell each of them separately, but a group discussion on the matter was out of the question.

"Oh, you know. I just Marigold-ed out on him."

"We're verb-ing your name now?" Ashe asked.

She lifted her hands and then let them drop. "Why not? If the shoe fits."

Sebastian shifted a little, facing her. "Tell us what happened."

She let out a sigh, rubbing her temple with her thumb and forefinger. She'd already endured humiliation today. What was a little more? "I guess I was a little wishy-washy today because I wasn't sure if I was ready to have sex with him yet, because it's...been a while."

"How long is a while?" Ashe asked, looking a little too interested.

She tightened her lips. "A long while."

"Mmm hmm," he said, nodding like a therapist.

"But then he said it'd been a while for him, too, so I thought we'd stumble through it together, and sort of get it over with."

Sebastian gripped her knee. "Hang on. Get it over with?"

She shrugged. "Yeah, I mean, I guess he wanted to spend time with foreplay. I mean, what guy likes foreplay?"

They held up their hands in unison. "Me."

She looked between them both. "Really?"

"Oh, yeah," Sebastian said. "That's the best part."

"Anticipation," Ashe said with an eyebrow waggle.

She took a sip of her wine and looked at the glass like it could tell her something. "What is this? It's wonderful."

Sebastian waved her off. "I'll have to look at the bottle. So what happened?"

She rested the stemless glass on her knee, swallowing her pride. "He was taking a really long time, kissing and touching, and all I could think was that I wanted him inside of me, and it was like my libido took over my brain and I just starting going for it."

"It, as in..." Sebastian trailed off.

Ashe tilted his head to the side. "His big toe. Of course she's talking about his penis. You're such a school girl sometimes, Bastian."

"Says the boy who walked away from this hot guy's twin brother the other night," Sebastian said.

Ashe lifted his chin. "I'm playing hard-to-get. Other-wise he would have been done with me that night."

"Has he been texting you?" Marigold asked.

"Oh, yeah. I respond to about every other one."

She backhanded him on the knee. "See. You're the exact kind of guy that I get myself in trouble with. I sleep with them, and then I get all attached and weird, and then they ghost me, and then I feel like shit. I'm incapable of being a normal person."

"You need to channel your inner Cassidy Anderson," Sebastian said.

Marigold turned to him. "What do you mean?"

"Do you think she lets herself get in a tizzy over men she sleeps with who don't call back?" Ashe asked.

Marigold thought about it. "She wouldn't, would she?"

"Hell no," Ashe said.

She clenched her free fist. "I'm just so not cool like her. Why can't I be cool?"

Sebastian squeezed her knee. "You're perfect exactly how you are."

"I have perfect friends, for sure."

"That, too," Ashe said, and then squinted at her. "You do know that you totally self-sabotaged this afternoon, right?"

She pursed her lips. "I guess."

"I think we need to analyze why you wanted it over with so quickly," Sebastian said.

Ashe considered her. "I think you didn't want to let yourself actually enjoy the whole thing because you were punishing yourself for giving in and having the hot sex with the hot guy. I think your rushing it was a way to go ahead and get to the part where you start the disappointment and heartbreak."

"Yeah, but who's to say Dane Knight would have been one of those guys who didn't call back?" Sebastian asked.

"Exactly," Ashe said. "He very well could have been a guy who wanted to keep seeing you because you're wonderful."

"I'm wonderful to you two because you love me and don't have to put up with my neurosis." They both gave her a look. "Okay, so you have to, but not out of obligation because we're dating."

"I think you manufacture your neurosis to protect yourself from situations, including possibly letting yourself fall for a man who might break your heart," Ashe said.

"Nice, Dr. Phil," Sebastian said.

"But that's just self-sabotage," she said.

"Exactly," they said in unison.

She glanced between the two of them. "So it's not the guys who are assholes. It's me."

"Bingo," Ashe said with a smile.

Marigold let her eyes dart around the room as her mind spun. "I'm exhausting."

"But wonderful," Sebastian said with a hug. "Now, before this turns into a big ugly ordeal, get your behind back over to this guy's house and apologize for any confusion and let him know he can play with your body all night long if he wants."

She looked between them. "What would I do without the two of you?"

Ashe patted her leg. "Be sex-free for the night. We can't let that happen. Off you go."

She kissed them both on their cheeks and stood. "I'm going back in, tail between my legs."

"There's getting ready to be something else between those legs," Ashe said out the side of his mouth.

Marigold pointed at him. "I'll report back and let you know if it's worth your while with Ethan. They're identical twins, you know."

Ashe rubbed his hands together. "Oh, this is good." He waved her away. "Go."

She grinned. "I'm gone!"

Chapter Eleven

Dane sat in front of his television with a beer but was too dumbfounded to drink it. He kept replaying the day, wondering where he went wrong. They'd been so in sync all day, all last night, too. But they'd been completely out of sync when it came to sex, or lack thereof.

What had been so bad about a hot girl trying to get in his pants, anyway? What kind of man was he to try to pace her? She wanted him, and for fuck's sake did he want her, but somehow he thought the right thing to do was to slow her down.

It was just that he'd not had sex in a whole year. If he was being honest with himself, the reason he'd slowed her down was because if he would have let her go for it like she was trying, he'd have done the same exact thing he did the first time a girl tried to have sex with him when he was seventeen years old, and he couldn't hack that kind of humiliation, not with Marigold.

He wanted to impress her, not make her think he

was as capable in bed as a twenty-nine-year-old male virgin. He wanted to ease his way around her body, touching and tasting every inch of her before he made his way inside of her. They were still in the early parts of the hotel bidding. Once that swung into high gear, she may never want to see him again. He couldn't stand the idea of having a quickie with her and that being the end of it.

What a dick he must have come off as, asking her to slow down. She wanted him and was showing that in the most awesome fucking way ever, but he was too afraid of losing control to let things progress naturally. This was what he got for letting a whole year go by without having sex.

He needed to apologize. Explain. Fuck, he didn't want to explain. But he needed to so she could make sense out of it. And then he needed to throw her down on the goddamned bed and show her exactly how ready he was for her.

As he picked up his phone to call her, a knock sounded on his door, startling him. He grinned. She was back. He set his phone down, ready to go grovel before she had the chance to tear him a new one.

He slung open the door, and his heart dropped when two little blond heads shouted, "Dane!"

He wrapped his arms around both of their backs, his instincts replacing any logic and sense, and then dropped to his knees to bring the two of them in for a bear hug. His eyes closed for the briefest moment as he drank in their little boy stink, their sticky hands all over him.

"We saw the alligators at Fudpucker's," Noah said,

like it hadn't been three months and one week since they'd seen each other.

"Chris held one," Jaden added. "It was huge and it had all these teeth."

"Yeah, it was like..." Noah made a big chomping motion with his mouth and arms all together.

Dane peered out into the hallway, but came up empty. "What's going on with the two of you? Where did you come from?"

"The hallway," Noah said, informationally.

"Yeah, I figured that, but what are you doing here?"

"Mom said she texted you," Jaden said.

Dane stood and peered out the doorway, but no Erin. That same old familiar pull at his heart stung his chest. He'd worked so hard to get over the loss of these boys in his life, and there they were, back in his apartment like they'd just been there yesterday.

Even though they'd been apart for a year, Erin had made a practice of continuing to dump them off on him at her will. Sometimes he would protest, and other times he was just so damn happy to see them that he wouldn't even say anything. But the last time she'd done it, she'd stayed gone for three days. She'd not given Dane any notice, and he'd lost an important deal because he'd had to miss the meeting he'd set up. After that, Ethan had laid down the law, and Dane had conceded. He'd let Erin know in no uncertain terms that the days of drop off were over. She'd flown off in a rage, shouting that he didn't love them like he'd once claimed and throwing out the big guns, saying she didn't understand how he could turn his back on them like his father had on him. It was classic manipulation, but it'd done him in. He knew he needed to detach for good, and he'd done that. Yet somehow, here they were.

The door to Ethan's condo opened, and Dane winced, waiting for the other shoe to fall. Ethan had no time for Erin and her bullshit, and definitely no time for Dane's putting up with it.

Ethan came into the doorway with a plastered-on smile. "Well, look who it is. If it's not Zack and Cody."

Jaden frowned. "Who's that?"

"Mr. Ethan!" Noah, who hadn't gotten the memo that Ethan wasn't into little kids, especially ones whose mother used them as pawns, ran over and wrapped his arms around Ethan's legs.

Ethan breathed in. "What is that scent, eucalyptus, or is that alligator dung?"

Dane gave him a tempered smile. Of course, he'd heard the whole exchange.

"We petted an alligator!" shouted Noah.

"Mmm hmm." Ethan put his finger to his chin. "Don't you mean you wrestled an alligator?"

Noah giggled. "That, too."

Jaden was old enough to sense Ethan's restrained concern, so he held tentatively back.

Ethan looked around. "So, where's your mom?"

"She texted Dane," Jaden said.

Ethan lifted his eyebrows. "Did you get a text, Dane?"

Dane went for his phone that he'd left on the end table, cringing when he saw her name come up on his screen.

We were driving back through from Destin. They were begging to see you. It's only for tonight.

Dane just handed Ethan the phone and then went to the kids. "So, tell me about this alligator you slayed."

Ethan picked up the remote. "First, we're going to put it on a little cartoon and Mr. Dane and I are going to have a word." Ethan walked out into the hallway, and tried to go into his apartment.

"I've got to stay where I can see them," Dane said.

Ethan pursed his lips and then came back into the hallway. "You can't let her start this up again."

"What do you suggest I do? Load them in the car and drive to Panama City? I don't even know where they live now. They were moving somewhere last I saw them."

Ethan handed Dane the phone back. "Call her to come get them, now."

Dane humored him, knowing she wouldn't pick up. And she didn't. "Not answering," he said, pocketing his phone.

Ethan pulled out his own phone. "I've still got her number in my phone."

"I'll text her," Dane said.

Ethan stood there, eyebrows up, waiting. Dane let out a heavy breath, trying to think of what the hell to even say.

"How about no?" Ethan said, reading his mind. "How about come and get your—"

Dane gave him a look that shut him up, and then peered into the apartment. The boys sat on the couch, watching a cartoon. Jaden glanced at him, and Dane held up a thumbs-up. Jaden returned it with a sad little smile.

Dane pulled the door almost all the way shut. "She said in her text it was just for the night. Let me make these next couple of hours okay for them, and then I'll let her know that if she does this again, I'm calling the police or the department of child services, or whoever the hell you call for stuff like this." Ethan shook his head, a huff of air coming out his nose like a dragon. Dane put his hand on Ethan's shoulder. "I got this, okay?"

Ethan shook his head and walked back into his apartment. There were perks and problems with his brother living next door. Ninety percent of the time, the perks won out. Tonight, though, Dane wished Ethan was on the other side of the earth. Or at least the other side of town.

Dane went back in and headed for the couch. "So you all just ate, huh? Fudpucker's?"

"Yeah, Chris works there. He gives Mom and us free drinks," Jaden said. The picture was becoming crystal clear.

"He left his shift early so he could come hang with us," Noah said.

"He did it so he could be alone with Mom, stupid. Why else would we be here?" Jaden said.

Dane's chest heated. Erin wanted a night with her boyfriend or date of the week. That's why they were here right now. She had the gall to dump her boys on her ex to sleep with some guy. If Ethan had this piece of information, he'd lose his goddamned mind.

"Nobody's stupid. We don't talk like that, okay?" Dane said.

"Mom lets us call each other that," Noah said.

"Well, I don't," Dane said.

"You're not our dad, you know," Jaden said.

Dane rubbed his forehead, not able to believe he was right back in this nightmare. There were so many times he wished he was their father. Once Dane had even looked into adopting them before Ethan found out about it and put a stop to that, threatening Dane with everything in his arsenal. In the end, Ethan had been right, and Dane had been grateful for his interference. But moments like this one reminded Dane how powerless he was to actually help these boys he loved.

"What about dessert? Did you have that at the restaurant?" Dane asked.

"No," they said in unison, eyes wide.

Dane walked to the freezer and opened it. He thought he had a half gallon of ice cream in there, but a glance inside the carton revealed freezer burn.

"How about Blue Mountain Beach Creamery?"

"Yes!" they both yelled, and jumped up.

Dane grabbed his wallet and his keys. He needed to get the hell out of that apartment, anyway. This would keep them doing something until Erin got back, whenever that may be. She said it was just for the night, which could mean until nine or ten, or it could mean tomorrow morning. He was hesitant to tell her he had to be somewhere at eight in the morning, because then she'd assume it was fine for them to spend the night, which it wasn't.

He pulled out his phone, gritting his teeth.

Be here by nine tonight to pick them up.

He left it at that, for now, deciding not to threaten to call the police or whoever the hell dealt with this shit unless she didn't respond. But the ellipsis came up immediately.

Yes sir!

That was so typical of her. Make a joke out of it. *Isn't it so cute that I've dumped my kids on you, reopening the wounds it's taken months to get over? Aren't I so funny?!*

"Come on," he said to the boys, herding them through the doorway. As he was locking the door, the elevator dinged.

"Can I push the button?" Noah asked.

"You can push it now, then Jaden can push—" Dane stopped in his tracks when he realized it was Marigold who had come off the elevator. "Hey," he said, his heart thudding against his chest. Talk about his worlds colliding.

"Hey," she said, viewing the scene with an expression of utter confusion.

Noah shoved his big brother. "Dane said I could do it."

"He was talking about once we got on the elevator. You can push this one, too."

"But it's already lit up," Noah said.

"It was already lit up when I pushed it, dork." Noah went over to the button and pushed it repeatedly. Jaden was on the inside of the elevator now. "Come on, Dane." Dane just stared at Marigold, not believing this was happening.

"Dane!" shouted Noah, jerking him back to earth.

"Come out of the elevator, both of you." When they didn't mind, he said, "Now." They both walked out and focused on picking on each other.

Marigold blinked, her mouth open, looking between the boys and Dane. "I've clearly interrupted. I'm just going to slip away." She started toward the elevator, and then the boys followed her.

"I get to hit the button!" Noah shouted.

Marigold stepped off the elevator, looking like a deer in headlights. "Actually, I should probably just take the stairs."

Dane held up both hands. "Hang on. Just...wait a minute." He stood there, trying to decide what to do. He stared at the door to Ethan's place. Dane was going to pay for this dearly. He knocked on the door, and Ethan answered. Dane just stood there and let him view the scene a minute.

Marigold held up a hand in a tentative wave, glancing around at the boys like they were live snakes.

Dane pleaded with his eyes. "Two minutes."

Ethan glared at him. "They're not coming in here."

"Then hang out here with them for just a second."

Ethan opened the door farther, eyeing his brother like John Wayne in a showdown. He stepped out into the hallway.

Dane gave him a look. "Thanks." He motioned Marigold into Ethan's apartment.

She glanced around. "Wow. It's just like yours but...stylish."

"I'm so sorry about earlier today."

"Okay, let's totally get to that, but first, who are the two blondes in the hallway?" she asked.

He rubbed his temple, hating the words he was getting ready to have to say. "They're my ex's boys."

"Oh, I didn't realize you still had some sort of visiting arrangement, or whatever."

"I don't. There's no arrangement. She just dumped them off here a few minutes ago."

Marigold's eyes got big. "Your ex was here a few minutes ago?"

Every word out of his mouth made things worse. "She was, but she didn't come in. She just dropped them off and sent them up here."

Marigold scratched the side of her head, scrunching up her face. "So, is this something she does often?"

He inhaled a deep breath, looking at the floor, and then met her gaze in what was going to have to be a major moment of truth. "She used to do this, quite often in fact, but she hasn't in a while."

She narrowed her gaze. "How long's a while?"

"Three months." He supposed it would be too telling if he gave her the exact month/week/day count.

Her eyebrows went up. "But I thought you two broke up a year ago."

"We did. She just kept dropping them off, and then finally it affected my work, and Ethan laid down the law, and it was over."

"Ethan laid down the law to her?"

"No." He shook his head out of frustration. "To me, and then I laid it down to her."

"So, basically if it weren't for Ethan, you'd have kept on letting her do this."

He let out a sigh, resigned. He loved how forthright she was, just not at the moment. "Yeah, probably."

She nodded, glancing around the room like an answer to this mess was somewhere in the walls.

"But I'm going to talk to her when she gets here tonight to pick them up. She's coming at nine. We're not starting all this again."

Marigold blinked like he'd said something offensive. She pulled her phone out of her purse. "Looks like you've got three hours. What are you gonna do with them?"

He tossed up a hand in the direction of the door. "We were just getting ready to go to Blue Mountain Beach Creamery..." He trailed off when he saw the look on her face.

"You're going to Blue Mountain Beach Creamery?" she asked.

"Yeah," he said, holding back a smile, because clearly, this made her happy. "Do you want to come?"

"Oh, no. I couldn't intrude on your time with them."

"Actually, I could really use you being here with us. I don't need them reattaching to me, thinking I'm getting back with their mom. You could serve as a buffer."

She lifted an eyebrow. "I'm wondering who you are more worried about getting reattached, you or them."

He gave her a contrite smile. "You're probably right about that. Will you come?"

The door opened. "Two minutes is up, sweet brother."

"Just give me two more."

"You get one more, then I'm coming back in." He shut the door behind him.

"Ethan's not a *kid* person?" Marigold asked.

"Not at all."

She put her hand on her hip, grinning at the door. "I knew I liked him."

He took her hand, overcome with the desire to make things right with her. "I'm so sorry about earlier. I should have let you move as fast as you wanted."

Her face bloomed with color, and she looked down at the floor. "No, you were right. I'm so sorry I acted like a dog in heat. I just got a little overexcited or something."

He put both hands on her hips. "I love that you got excited. You have no idea how excited I was." Now it was time for his face to warm up. "In fact, that's one of the reasons I was trying to hold you off. I wasn't sure how quick on the trigger I'd be after being out of practice so long."

She met his gaze. "Really?"

"Oh, yeah." He squeezed her hips. "I've been...*excited*...ever since I met you. Like really excited."

She smiled, her whole face lighting up. She put her hands on his biceps and he tried to flex them a little. He went in for a kiss but the door opened.

"Time's up, lovers," Ethan said, coming back into the apartment.

"That wasn't a minute," Dane said.

"It was in Ethan time." He jerked a thumb toward the door. "Now scram. Good to see you, Marigold."

"Good to see you, too," she said. "I just left a mutual friend of ours, by the way."

Ethan grinned. "Oh yeah? A certain photographer?"

"That's the one. I hear you've been texting him."

"He told you that?" Ethan asked.

Marigold scrunched up her face. "Oh, I probably wasn't supposed to say that."

"Oh no, please continue," Ethan said, making a motion with his hand.

Marigold held up both hands, backing away. "I've said too much."

"Just tell me this, are the texts annoying him, or is he playing hard to get?"

Marigold made a motion like she was zipping her lip and then turned around and headed for the door.

"Then just answer this one question. Should I keep texting him?"

Dane opened the door for her, and she met Ethan's gaze with a quick, playful nod.

Ethan pumped his fist. "Yes! There's hope."

As Dane pulled the door closed he said, "You want anything from Blue Mountain Beach Creamery?"

"Not after this encouragement. Bye." Ethan picked up his phone.

Dane shut the door and met Marigold's gaze. "You know you just unleased a beast, right?"

"Ashe loves the attention, trust me. He's playing hard to get." She shoved Dane. "Don't you tell Ethan I said that."

"I'm not helping his ass out."

"Dane cussed! Dane cussed!" Noah shouted.

"He's an adult. He's allowed, doodie pants," Jaden said.

Noah pushed the elevator button repeatedly. "Your mom's doodie pants."

Marigold giggled, and then covered her mouth. "Sorry."

Dane held his arms out to the side. "Who wants to go get some ice cream?"

"Me!" shouted all three of them.

Marigold's smile was enough to get him through the rest of the night, whatever fate that held for him.

Chapter Twelve

Marigold sat snuggled up with Dane on the couch, the boys in the floor in front of them, their eyes glued to SpongeBob. "Lucky this happened to be on," she said.

"SpongeBob is always on," Dane said.

"Really?"

Dane nodded, eyes wide like he was going slowly mad. She couldn't wipe the grin off her face if she tried. She'd actually had a wonderful time with him and the boys. Of course, the offer of Blue Mountain Beach Creamery was all she needed to hear. She was flat-out addicted to their mango yogurt, and she'd already splurged once that day. Might as well top it off.

Sitting on the deck to the ice cream place, watching the boys run around in the gravel next to the fence painted with all kinds of fun art from flamingoes to sharks, made her wonder for the first time what it would be like to have her own kids. She had never been a *kid* person. She never assumed she'd have any sort of typical life.

She remembered a time in college in an economics class on the subject of female leadership in the workplace, a professor taking a poll of the class. "How many women in here plan to get married right out of college?" Marigold watched the hands go up. "How many of you plan to work when you get married?" A few hands went down. "How many plan to work once you have children?" More hands went down. The whole process had fascinated her. These women had been so sure of their fates, so seemingly in control of their destinies. Marigold had never assumed anything about her future, especially that she would meet the perfect man who would make enough money to support her and their children in such a robust way that she would be able to stay home without bringing in income.

She had known better. The parade of losers she'd dated in high school had disrespected and humiliated her in more ways than she could count. Her junior prom date had taken her to the back of their limo during the announcement of the king and queen for a *surprise*. He'd unzipped his pants and shown her his package, saying, "I want you to be the first girl who gives me a blow job." She'd been less than honored.

Marigold had sworn to herself that she wouldn't settle for one of those assholes, and she hadn't. Now, at thirty years old, she sat next to a guy who wanted to take his time with her, and she'd run out on him as a result. Who was the asshole now?

She checked her phone for the time. 8:45. "I should go."

"You don't have to. You're welcome to stay until after they get picked up." He raised his eyebrows, causing her belly to spin around.

"Thanks, but I want to go ahead and leave before she gets here." Was her nose growing? Because that was the fattest lie she'd told in a while. She desperately wanted to get a look at this woman. She was self-destructive like that. But more so, she was really curious. The woman's boys were adorable with beautiful, white-blond hair and blue eyes. She imagined their mother was equally as gorgeous. That's just what Marigold needed—a visual image of Dane's ex to torture herself with.

She stood. "It was lovely to meet you boys."

Noah turned to her with eyes like an *Oliver Twist* character. "You're leaving?"

Marigold looked at Dane for help, but he just winced.

"I need to get going so I can get my sleep for work tomorrow. You guys understand. You have school tomorrow, right?" she asked, realizing that was probably stupid. The inference was they needed their sleep, too, but how was that going to happen when their mother wasn't even coming to get them till nine. What time did kids this age go to sleep, anyway?

"Can you bring her next time, too, Dane?" Noah asked.

Dane scratched his head. "We'll see." God, this was torture. Marigold couldn't help wondering how often this really happened. He seemed to take it all in such stride, these children dropping in on his day. He'd said she hadn't dropped them off in three months, but she had to wonder if that wasn't a white lie. Dane stood. "I'll walk you to your car."

"No, stay. You can't leave them."

Dane studied the two of them, considering.

"Seriously, I got a great visitor spot, and it's Water-Color. It's virtually crime-free here. I'll be fine."

"I'll see if Ethan can walk you," he said, heading for the door.

"Dane, you're ridiculous," she said, following after him, but he was already out the front door and knocking on his brother's condo door. She had to admit, she couldn't decide if it was really cool or kind of co-dependent that the two of them lived side by side in addition to working together. But they were twins. Surely there was some super-duper connection there that she couldn't understand and probably didn't need to at this point.

Ethan answered, glaring at Dane. He held up both hands. "I was just wondering if you could walk Marigold to her car. I don't want to leave the boys."

Ethan eased up. "Of course. Let me get my shoes on."

Dane held Marigold's hand. "Thanks for coming back. Can we try again soon?"

She smiled. "Okay, but maybe a real date first?" If he wanted to take his time with her, she was going to get the full treatment.

"That'd be perfect."

Ethan shut the door behind him. "Do I need to hide my eyes while you two kiss goodnight?"

Dane punched him lightly on the arm and then gave Marigold a quick kiss before heading into his place where the boys were in the background wrestling with one another. The scene was surreal. It seemed so much like they were his that she had to remind herself that he wasn't their father.

Ethan hit the elevator button and the doors opened. "Shall we?"

She headed in. "This really isn't necessary."

"It's like five steps." He held up his wrist, showing off his tracker. "Besides, I get credit for them."

She held up her phone. "I know. Ever since I discovered the app on this phone that keeps up with steps, I don't take a single one without it." She smiled at him. "So, did you try again with Ashe?"

He gave her a sly grin. "I did, and he took the bait. Thanks for the tip."

"No problem." She winked at him. "I'm rooting for you."

"Nice to have an insider in my corner."

The elevator doors opened, and a brunette with wide hips and bright blue eyes stopped dead in her tracks wearing an expression like she'd seen a ghost. She looked Ethan up and down, and then relaxed, but became a bit cautious. "Ethan," she said, the word coming out in a mix of relief and irritation.

"Hello, Erin. Excuse us." Ethan put his arm around Marigold protectively, ushering her away.

Marigold's heart pounded wildly as they walked toward the car, her neck craning to see back to that elevator, but the girl was out of sight, the door closing.

"Holy crap, was that her?" she asked.

"Just walk. It's taking everything in me not to turn around and go off on her."

"Oh my gosh," she said, freaked out. The girl looked nothing like she expected. Marigold thought she'd be this natural blond bombshell. "She looks nothing like those boys," Marigold said.

"Don't get me started about her, please. I'm trying so hard to be good."

They pushed through the lobby doors and Marigold led them to her parking space, but she couldn't get in the car. "Wow. Look at me." She held out her shaky hand.

He grabbed it, stilling the shaking. "Oh, please. You are Beyonce and she is Voldemort. I know that's not nice, but after what she put that boy through, I'm justified, trust me."

Marigold looked up at the building. "How did they get together?"

He pursed his lips. "I'm not altogether certain of this, but I'm pretty sure she stalked him."

"What?"

"They met at the bar in our lobby. The local paper had done a piece on us." He waved it off. "We play up the twin thing when we can to get exposure. It got some social media traction, and the next thing we know, she's at our lobby bar." He shook his head. "She said all the right things. I was even charmed by her in the beginning, if you can believe it. She had this way of making you feel like you were the most special person on the planet. She seemed truly genuine."

Marigold had known people like that. She'd had someone in college attach to her who had that ability. It was like an addiction, being around that girl...until she turned out to be nutso.

"It all changed though once those boys got involved. Dane latched onto them like nothing I've ever seen. Once he was hooked, she started taking advantage. Dropping them off for him to watch with little or no notice, hitting him up to pay for this sport or that lesson. The more attached Dane got to those boys, the more one-sided their relationship became. You know, you'd think she'd be grateful for the help, but instead, she would hold the boys over his head like leverage."

"Wow," Marigold said, taking it all in.

"Mmm," he said, glancing up in the direction of their apartments.

She leaned in. "So is it true that he's not been with anyone else for a while?"

"Oh yeah. She scared him off all women. You've been like a ray of light, bringing him out of the dark."

She smiled, liking that inference, and then sighed. "I guess I better go before she comes back down."

"Before you go, tell me two things about Ashe that I can use to hook him."

She thought about it. "He loves brunch and Vampire Weekend."

He nodded, smiling. "Noted. Thanks."

"So what are your intentions with him, anyway?" she asked.

"I'll be honest, before I met him, they were purely carnal, but now..." He trailed off, shaking his head. "I'll be lucky if don't end up proposing to him before it's all over."

She smiled. "He's pretty fantastic. Worth so much more than a one-nighter."

He gauged her. "Is he bi, by any chance?"

"Not that I'm aware of, why?"

"His Instagram is full of pictures of a beautiful woman."

"Looks like the love child of Zoe Saldana and Jason Momoa?"

He gripped her arm. "Oh my God, yes."

"That's Desiree."

"Are they together?"

She considered the question. "I'm not sure how to answer that. They're very close, I'll say that."

"Ya think? He gushes over her."

"She's all that. They have a unique relationship none of us can really figure out."

"Is she my competition?"

"Not at the moment. She's dating someone right now."

"Thank God, because it sounds like it'd be hard to compete with her."

"Are you competitive?" she asked.

"To a fault. When I get my mind set on something, I can be pretty obnoxious getting what I want."

She smiled at him. "Well, I think that's a good quality."

They stepped out of the way while a couple got into the car next to them. She glanced up at the building. "Still in there, huh?"

"Trust me, he's not having any fun."

"What do you think they're talking about?"

145

"I hope he's laying down the law, but I'm guessing if she was brazen enough to do this today, she'll do it again."

"Does she do this often?" she asked, feeling guilty for double-checking Dane's word, but the stakes were too high not to.

Ethan pursed his lips. "Not in a few months. Not that I know of, at least."

Marigold nodded at the building, and Ethan took her arm. "Don't blow him off because of this, okay?"

"Okay," she said, but without the requisite enthusiasm.

His expression dropped. "Oh, shit."

"No, I won't, really." Not at this point, at least, but if this became a thing, it'd be hard for Marigold to be a part of this kind of drama. Not that she didn't enjoy a little drama, but she wanted to be the one creating it, and it definitely wouldn't include kids. "I better get going."

He studied her, playing with her hair. "You know, if I were straight, I think you'd be exactly my type."

She gave him a look. "I bet you say that to all the girls."

"Just the ones I really like," he said with a wink.

It was strange looking at this guy who was so similar yet completely different from the guy she was starting to fall for. She went in for a hug, taking in his smell, which was clean and fresh, while Dane's was sort of earthy—both delicious, though, in their unique ways.

She pulled away. "Have a good night."

"You, too, firewoman," he said, before closing her door.

Driving the short distance down 30A toward Fiona's

place, she couldn't help wondering what was going on in that apartment. This was Dane's ex, and all signs pointed to her being horrible, but he'd once loved her, hadn't he? He for sure loved those kids, and they were who bonded him to her for longer than he'd liked. And here they were back in his life.

The last thing she needed was to get attached to a guy who was getting ready to be attached elsewhere, even if it was to kids. But these kids came with a mom, and one who had powers of persuasion, apparently. And worse, she didn't use her looks as part of those powers. She used her personality. Marigold could compete with her looks, but her personality was always how she lost out where guys were concerned. She was too much. Apparently Erin knew how to reel them in using her charm. Marigold's charm was about as useful as a pet rock.

She stopped at a crosswalk to let a couple holding hands cross the street. Lucky bastards. They were already hooked up—in love likely and on vacation where they weren't carrying a stressor in the world. At least she hoped for their sakes that they weren't.

She, on the other hand, was headed to a home that wasn't even hers, away from a guy who wasn't hers either. She needed to get her shit together, quit focusing on Dane and start focusing on this hotel—polish that business plan and present the goods. She'd take the night to get it perfected. And she would not sit around wondering when Erin would be leaving Dane's apartment.

Chapter Thirteen

Dane could not believe Erin was sitting in his living room between her boys, smiling and laughing as they regaled her with their adventure to get ice cream. Why had Dane not answered the door with the boys in tow and ushered them out along with her? She'd made herself at home instead.

"Miss Marigold let me try her mango yogurt," Jaden said.

Erin slid a look in Dane's direction. "Oh yeah? How did you like it?"

"It was actually good, even though I don't like fruit. She has a shop called Apples to Oranges."

"Oh," Erin said, looking at Jaden. "What about a store with a fruit name? Is that okay, or do you dislike that, too?"

Dane had royally fucked up here. He should never have let Marigold come along. Even though he'd offered for her to stay while Erin picked them up, he was relieved as hell when she'd said no. He didn't want Marigold and

Erin on the same planet, much less in his living room together.

He wanted Erin out of his life, now, but he had to tread lightly because of the boys. The last thing they needed was to witness him being rude to her and think it was about them.

"You guys have school tomorrow, right?" he asked.

She rubbed Jaden on the back. "Yeah, but Mondays are late mornings. They give the students an extra forty-five minutes for start time so the teachers can have meetings and plan."

"We like Mondays," Jaden said with a grin. "Shorter school day."

Dane scratched the side of his head, not believing this was happening. "Erin, may I have a word with you on the balcony?"

She glanced up at him lazily. "Go ahead. The boys can hear whatever you want to tell me."

He'd had it. "Erin, now."

She hauled herself up with a little roll of her eyes at the boys like Dane was such a stick in the mud. He slid the door shut behind her, and she walked over to the railing. "God, I miss this ocean view."

He couldn't believe that just hours earlier, Marigold stood in that same spot, revving up his engine. Now she was replaced by his worst nightmare. "Erin, what the fuck?"

"Don't cuss at me, Dane."

It was all he could do to keep himself calm. "This can't happen again."

She leaned against the railing and shrugged. "Okay."

"I'm serious, Erin."

She held up both hands. "Okay. I get it." She looked him up and down. "How are you?"

"If you do this again. I'm calling someone," he said, ignoring her attempt to derail him. He should have Googled who you call when your ex drops her kids off at your door so he could have been more specific, but he'd been a little preoccupied.

She grinned. "Who are you gonna call, Dane? Ghost-busters?"

He crossed his arms over his chest. "I'll do it."

She chuckled. "Oh, okay."

"You think I won't?"

She dropped her head to the side lazily. "Come on, Dane. You know you enjoyed seeing the boys as much as they liked seeing you. You know, I wouldn't be opposed to a bi-weekly arrangement. Every other Sunday afternoon?"

He couldn't believe he was having this conversation. "We're not doing anything like that. We were supposed to have had a clean break here. Why open all this up again now?"

She grinned, looking behind him at the sliding glass door. The boys had their faces pressed against it, licking it with crazy eyes. He couldn't laugh. It would set him back eons here. She motioned to them. "How can you not love those faces?"

Dane opened the door and pointed. "Go sit on the couch. Give your mom and me five more minutes, okay?" They tripped over each other, heading back to the couch and then plopping down.

She shook her head. "God, you're such a good dad. They don't mind anyone the way they mind you."

He rubbed his forehead, the manipulation bearing down on him, just like before. "This wasn't fair to do to me."

"I know it wasn't, but I have no help. You know that. I just needed a couple of hours to myself. And the boys needed a minute with a good male role model. They have no one."

He knew he needed to clam up here, but he couldn't help himself. "What about Chris, the alligator wrestler?"

That triumphant smile of hers that made worms crawl up his chest spread across her face. "Jealous?"

He went for the door. "It's time for you to go. Don't call my bluff on this. When you leave here, I'm gonna figure out who I need to call next time you drop them off, and you can plan on picking them up from wherever that is. Child Protective Services, or whatever."

"She's a knockout. Congratulations."

He stopped cold in his tracks and slid the door shut again. "Excuse me?"

"Marigold? Is that her name? The boys seemed to like her."

"How do you know what she looks like?"

She put one hand on her hip. "I saw her coming out of the elevator with Ethan. What a beauty. How long have you two been together?" She glanced through the glass door at his living room. "Doesn't look like she's moved in yet."

"She's none of your concern."

"Oh, she absolutely is my concern if my kids just spent the evening with her."

"You have no choice who they spend the evening with if you drop them at my house unannounced. What if I hadn't been home?"

"I saw your car."

"I could have been out with Ethan."

"I saw both of your cars. Besides, I waited in the stairwell and made sure they got inside. I'm not a monster." Dane shivered, realizing she'd been right there, hiding in the shadows earlier. She looked him up and down. "She's a little skinny for you, don't you think?" She turned to the side, rubbing her ass cheek. "Remember how much you loved my curves? I can't imagine an ass-guy like you with a girl like her."

He slid the door open. "Bye, Erin."

She held his stare, hard, a small smile creeping over her lips. "Apples to Oranges, huh? That's Miss Marigold's shop?" she asked the boys. "What kind of shop is it?"

"She has Halloween stuff up all over the place, and she's passing out candy all day on Halloween to trick-or-treaters. Can we go see her then?" Noah asked.

Erin gave Dane her worst *Fatal Attraction* smile. "I'd love to go see Miss Marigold. She sounds wonderful."

"You guys need to get home now."

Noah attached himself to Dane's legs. "No, I don't want to go. I want to live here."

Jaden's expression dropped, and a flash of anger went over his face. "We've got to go, Noah. He's not our dad."

Dane hated how mature Jaden had been forced to

become. He couldn't even begin to wonder what all had transpired since he'd been out of their lives with Erin and her boyfriends. But the fact that they had been so excited to see him and had expressed no anger toward him since they'd been there made him believe Erin had been careful about how she'd framed her relationship with Dane...likely because she wanted to keep the door open for a time like tonight when she wanted to dump them off.

"We'll see Dane soon, right Dane?" Erin asked.

"Really?" Jaden asked, his innocent hope breaking Dane's heart all over again.

"I'm not sure, actually," Dane said.

"Why can't we live here?" Noah asked, the tears starting to fall.

Erin knelt next to Noah. "It's okay, sweetie. Dane's got his own life. We need to let him move on from us."

Jaden's expression fell again. "That's what I thought. Come on, let's go." He started walking off, and then turned around and met Dane's gaze. He held up a hand in a half-wave. "Bye. Thanks for the ice cream."

Noah wailed. "No! I want to live here with Dane. I want to live here!"

Erin shouldered her bag and then picked him up, ushering Jaden out the door. Dane waited for them to get on the elevator, and then he shut the door behind him. Leaning on it, he slid to the ground, head in hand.

In just a moment, Ethan's door opened and closed, and Dane waited for the knock. "I promise I'm not here to judge. I'm just here to listen this time."

Dane shut his eyes, tightly. His brother knew him so

well. He stood and opened the door, letting Ethan wrap him in a hug. They didn't indulge in hugs often, but they both pretty much knew when the other one needed it.

They pulled apart and both collapsed on the living room couch and chair. "How was Marigold about all this?" Dane asked. Ethan never pulled punches, and by his expression, Dane was getting ready to get one in the gut.

"Freaked out. God, I forgot how scary Erin is."

"She's not scary," Dane said. "Just destructive."

"Poor Marigold was shaking after we saw her."

"What did Erin say to her?"

"Nothing. She barely even looked at her. Just acted irritated to be running into me. We exchanged icy hellos and moved on."

Dane mussed his own hair. "I just hate that I'm right back here. I thought I was done with all this."

"You are done with it. Remember that."

Dane held both hands out to his sides. "How can I be done when I'm sitting here a year out and look who's at the door?"

"Why don't we file a restraining order."

"On what grounds?"

"Freaking stalking," Ethan said.

"I let her in here. What's a judge gonna say about that?"

Ethan let out a heavy breath, looking even more worried than Dane felt. Dane reached over and patted him on the knee. "Don't worry about it. I got this."

Ethan cut his eyes at Dane. "You're putty around those kids and she knows it."

"I know. But I stood my ground tonight, just now when they were leaving. She said they'd see me soon, and I said they wouldn't. About fucking killed me, too. But I had to."

"I heard the wails," Ethan said.

"They were nothing compared to the look on Jaden's face."

Ethan shook his head. "Goddammit."

Dane knew it was bad. Ethan didn't cuss nearly as much as he did, and he rarely said that word. Dane considered him. "Did Marigold say anything I should know?"

Ethan tightened his lips into a thin line, and Dane knew he was done for. "She didn't say anything, per se, but she did look concerned."

Dane shook his head. "Can I blame her?"

"I think she just got a little freaked out."

"I'd be freaked out if the tables were turned."

Ethan was the one to pat Dane on the knee now. "I'm sorry, brother."

Dane waved him off. "Let's just get some sleep. We've got a big day tomorrow."

"Oh, yes. Our first client meeting since the announcement. We should stop at that bakery and pick up some muffins or something."

"I'll have Ginger find out what his morning drink is," Dane said.

"Good idea." Ethan stood. "You gonna be good here?"

"Yeah. Thanks."

Ethan headed for the door. "Love you."

"Love you, too." Dane collapsed back on the couch, running his phone between his thumb and his middle finger. He picked it up and stared at it, wanting so badly to call her. But he needed to give her some space. She was freaked out. The last thing to help his situation would be to smother her with a phone call or text, but he felt like he needed to say something to her—end this whacked-out day with something positive.

He pulled up a text to her.

Sleep tight.

He held his breath for a long moment until he saw the ellipsis moving across the bottom of the text thread, and he exhaled.

A gif populated his screen of a princess falling backward onto a bed and then getting swarmed by bugs. He grinned, wanting to respond, but knowing he needed to end it there if he had any hope of playing it cool with her.

Chapter Fourteen

M arigold peeked into the back room. "I'm sorry," she whispered. "I don't know where these people came from."

Sebastian waved her off. "Go, make money. I've got this."

Marigold was the luckiest girl in the world to be able to call Sebastian Peyton her friend. He was a financial and business whizz. He did consulting for a living, but Marigold knew he was independently wealthy due to some brilliant investments he'd made in his twenties. So he worked for fun. Marigold couldn't understand that concept. Sure, she enjoyed her shop, but if she could afford to pay someone to work with her year-round, she'd be there about once a week.

Marigold chatted up a group of sixty-something women who were in town from the Memphis area. She was able to chat them right into a cozy, furry white blanket, a set of cocktail plates with decked-out fish on them, and a scented candle reminiscent of salty beach air. She was even able to sell one of her last pieces of local 30A art —one of Desiree's pieces. Her sweet friend was the last of the local artists willing to go consignment with her. She couldn't blame the rest of them though. They couldn't let her hold their pieces hostage back here in this rotten location. If she ever got the customers to actually come into her store, she could sell them.

Marigold had minored in art history in college. Art had been her true passion—not creating it herself of course. When she painted it looked like something out of a kindergarten classroom. But she did love experiencing art—the stories behind the colors, the beauty, and the awe of talent. She saw the customers out, and then headed back to check on Sebastian. "How's it coming?"

"Oh, sweetie. I so hope you can pull this off. This shop is going to be incredible."

"I know, right? I was just playing with that software last night and got carried away. I was up till like two messing with it."

"The lobby has a really cool setup."

"That's based on one of my dad's current hotel layouts. I can't take credit for that."

"I love that the bar opens up to the shop. That way while people are getting hammered, they can see all the fabulous things inside and slide on over."

"Exactly. I'm going to feature local 30A art in the window to start conversations."

"I love it. When are you going to talk to your dad?"

She took a deep breath. "I guess I could do it now. Would you mind watching the shop for a minute?"

"Absolutely not." He handed her a piece of paper. "Here's your talking points for the business plan. If you need me, I'll be right out there."

She hugged him tightly. "I love you."

"Love you, too, sweetie." He kissed her on the cheek and then wiped it off like it was lipstick. "Good luck, okay?"

"Thank you." She collapsed in her chair and pulled up her father's contact. Marigold was not the daddy's girl in the family. Camellia had filled that role with flying colors. But this wasn't about getting her dad to do her bidding. This was about offering him the opportunity to open a hotel in a prime tourist spot he'd been eyeing since they came to 30A on vacation when she was in college.

Her dad picked up on the second ring. "Buttercup, how are you?"

Marigold smiled, her dad always being so much less daunting than she made him out to be in her head. "I'm good. Are you busy?"

"Well, I'm usually busy, but I'm available to talk to you."

"I just wanted to see if you'd given thought to making a bid on this land for a hotel."

"Absolutely. We've already got it submitted. Thanks for letting me know about it."

She blinked, not realizing how fast things would move. "Oh, great." She swallowed hard as she held the talking points out in front of her. "I have my business plan ready for you."

"Oh," he said, sounding taken off guard. "For the..." He trailed off.

"Gift shop?"

"Oh, sure. I'll tell you what though, what I really need is someone to manage it for me."

The air flew out of her inflated balloon. "The hotel?"

"Sure. It's what you went to college for."

"Dad, I haven't worked in a hotel in seven years."

"Yes, but you worked at one from the time you were fifteen until you left here at twenty-three. You majored in hotel management in college. You're more qualified than most candidates who would apply for the job. It's going to take a while to get the hotel built. If you come on home now, I can put you on staff here at our Savannah location letting you shadow our manager there for the next several months, then you'll be ready to go once the 30A location is built."

She rubbed her forehead, recalibrating. "But Dad, what about my gift shop? I've got the business plan for it and I used some software to put together a design I'd like to send you."

He let out a sigh that could go either way, and she held her breath. "Send me the plan and the design."

Her heart soared. "Really?"

"Sure, and copy Malcolm."

She stilled, her stomach going sour. "Malcolm?"

"Yeah. He's my right hand now. I'll tell you what, I'm so thankful you brought him on when you did. He's been a true asset for this company."

"Great," she said through gritted teeth. "So he's handling this whole deal?"

"Oh, hang on. Your mother's grabbing for the phone. I've got a meeting anyway. Love you."

"Love—"

"Angel?" Marigold's mother's voice came over the phone.

Marigold sighed. "Yeah, hey."

"How are you, honey? I haven't talked to you in weeks."

Marigold winced. "I know. I've been meaning to call. What's going on with you?"

"Well, we've got some pretty big news to tell, and I just want to make sure you're going to be okay with it."

Marigold closed her eyes, pinching her temple. Her mother did love the dramatic. "I'm sure I can handle whatever it is."

"Well, as you know, Malcolm has been with Heather, who is lovely, for almost eleven months now."

Heather, who is lovely. This was how her mother always referred to Malcolm's girlfriend. Marigold was not aware of the exact month count, but still, she mumbled, "Mmm hmm."

"Last night, we were all out to dinner at Elizabeth's, and right there, in front of all of us, he stood her up, and got down on one knee."

"Wow, that's great," she said, meaning it mostly. But she couldn't help a little irritation at yet one more person in her life who was getting engaged.

"Are you okay, honey?" her mom asked, like she had just found out she'd developed incurable cancer.

"Of course, Mom. I'm very happy for him. He's a great guy. He deserves a happy life."

"Yes, he does. And so do you. I'm just sorry you couldn't find that with one another."

If Marigold had a dime for every time her mother had made that statement, she'd be able to pay all her creditors and buy a yacht with the spare change. Of course Malcolm was a nice guy. He checked off all the proper boxes and got an A+ on paper. But he was also more locked in with her parents than she was, and that alone was enough to send her four hundred miles away.

"He must be happy if he's proposed to Heather," Marigold said.

"Well, I suppose that's true. Oh, speak of the devil. He's right here, passing by. Would you like to say hello?"

Marigold's blood pressure rose. "Actually, I'll just text—"

"Marigold?" came that familiar voice.

She winced. "Hey, Malcolm. Mom says congratulations are in order."

"Yeah, I guess so. She said yes. I was sweating it for a moment there."

Marigold didn't believe that for a second. Malcolm's *aw shucks* personality was part of what drove her crazy about him. "When's the wedding?" Marigold asked, knowing it was the cliché question, but not sure what else to say.

"We're going to wait a while. If we get this hotel on 30A, I'll be traveling quite a bit until it's ready."

"Dad just let me know you're heading up the proposal. I've got a business plan I'd like to send you regarding the hotel gift shop. Dad said to route it your way."

"Sure thing. I'll take a look."

Something sludgy rolled around in her stomach. Malcolm had her family wrapped around his pinky, but Marigold had never really fallen for his charms like they had.

"Great. I'll email it to you."

"Hopefully we can have dinner when I come to town."

"Of course. Sounds like a plan."

They hung up and she sat and stared at the wall. Now that Malcolm was involved, something told her the gift shop plan had just gotten ten times more complicated.

Sebastian appeared in the doorway. "That bad, huh?"

She dropped the phone down to her leg. "No, it was fine. It's just, the guy who I've got to go through on this is...well, there's history there."

"History. Sounds intense."

She shook her head, the old garbage from her past littering her memory. "He just sort of helped me out of a jam once, so I repaid him by ingratiating him to my father."

"What kind of jam, sweetie?" Sebastian asked, a look of concern crossing his features.

She rolled her eyes. "It was stupid, really. I was dumb, of course. Imagine my stupidity now but I'm nineteen. So dumbass-ness with even less maturity."

He squeezed her shoulder with his sweet, loving touch, reminding her that she could tell him anything and he wouldn't judge. Still, she couldn't talk about that right then.

She waved him off. "It's no big deal. It's just, he wanted to be together with me, and I tried, but I couldn't. Anyway, he just got engaged, so he should be all happy and in love. I'm sure it'll be fine." She forced a smile to put the topic to rest. "I better go ahead and send that email."

"Okay. Good luck."

"You're good to hang a minute while I do that?"

"Yep."

"Thank you, my sweet friend," she said and turned toward her computer. She drafted the email, and then, cringing, she hit send. It was like opening the door and letting a ghost of the past into her house.

These were a weird couple of days, between Dane's creepy ex Erin and Malcolm. She guessed she shouldn't judge Dane for having attachments to his past. Looked like she had them just the same, except hers wasn't dropping in unannounced with two little boys.

As Marigold came back out front, both her phone and Sebastian's dinged simultaneously. Sebastian pulled his out. "Group text, I presume." He read it while Marigold greeted a customer who walked in the door.

"Barbecue at the O'Neils' house," he said.

"You mean at Chase's house?" Marigold said with a smile. "They're not married yet."

"Oh, but they will be. Give it ten more seconds."

"They just got together a few months ago."

"Yes, but they're in their mid-thirties." He tapped on his wrist. "Time's a-tickin'."

"Shayla doesn't strike me as the type who would let a biological clock make decisions for her."

"I'm not talking about Shayla. I'm talking about Chase. I caught him at the Target in PCB the other day looking at baby furniture."

"He was probably buying a gift for someone."

"Oh, no he wasn't. His face went beet red when I saw him and he sang like a canary. Told me it was all he could do to keep his cool in front of Shayla, because he didn't want to rush her, but that he was ready to have a house full of kids with her."

She leaned against the counter, crossing her arms over her chest. "God, how nice would it be to be adored like that."

"You don't want kids right now though, do you?"

"Me? Oh, hell no. Although, those boys that were at Dane's place last night were pretty fun to be around."

"Boys at Dane's?"

The customer approached the counter with a neck-lace. "I'll tell you later," she said under her breath. Smiling at the customer, she said, "You ready?"

When Marigold got home from the shop, she was surprised to find Fiona home and Bobbie there. Still there? Last night, they'd been in Fiona's room, mostly silent with the occasional moan or giggle seeping through the wall. Marigold had put in her earbuds while she worked on the software, letting the sounds of St. Vincent and Jade Bird drown them out.

Fiona typically worked the bar on Monday nights. She worked it every night pretty much, giving herself the occasional Sunday night off, which she'd done last night. But two nights off in a row? This was getting serious.

"Hey," Fiona said from the kitchen with a dreamy smile. "Come have dinner with us. You're just in time."

Bobbie wrapped a long, thin arm around Fiona's waist. "We experimented. Sort of a Mediterranean thing."

Marigold pointed to her bedroom. "I actually just stopped by here to put some workout clothes on," she lied.

Fiona eyed her, knowing this wasn't something Marigold did unless she was on a kick, and there was no such sign of a kick. "Come on, eat with us. We'd love to have the company."

Bobbie bit Fiona's ear, causing her to grin like mad. Fiona shooed her away, clearly for the sake of Marigold only. Marigold loved affection as much as the next gal, but she had to wonder how much nonstop touching two people could do before it got old.

"Save me some. I'll get it after my run." Walk. She'd definitely be walking. But the word *walk* seemed too easy to be talked out of.

Bobbie popped something into Fiona's mouth and Marigold took that as her cue to head into her room. Five minutes later, she was suited up and headed out. "Bye!" she said as she shut the door, their reply delayed as the two of them probably forgot she existed for the moment.

She kicked off her shoes and left them on the deck before hopping down the stairs to the beach. She stood there breathing in the ocean air a moment like it could take her stress away. Sometimes it could.

She glanced in both directions. *Go right*, she told herself, *Go right*. Right was safe and far from any temptation. But left was so alluring. She was just walking by. It wasn't like she was going to stop in at his house or throw seashells at his window. She was on a walk. That was it.

As she got closer, she found that she had gravitated away from the shore, gradually moving inland. He wasn't outside, of course, but his sliding glass door was open, and his TV was on. The idea that he was right there sent a sweet shiver through her chest. That was probably just the evening chill.

Her feet took her closer to his place. Just as she was getting ready to walk away, she saw movement in his unit as he walked into the living room from one of the other rooms. Her belly did a backflip as he looked up and caught her gaze. He stopped in his tracks, and then headed out to the balcony.

She pulled out her earbuds. "Hey, I had no idea this was your building," she lied.

"I had no idea you were a beach-walker."

"Oh, yeah. Every night. Sometimes two or three times a night. Sometimes I don't even sleep I'm walking so much."

He smiled at her. "How come I've never seen you out here?"

She put her hands on her hips. "Hum. That's odd. You should have seen me. You're probably just too busy watching *Twilight* to take a look out your balcony."

"Ah, that's it," he said.

This was all very Romeo and Juliet with him on the balcony and her on the beach. Except for it seemed she was Romeo in this scenario. Story of her life. "Have you gotten your exercise in for the day?" she asked.

"You mean besides those eight hours I spent at the gym bench pressing triple my weight? No, I don't guess so." She loved that he was playing along.

She tossed her hands out to the sides. "Well?" Her heart skittered as his smile widened.

He held up a finger. "Hold that thought."

She flipped through her phone while she waited, keeping her eyes trained on it as he finally approached her. She looked up at him like she was shocked. "What a coincidence, the two of us bumping into each other like this."

He pocketed his hands, the cutest closed-mouth grin on his lips that she could just eat. "Mmm hmm."

"So I see you're a survivor. Night with two cute little boys in the books, huh?" she asked.

He pulled his hands out of his pockets and squeezed her upper arms. "I'm so sorry about all of that."

"You have nothing to apologize for, Dane."

"I wasn't sure how you'd be feeling about all of it today. That's why I didn't text. I was trying to give you a little space."

"And I end up on your doorstep." She pointed at him. "See, I told you I overstepped."

He wrapped his arms around her waist and pulled her in. "I'm really happy to see you, Marigold."

Her heart free-fell at her name on his lips. "It's nice to see you as well."

"Wanna...come up?" he asked, eyebrows raised.

No freaking way was she coming up right then. She'd

been at work all day, and then she'd just walked down the salty beach. No doubt that she stunk. And she would not be having him all up in her stanky business.

She wiggled away from him. "I thought we were getting some exercise."

He let his head drop back with lazy eyes. "Really?"

She took his hand. "Sure. We live on the beach, Dane." She motioned broadly with her arm. "The Gulf of Mexico is our playground."

He followed her toward the ocean. "Then let's play."

Oh, crap. What kind of trouble was she getting herself into? "Define play," she said.

He scooped her up into his arms, honeymoon-style, and twirled the two of them around in a circle, her squealing in delight like a ridiculous rom com cliché—the obligatory montage scene where the characters were still in that pre-love, hazy phase where they couldn't get enough of one another. Except for she and Dane were nowhere near that phase yet. Where were Bobbie and Fiona? They belonged in one another's arms. Not Marigold.

He came to a stop, staring at her in that *I'm so going to kiss you right now* way, which of course, she had to blow up immediately. She flung her head back. "Okay, I get the picture." She squirmed, her signal for him to put her down, and he obliged. She stumbled away from him. "You should be embarrassed." She motioned to all the condos behind them. "You live here."

"Yeah, but none of the people here do. They're all renting. A new crop of renters will be here next week."

She made her way to the shore, him in tow. "You're

supposed to be an astute businessman. Show some decorum, please." She tried to hide her smile, but she could feel it coming through.

He held his hands up high as their feet penetrated the cold water. "I promise not to touch you again."

She cut her eyes at him as she drew in the wet sand with her foot. "Well, let's not get crazy."

"Has anyone ever told you that you're a complex woman?"

"Ha! That's a nice way of putting it."

He just smiled, staring out at the ocean, his hands pocketed. She'd gone and scared him off. She had the feeling it'd be up to her to make any further moves. That's what she got for not letting him kiss her. It was just that kisses led to other stuff, and she wasn't currently ready for other stuff—not without a shower, and even then, she still didn't know.

"So, last night went okay? After I left?" She knew she shouldn't have asked, but she couldn't help herself.

He let out a hard breath through his nose. "Yeah, as good as could be expected."

She lifted an eyebrow. "I imagine you didn't expect it to go well."

He shrugged wordlessly while they both studied the ocean.

"I saw her, you know," she said, looking at him for his reaction.

He nodded. "I heard."

"I was expecting a blonde. Where do the boys get that blond hair?"

"Their dad's blond. I saw a picture once. Can we not—"

"Sorry," she said.

He shook his head. "No, you have every right to be curious about all of it since you got unwillingly thrust into the situation. I'm sure that was weird. It's certainly weird for me."

She touched his arm. "I'm sorry you had to deal with that. I know you love those boys. It can't have been easy to say goodbye again."

He gave her a closed-mouth smile. "Thanks. I just hope she doesn't do that again."

She stilled. "So you think she will?"

He let out a hard breath. "I don't know. I threatened to call the cops if she did."

"And are you prepared to move forward with that if it happens again?"

He hesitated for way too long, mouth open, looking for an answer.

She nodded. "I see."

"I don't know. It's just so fucking complicated."

She winced at the hurt in his eyes. "Come here," she said, bringing him into her arms. As she held him there on the beach, his inner turmoil over this situation seemed to permeate out of him.

This was all wrong on so many levels, and she was not helping him with her back and forth. He needed a friend right now to get him through this, not the waffling tease of a girl she had been being.

He pulled away first. "Thanks." His hands slid down to her hips, making her insides go mushy. "I know this is really bad timing. I can't believe all this is happening now, just as I've met you."

"I know." She thought about Malcolm and the email or phone call that was destined to drop into her phone at any time now. "I've got some weird stuff going on, too."

He looked concerned. "Weird stuff?"

She shook her head. "It's fine. Not nearly as weird as your stuff. Just something unpleasant I'm going to have to deal with."

"Something or someone?"

She inhaled a deep breath, knowing she wasn't ready to talk to Dane about Malcolm. For sure not now while he was dealing with all of this. She pulled his hands off her hips, squeezed them, and then let them go. "I've got a proposal for you."

"Okay," he said with caution.

"We've both got a lot on our plate right now. What would you think about calling what's going on here a...friendship?"

"Oh!" he shouted, hands clutching his chest like he'd been shot. "The 'F' bomb."

She shoved him. "I'm serious. I'm sort of a mess right now, well...always, but you're kind of a mess, too, and I think if we tossed sex into this blender, it might explode," she said as she poked him in the chest, "and not in a good way."

He grinned. "I'm totally good with being your fff... your fff...I can't say it."

She stood there smiling at him, head dropped to the side. "Dane."

"No, seriously. Let's do it. Let's be friends."

She nodded. "Good," she said. But what she hoped would be a sense of relief was overcome by a stabbing pain of want. It would subside with time, surely.

He jabbed a thumb at his apartment. "We've still got the rest of the movie to watch."

She scratched her cheek, deciding whether or not she could trust herself.

He held up both hands. "I swear, Marigold, I'm not going to touch you. I like this idea, a lot. I could really use a friend right now."

"You could?"

"Yeah, absolutely. Ethan's way too close to the situation for advice, and Jesse's good to talk to but impossible to pull away from the bar."

"Are those your only friends?"

"Close friends, yeah, pretty much."

"What about Chase?" she asked.

He shook his head. "I don't know Chase all that well." He squinted at her. "Wanna go finish the movie?"

"I haven't eaten dinner yet. Do you have popcorn?"

"I have a boatload of it. Don't ever buy from a Boy Scout unless you've got a lot of cabinet space."

"How much did you buy?"

He looked guilty. "A lot."

She smiled, realizing he'd probably bought it from the boys to help support them. But every time she thought of him and them, a prick of unease got her. She definitely needed to keep this thing in the friend zone. She scrunched up her face. "I'm kind of gross. I mean, I've been at work all day, and then I've been out here walking."

He waved a hand in front of his nose. "I knew something out here stunk."

She shoved him, hard, then shoved him again, then played punching bag on him as he tried to combat her, laughing too hard to defend himself properly.

Chapter Fifteen

Fucking friends. Dane didn't want to be Marigold's friend. He glanced at her out of the corner of his eye, sitting at the other end of the couch, bowl of popcorn in her lap, feet tucked in beside her watching Robert Pattinson sparkle.

She took a sip of her beer, glued to the TV. He put his gaze on the screen just as he felt her getting ready to look at him. He acted like he was so engrossed in this stupid movie that he didn't see her look. But he was aware of her. Oh, how he was aware of her.

She wasn't wrong about wanting this *friend* label on their relationship. With last night's fiasco, the last thing he needed was to start another relationship, dragging her into his drama. But he couldn't help himself. He just wanted her so goddamned badly. Her sitting there in those knee-length, skin-tight workout pants and that tank top was more than he could handle. He'd almost asked her if she wanted a blanket a few times, but he didn't want to block the view.

She shuddered a little, and he caved. "Are you cold?"

"Hmm?" she asked, eyes wide. God he wanted to kiss her. "Oh, no. Well, maybe a little."

"You want a blanket? Or a hoodie?"

Her eyes got big. "Can I have a hoodie?"

He was unable to contain his smile around her. "Sure thing." He went and found one in his closet and brought it to her. She slid it on over her tank top, the thing swallowing her whole. But she couldn't have looked hotter in it.

She cozied back into her spot on the couch, her toes digging in between the cushions. She'd borrowed a pair of his socks, and her little feet were so cute in his big white socks, so in contrast with her stylish workout clothes. Why couldn't they just be past this irritating, uncertain part of their relationship and to the part where they were sharing that bowl of popcorn, her snuggled up to him.

He remembered why. Erin. He started paying for that relationship the day she stepped into his life, and he realized now that he may never quit paying.

But it wasn't just Erin. Marigold had mentioned that she was going through something. Weird stuff, to be exact, and she'd ignored him when he'd asked if it was a something or someone. So it was probably a guy. He should have known. How arrogant was he to think a girl like this was truly single, no matter how self-deprecating she was.

The ringer on her phone went off—a call, not a text. She picked it up and then stilled, closing her eyes like she'd just gotten news of the death of a loved one. He was pretty sure she mouthed the word *fuck*.

"Take that if you need to," he said.

"Do you mind?"

"Not at all. I'll pause it."

"No, don't pause it." She stood, bringing the phone to her ear.

"You can talk in my bedroom."

She nodded at him and then said, "Hey," with tempered enthusiasm, and then the door shut behind her.

He would not listen in. He paused the movie though, so she wouldn't miss it. The silence left her voice muffled, but understandable. *Put it on Sports-Center*, he told himself. But he was too curious to be good.

"Great. No, that's awesome. I appreciate you taking a look." She paused. "Oh, wow, I didn't realize you'd be coming so soon. Is Heather coming with you?" Another pause. "Oh, well, that's too bad. I'd like to meet her." Pause. "Yeah, definitely. I'll pick a good local restaurant for us to meet, so you can get a taste of 30A. Listen, I'm at someone's house, so I can't really talk, but I'll see you Friday, okay?"

He flipped the TV onto *SportsCenter* to mask his eavesdropping around the time she opened the door and came into the room, looking deflated. "Everything okay?" he asked.

She waved him off. "It's fine. Just a minor annoyance." She nodded at the TV. "As you were."

He turned the movie back on, but she didn't seem nearly as focused on it as she had been. He wanted to talk to her about whoever that was on the phone, but he didn't want to overstep. She lifted her hand to her mouth and ran her knuckle along her lips, making him wonder if she was a nail biter trying to resist.

He nudged her in the leg. "You sure you're okay?"

"Hmm?" she asked, looking up at him, and then let out a sigh once she met his gaze. She shook her head. "It's nothing, really, I promise. Just someone I've got to work with that I'd really rather not."

He nodded, wishing he could get more out of her, but she clearly wasn't ready.

She smiled. "Thank you for being so concerned. But I'm a big girl, and I got this. Now hush up before you make me miss the fight scene." She tossed a piece of popcorn at him and then put her attention back on the movie.

He settled back in, trying to watch the movie but barely able to keep his eyes off her.

Chapter Sixteen

M arigold followed a hostess to the rooftop bar of one of her favorite 30A restaurants, wishing she was coming to this place she loved with friends or, really, with Dane. They'd been texting one another all week—all silly memes and jokes, one night staying up until one in the morning texting. It was like the introduction of the *friend* word had loosened everything. The pressure between them had subsided. A little innuendo had snuck into their texts, of course, but it had remained natural and fun the entire time.

But instead of it being Dane she was meeting, it was Malcolm who awaited her. He wasn't that bad. He was just...too much. Too clingy. Too subservient to her father. Too always available for her. So available that she'd screwed up and slept with him a few years back.

That had been the straw that broke the camel's back. The whole night had left her feeling icky and ashamed of herself. She'd been transported right back to her college years where she'd sought solace in him after that cursed night...except the solace never came.

The hostess grinned at her and then motioned. "I believe this is your party?"

Marigold stumbled to a halt when she set her gaze on Malcolm sitting at a table with her mother, her father, Camellia, and her brother-in-law Pete. They finally took note of her, and then her dad grinned from ear to ear. "Surprise!"

Marigold stood there stunned, wondering why someone hadn't made teleportation a thing yet. "What are you all doing here?"

Everyone stood for hugs, and she made her way around. "It was a last-minute decision," her mother said. "We missed you."

Marigold gave her sister a look that asked for the real story. "We also wanted to see the land."

"Ah," Marigold said, appreciating Camellia's honesty. It did come in handy from time to time.

It was Malcolm's turn for a hug. "Hello, Marigold," he said in that slightly condescending tone of his. Nothing overt, but just enough to irritate her.

They all took their seats as Marigold realized the one designated for her was between Malcolm and her father. Perfect. She hesitated to sit. "Um, actually, I was planning to just have a drink with Malcolm. I'm going to a barbecue after this."

"Sweetie, we're here," her mother said, guilt in full swing.

"If I had known I wouldn't have committed."

"The party can't go on without you?" Camellia asked. There was that sisterly backup Marigold treasured.

This was so typical of her family. They wanted to *surprise* her. Marigold was calling bullshit. They were assuming that she would dump any plans she had the second she laid eyes on all of them. It wasn't a fun surprise. It was a sabotage.

Marigold rubbed her forehead, eyes closed, and Malcolm said, "Let's just do drinks and appetizers with Marigold and then let her slip away to her party. Sound good?"

Her father mumbled something as he looked at his menu, and then everyone else followed suit. Marigold met Malcolm's gaze. "Thank you," she said softly.

He gave her a smile that lingered a bit too long for her liking. "Sure."

She cleared her throat. "So, where's Heather?"

"She couldn't make it. She's a kindergarten teacher, and they don't get a lot of days off. She's saving hers for the wedding."

"Congratulations on that, by the way," Marigold said.

Camellia set her menu down. "We love Heather. She's precious."

Marigold couldn't be sure, but she thought she might sense a challenge in her sister's tone. "That's fantastic," Marigold said, wishing she hadn't sounded so enthusiastic. She was overdoing it. This is what her family did to her. They made her overthink everything. "So how long are you all in town?"

"Just till tomorrow morning," her mother said. "We

thought about heading back this evening but David has friends at Eglin Air Force Base. He's with them now. I'm sure he says hello."

David, her family's long-time personal pilot, was nothing if not formal and stoic. Marigold was certain he didn't say hello.

"I'm here for a few extra days, looking into some things for the possibility of this new hotel," Malcolm said.

Marigold nodded, wishing for some reason that he was headed back with the rest of them tomorrow. "So when are you all going to view the land?"

"Did it already...just before we came here," her father said.

She wasn't sure why she was shocked by this. "I would have gone with you if you'd have called."

"You had the shop to tend to, right?" Camellia asked, definitely a challenge.

"I can flip the sign to CLOSED when I need to."

Her dad waved her off. "You've already seen it, I'm sure."

"Yeah, but..." She would have liked to have imagined the space with him there, heard the insider info that was no doubt exchanged between them all when they were there.

"We can go back with you tomorrow morning if you like?" her mother asked.

Marigold closed her eyes and scratched her eyelid. "No, it's...fine. What did you all think?"

"Great location," her father said. "We debated whether we made the bid aggressive enough, but I think it's pretty solid as is."

"Me, too," Malcolm said, always the suck-up.

The server came over and her dad ordered on behalf of the table—several appetizers and two bottles of wine. Marigold cut her eyes at Malcolm and he just responded with an irritating smile. They were supposed to be talking business tonight. They were going to go over her plans for the store. But now with everyone here, that was out of the picture. She wasn't about to make a public presentation, not without notice.

She scooted back her chair. "I'll be right back." She went to the ladies' room and breathed deeply, pulling herself together. Shouldn't a person be happy to see their family? And these people weren't awful. They just had a way of making her feel inferior with every word out of their mouths...which was ridiculous. Didn't Eleanor Roosevelt say that no one could make you feel inferior unless you let them? So why was she letting them? And were they even trying?

She closed her clutch and headed back out of the bathroom to be confronted with Malcolm lurking there in the hallway. "Hey, I'm sorry. They made me promise not to tell you they were coming."

She let out a hard breath. "It's fine. I'm just a little... disappointed. I was hoping we could talk business."

"We can. We should. We could have a glass of wine with them and then scoot off somewhere?"

Marigold narrowed her gaze, not exactly sure how to take that.

"I mean, to another restaurant or wherever you're comfortable."

She checked her phone to see what time it was. "I've

got that party to get to." She could cancel. Chase and Shayla would forgive her. But she couldn't be sure of Malcolm's motives, so a set schedule for the night seemed in order. "But maybe we can connect in the next day or two. You are staying for a few days?"

"Yes, I am. That sounds good." He just sort of stood there staring at her, and then he motioned toward her. "You look great, by the way. I guess I haven't seen you in a few years, right? You're always in and out of town so quickly at Christmas and Thanksgiving."

"Well, you know. I can't afford to be away from the shop long. Day after Thanksgiving and Christmas are two of my busiest days of the year." Owning a gift shop had always come in super handy for getting out of long visits. "If this hotel works out, I'll be open 365 days a year. I'll have to eat my turkey at the register."

"Your dad mentioned you might want to run the hotel."

She waved him off as she walked out of the hallway into the open air where she didn't feel like she was conspiring for an illicit affair or something. "No, that's what he wants. I never said I wanted that."

"You could train under me in Savannah. I've been running our flagship location up until just recently. You'd be up to speed by the time this location was built. Or if you like, you could run the Savannah location."

What was he going on about? She forgot how *Malcolm* he was...figuring out her life before she could even think about it herself. "Why don't we just see if we get the bid first, then we'll take it from there. Don't you think?"

"Sure," he said, looking a little hurt. "What's the story with your lease, anyway? How much longer do you have in that spot?"

"Oh, um..." She scratched her scalp, wishing she was a better liar. "It's over at the end of November." She hated how his face lit up. "But I was thinking about seeing if he'd go month-to-month, at least until the place is rented. But enough about that. Let's get back to the table."

"Of course." He held out his arm, motioning her toward the table. As they walked that way, her phone dinged, and she pulled up a text from Dane.

I'm not stalking you, I swear. But Chase invited Ethan and me to his cookout and so...

She waited a second and then a picture populated her screen of Dane's beautiful face with the backdrop of Chase's pool with some familiar faces in the background. She grinned, her heart warming up for the first time all evening. He texted again.

Where the heck are you?

She glanced up to find herself staring at her family, who were sipping glasses of wine and staring at menus.

"Sit down, honey," her father said, a command, not a request. "We've decided to order dinner. You can eat with your friends anytime. We're here now."

She glanced at Camellia who had a wine glass close to her lips as she looked around the place like she was bored out of her mind, and at her mother who was pointing at the menu and consulting Peter about something.

She tucked her clutch up under her arm. "As I said, I

have plans. I hope you all have a safe flight home tomorrow." She turned to Malcolm. "I'm happy to do a call or even a video chat with you about the plans when you're ready." She held up a hand in a wave and exited before anyone could guilt her otherwise.

Chapter Seventeen

Dane was starting to regret having come to Chase's barbecue. He and Ethan had gotten the invite just yesterday when they ran into Chase at lunch at MarketCafé in Seagrove. Chase had been in the best mood, mentioning his new girl, Shayla, about ten times during the one encounter. Dane had been envious. He had someone he was excited about, too, but his someone had thrown him the F-bomb earlier in the week.

At first, Dane had tried to play it cool and not text or call her. That lasted about six hours into Monday. When he decided he couldn't take it anymore, he texted her his favorite joke about the three-legged dog that walks into a saloon looking for the man who shot his paw. Of course, that joke was better told than written, but she still got it, and the floodgates opened to a week full of texts.

He hadn't mentioned anything today about coming to Chase's barbecue. She hadn't mentioned it to him all week, but he knew she was invited. She was in Chase's inner circle of friends, and he'd overheard someone asking where she was and her friend Sebastian saying she'd be t here soon.

He was probably overstepping. He started getting paranoid and sent her a text letting her know he was there, just because he didn't want her to walk in and see him and think he was stalking her. But she hadn't responded, which had made him all jittery and nervous.

"She's prettier than I am, isn't she?" Ethan asked, staring at the beautiful girl who Ashe Bianchi often posted on his Instagram.

"God, I hope so," Dane said.

Ethan nudged him. "No, seriously. Who's hotter, her or me?"

Dane gave him a look. "How am I supposed to answer that objectively?" Ethan waved him off like Dane was the one not making sense. Dane nudged him. "Go talk to him."

"I can't be the first one to approach. Whoever approaches first loses the upper hand."

"I think you lost that the first night we met him."

"I lost some ground, but I've been working on gaining it back. We've been playing this game over text. Whoever texts last loses."

"Sounds mature," Dane said, and then took a drink of his beer.

The door to the house closed and Chase hustled down the stairs and toward them. He'd been tied up when they came in and had directed them to the beer by the pool, so they'd been standing there solo for a few minutes. Chase held out his big banana hand for Dane to shake. "What's up, man? I'm so glad the two of you made it."

"Thanks for the invite," Ethan said. "Your house is amazing. Your kitchen's new, huh?"

"About a year old," Chase said.

"Who did it?" Dane asked.

Chase pointed his beer bottle toward a woman across the pool standing with Cassidy Anderson of Seaside Sweets fame. "Seanna Evans. Perry at the time. She just married Blake Evans last summer. You guys know him?"

"I've seen him around," Dane said, Ethan nodding along. "Have we met her?"

"Probably. She works with me now. She was looking for work and I was looking for someone to get me organized. Win-win." His girlfriend, Shayla, stepped up beside him, and he took her into his arm, beaming. "Have the two of you met Shayla Harrison yet?"

The dark-haired beauty squinted, searching them, and finally landed on Dane, pointing. "We've met, right?"

Dane nodded with a smile. She was good.

Ethan held out his hand. "We have not. Hello." He looked her up and down, pleased. Ethan was so superficial sometimes, drawn to attractive people like a magnet.

Shayla shook his hand. "You guys work together, right?"

"Yes. Property development," Ethan said. "What do you do?"

"Pool cleaning," Shayla said, and Ethan turned his

head to the side like a dog trying to make sense of an odd sound.

"Harrison Pool Supply?" Dane asked, making the connection. He'd thought it was a guy named Bo who owned that business, but he could have had it wrong.

Shayla nodded. "Right."

"Ah," Ethan said, as if it all made sense now.

"It's not my business though," Shayla said. "My brother owns it." She pointed to a guy tending to the grill in the outdoor kitchen.

"Mmm," Ethan said, looking the guy up and down. Dane was this close to shoving Ethan in the pool to cool him off. Dane had to admit the guy was buff and had a certain *likability* about him, but Ethan needed to cool it. Dane figured Ethan's inability to land Ashe Bianchi was more than his libido could take.

The door opened, and a woman with short blond hair stood in the doorway. "Chase, where are your salad tongs?"

Chase looked lost, and so Shayla said, "I'll be right there." She turned to them. "It was really nice meeting you. I hope you're hungry. We've got more food than we can shake a stick at in there."

"Chase, go get that clean platter on the counter inside," Shayla's brother shouted, looking down at the grill. He glanced up distractedly, then did a double-take when he saw Ethan and Dane, their presence seeming to take him by surprise. He waved with his spatula in acknowledgment of them.

"Aye aye," Chase said. "I'll be back."

"No hurry," Dane said, making sure Chase didn't feel the need to babysit Ethan and him.

Ashe Bianchi caught Ethan's eye and held up his cup in greeting, smile in check.

"Oh, he so wants me," Ethan said, holding up his beer in return.

Dane shook his head at his brother. "We need to go talk to someone before these people think we're anti-social."

"Let's go talk to Cassidy. We know her."

Dane shrugged and they headed that way. He couldn't help but wonder if Marigold had come in the front door and was inside talking to Shayla and that blond woman. But he was no better than Ethan. He knew he had to play it cool. As stupid as it was, the overeager one was the one to lose. She'd been the one to declare them friends, so the ball really was in her court.

They approached Cassidy, who was deep in conversation with Seanna and another guy Dane thought looked familiar. When Cassidy caught their approach, she smiled. "Hello there. I was just getting ready to head your way."

"That's what all the girls say," Ethan said, smiling and giving her a side-hug. Dane hated how familiar Ethan got with people so quickly. It made Dane uncomfortable because then they would look at him like they might have to hug him, too. But in this case, Cassidy just smiled at him genuinely, no awkwardness. He'd rarely seen a person so comfortable in their own skin.

Dane held out a hand to Seanna. "I'm Dane. I'm not sure we've met."

"Seanna. I definitely know who the two of you guys are," she said, shaking Dane's hand and then Ethan's. She grinned at Dane, and he wondered if she was a friend of Marigold's and knew something he didn't.

The well-dressed guy next to her held out a hand. "Sebastian Peyton. We met the night of the bonfire." He turned to Ethan. "We have not met yet."

"Ethan Knight," Ethan said, shaking his hand with interest.

Sebastian looked him up and down. "I definitely know who you are." He glanced discreetly at Ashe Bianchi and then back at Ethan with a small grin. Ethan's eyes sparkled. Point Ethan.

"These are the guys bidding on Marigold's hotel?" Seanna asked.

Sebastian looked them up and down. "Yes. The competition. I've been researching the two of you."

Ethan raised an eyebrow. "Hope you haven't found any skeletons."

"Unfortunately not. You two appear squeaky clean and like you do excellent work," Sebastian said, pursing his lips.

"How do you factor in here?" Dane asked.

"I'm Marigold's business consultant," Sebastian said.

"Ah," Dane said, recalling Marigold telling him about Sebastian. "She speaks very highly of you."

"She should for what I charge."

Cassidy nudged him with her elbow. "Oh, I'm sure you're not charging her anything."

Sebastian held a finger to his lips. "Shh, don't tell these two our secrets. I'm going for intimidation here."

He let a smile peep through at the two of them, and Dane could see why Marigold liked him so much.

"Speaking of, there's our favorite gift shop owner now," Seanna said.

Dane turned to find Marigold walking down the steps, his stomach like a kite being caught by the wind. Bo, the guy at the grill, turned around at the sound of the door shutting and grinned from ear to ear at the sight of Marigold. She went to him and he took her into his arms for a hug, picking her up off the ground as they embraced.

Dane swallowed hard, trying not to let the little green monster invade his brain. He knew Marigold was close with this group, and he also knew how likable she was. Of course these guys loved her. Dane just had to swallow that pill. What he couldn't understand was why she wasn't hooked up with any of them.

After the two of them spoke for a moment, Bo pointed at the cluster Dane was standing in, and Marigold turned toward him. She scanned the group, and then locked gazes with Dane with a smile that erased all of his neurosis from the past few minutes.

She walked around the pool, stopping at an open cooler full of drinks and retrieving a white can before heading their way. Hugging her way through the group, she hit everyone else first before coming to him. He, for some reason, didn't get a hug.

"Hey, stalker," she said, grinning at him.

Dane pretended to sniff his underarm. "Do I stink?"

She leaned in close, taking a whiff of his neck, waking up his midsection which he batted down with a quick image of Jabba the Hutt. "You actually smell pretty nice for a boy. Why do you ask?"

"Everyone got a hug but me."

"Did you want one?"

"No. Well, maybe."

She reached around him, pressing her body against his, finishing off with a kiss to his neck that made him want to pick her up and whisk her right out the door with him. She pulled away. "Will that suffice?"

"I guess I'd call it adequate."

She lifted her drink to her lips and took a sip through a smile. God he wanted her. Her gaze focused on Ethan who had apparently made his way to Ashe at some point. "Looks like that's finally coming together."

"We'll see how Ethan does."

"You don't have much faith in your brother, do you?"

"He usually gets what he wants, but I think he's met his match this time."

She giggled. "For sure. But I think Ashe is super interested. I've never seen him work it like this before."

"Good for him."

She nodded and sipped her drink.

"What are you drinking?"

She looked at the can. "Oh, it's one of those seltzer things with alcohol. You wanna try it?" She offered him her can and he sipped from it just to accept her offer of familiarity.

"That's pretty good."

"Mmm." She nodded, glancing around with that grin that made him feel like he was back in middle school with a crush on a girl for the first time. "So," she said, giving him a look. "How has your week been?"

He lifted an eyebrow, not sure what she was getting at. "Good."

"Did you have any...surprise visitors?"

"Ah," he said, catching on. "No."

She squinted at him. "You sure?"

"You don't believe me?"

"I'm just trying to help, as your friend...or maybe I'm trying to understand. I don't know. I'll butt out." She shifted, glancing around.

He squeezed his eyes shut, and then shook his head. "No, don't...butt out that is. It's confusing, and it's messy. It's a lot, and I wish I had clear answers for you."

"It's not for you to explain to me. The whole point of this friendship thing is for me to be there for you when you need to talk about it, or whatever."

He stared at her, wanting to tell her that he didn't want her as a friend. He wanted her in his bed, and in his life. He wanted to know her. He wanted to play putt-putt with her and walk on the beach with her and take her out to nice dinners and cuddle up on his couch with her—all those things people did when they were in new relationships.

But that wasn't his life. His life was...complicated. His life included two goofy kids who he loved more than anything on the planet, and it included their mother who was capable of throwing pipe bombs into his life at any moment, just as she'd done that week.

A loud whistle sounded and everyone turned to find

Chase standing by the door to his kitchen. "It's all ready. Come make your plates inside and we'll eat out here."

Dane exhaled a deep breath, partially thankful to be saved by the bell, but also wishing he had decent answers for her. "Are you hungry?" was all he could think to say.

"Yep," she said, and headed that way, leaving him behind with a heart that was becoming heavier by the moment.

Chapter Eighteen

The girls plus Sebastian all sat on Shayla's king-sized bed, having just watched a bit from a comedian Seanna had discovered that she'd been dying to share with everyone. "Is she not hysterical?" Seanna asked.

"I'm watching the rest of that when I get home," Sebastian said. "I may have peed a little."

"Wouldn't be the grossest thing on this bed," Seanna said, and Shayla knocked her on the head with a throw pillow.

"I changed the sheets this morning, not that we're even sitting directly on the sheets here," Shayla said.

"Didn't your housekeeper come today?" Sebastian asked.

Shayla winced. "I'm still not comfortable with that."

Desiree nudged her. "Girl, just relax into it. Let someone clean your house. You're providing a job."

"That's the main reason I haven't canceled yet. I hate to take someone's job."

"Money takes a little while to get used to," Sebastian said. "Give it a year, you'll be paying someone to give you in-home spa treatments."

Shayla rolled her eyes, a little smile on her lips. She put her attention on Marigold. "So what's going on downstairs?"

Marigold glared at her. "I see your attempt to divert the attention elsewhere."

Seanna nudged her. "It's working. So tell us about Dane."

Marigold narrowed her gaze. "You know he's not my date, right?"

"You may not have come here with him, but I'd be willing to bet my right arm you're leaving with him," Seanna said.

Marigold rolled her eyes, her cheeks heating up. "You're ridiculous."

"Oh, yes. So ridiculous," Desiree said, glancing around at the group. "The two of them clearly have zero chemistry."

"For sure," Sebastian said, rolling his eyes. "I think I got a contact high just from sitting across from the two of you at dinner."

"I haven't seen two people with happier smiles on their faces since we took Bo's nephews to Disney World," Maya said.

"We're just...friends," Marigold said, feeling her nose growing.

"Oh, please," they all said in one form or another.

She couldn't help her grin. "What? We are." She dodged a throw pillow flying at her.

"Seriously," Seanna said. "What's the holdup here?"

She exhaled a deep breath, not wanting to get into it all, but these were her closest and dearest friends who she trusted implicitly. "He's got some...baggage."

"Ha!" Cassidy said from the peanut gallery.

Everyone got quiet and waited for her to expound upon her harrumph. Cassidy was a woman of few words, and when she spoke, people listened up.

She glanced up from her spot on the ottoman at the end of the bed where she was flipping through a magazine. She closed it and gave Marigold a kind smile. "I think once you reach your thirties, baggage is inevitable. It's just a matter of whether or not you can carry it."

They all swung their gazes to Marigold. "Well," Seanna said. "Can you carry it?"

Marigold rubbed her forehead, thinking. "It's baggage of the kid-type."

Shayla looked confused. "I didn't realize Dane had kids."

"He doesn't. They belong to his ex."

"He's not the father?" Maya asked.

"He's not, but you should see him with these boys." Marigold covered her heart with both hands. "He's fantastic. I mean I don't want to think about kids now or maybe ever. But man, if I wanted them, my ovaries would be pulsing right about now."

"You met the kids?" Shayla asked.

"Not on purpose. She dumps them off on him unexpectedly, apparently. I was over there...well, I had been over there, and it all went wrong so I left, and then I went back to apologize, and there they were. I thought I was on

Planet Zotar for a minute until he explained it all. I mean, he's not explained all of it, but enough to where I get the picture." She exhaled a deep breath. "I just don't know if I can get into something like this. There's a lot going on there."

Maya's eyebrows went up. "Sounds like it." Maya was the sensible one of the bunch, the one who had all her ducks lined up perfectly until she met Bo and he threw a wrench the size of Texas into her world. If Maya could upend her life for a fantastic man what hope did Marigold have to resist Dane?

Sebastian squeezed Marigold's leg. "Take your time, sweetie. You're in no rush here."

Marigold nodded, but all she could think about was the ticking clock. Her shop was only going to be open in its current location until the end of November. That was a fact. She had not renewed her lease. If she knew the hotel would be built, she could limp along until that was done and take out a cheap lease on an apartment in Panama City or Fort Walton. She could work at a grocery store or a department store for the interim. But if the hotel wasn't happening, she was going to have to fall back on her family.

Sure, it felt wonderful to put them in their place earlier that night, but she had to face facts. No matter her path forward, she needed them. Either she was going into business with them—a partnership with her shop and their hotel, or she was going home to work in their business if she couldn't get a decent job soon. The thought did not bring joy to her heart. And if she was being honest with herself, getting in bed with them, even if it was through a partnership, may not be the wisest choice. She just didn't know what other realistic choice she had.

Seanna started talking to Sebastian about something, and the group sectioned off into separate conversations. Marigold nudged Desiree. "I've got your check for the piece I sold. It's in my purse downstairs. Don't let me forget it."

"You know you've sold more of my paintings than anyone?"

"Seriously?" Marigold asked.

"Oh yeah. I make most my money off graphic design."

"But painting is your real passion," Marigold said.

"Definitely. How do you get them sold?"

Marigold shrugged. "I love them. It's easy to brag on them and point out the emotions they evoke in me."

Desiree narrowed her gaze. "When one of us wins the lottery, let's open an art gallery together. I'll paint, you sell."

"Deal," Marigold said with a smile, genuinely thinking she'd love nothing more. As they joined in a conversation with Shayla and Maya, Marigold zoned off into la-la land imagining herself selling art exclusively. She wouldn't compete with the uber-classy galleries around town. She'd go for quirky and down to earth. Sure, this was an area that attracted people with lots of money, but the more affordable communities like Seagrove and Seacrest attracted people who couldn't afford to spend thousands on one art piece. She'd love to serve that clientele. It meant more paintings for less money, but how many starving artists would love to sell a piece for a couple hundred bucks?

She imagined herself locking up the gallery like she did her store, and then shouldering her purse and walking down a little imaginary path to a house up on the cliff of the sand dunes overlooking the beach. She'd get a glass of wine, kick off her shoes, and meet Dane on the covered deck where she would cozy up to him on a loveseat.

"Right, Marigold?" Shayla asked.

"Hmm?" she asked, looking around. "Oh, yeah." They all started laughing. "What?"

"Where were you just then?" Seanna asked. Marigold hadn't even realized she was a part of the conversation.

Marigold shook her head. "An impossible dreamland."

Chapter Nineteen

As Dane found was the case with most parties that had mainly couples, the women and men separated like they were at a middle school dance. Chase's girlfriend had taken the women along with Sebastian upstairs, and they had not returned. Ashe and Ethan had mysteriously disappeared, leaving Dane glad he'd been the one to drive Ethan and him to this party so he wasn't stuck.

Chase, Bo, Blake, and Dane had all been working to clear the dishes and clean up the kitchen, which didn't take long with them all pitching in. Chase started the dishwasher and then scrubbed his hands together. "Well, that's all that can be done for now. Let's play cards while they're tucked away up there."

Bo, who was clearly quite at home in Chase's house, opened a kitchen drawer and pulled out a deck. Surveying the room, he said, "How many do we have, four of us? Perfect. We can play Spades."

"I'll only play Spades if I can be partners with Bo 'cause he cheats," Blake said.

"I do not fucking cheat," Bo said, pulling a chair out. "I just overlook a card from time to time."

"If you'd line 'em up alternating red and black you could see 'em better," Blake said.

"You line your cards up how you want and quit worrying about how I do mine."

"We'll play Hearts," Chase said, glancing at Dane. "Have you played Hearts?"

"Once or twice, but I'll figure it out."

"It's easy," Bo said. "We're gonna lay cards in rounds of tricks. Just remember you don't want to drag a trick unless it's free of hearts."

"Or the Queen of Spades," Blake said.

Bo widened his eyes at Blake. "Will you let me tell it, asshole?" Blake shrugged, and Bo turned back to Dane. "Hearts are worth a point each and the Queen of Spades is worth thirteen points. You don't want points in this game, so if you can avoid it, don't win any tricks with hearts or the Queen of Spades."

"Unless he wants to shoot the moon," Chase said.

Bo tossed a beer cap at Chase who batted it away. "Will the two of you—"

"Just deal the damn cards before we all die of boredom," Chase said.

Dane smiled to himself as Bo dealt. These guys reminded him of his buddies from college with whom he'd done a bad job of keeping in touch. He missed close friendships with guys who felt like brothers, which was clearly how these guys were with one another.

"So, Dane," Bo said, dragging his cards but not looking at him, "what's going on with you and Marigold?"

"Subtle as a rhino," Blake said, organizing his own cards.

"Well, beating around the bush just wastes time, and so does having to deal with your unhelpful comments," Bo said.

"Leave him alone," Blake said.

"Oh, 'cause you're not curious at all."

Blake raised an eyebrow, staring at his cards.

"That's what I thought," Bo said.

Dane smiled, keeping his mouth shut.

Bo stared him down. "Well?"

"Hmm?" Dane asked, playing dumb.

Bo gave him an exhausted look. "Well at least tell me how long you've been dating."

"Well, we're not really dating, I don't think."

"You don't think?" Blake asked.

"Oh, so now you're interested," Bo said, and Blake gave him the finger.

"They're getting to know each other," Chase said. "Give him some time."

"She actually just wants to be friends," Dane said.

Chase looked up at him. "She said that?"

"Well, yeah," Dane said.

Chase looked back at his cards. "I'm gonna keep my mouth shut."

"Can we get that in writing?" Blake asked.

Chase laid down a card. "You can get my foot up your ass."

They played a couple of rounds in silence, and then Bo dragged a trick and looked at Dane. "Don't give up."

Dane nodded, and they all kept playing, Blake and Chase both looking as if they were holding back grins.

Seeing the girls and Sebastian coming down the staircase, Chase put his cards facedown. "There they are. The most beautiful women in Walton County."

Sebastian held his arms out wide. "Why thank you."

Chase winked at him. "You know you're my favorite."

"Of course I do. But Bo's my favorite."

Bo grinned. "I always knew I was."

Seanna rubbed Blake's shoulders. "You ready, good-lookin'?"

Blake set down his cards. "Sorry guys, she's way hotter than any of you."

Cassidy shouldered her purse. "I'm gonna head out, too."

Desiree jabbed a thumb at Cassidy. "She's my ride."

"Let me grab that check for you," Marigold said, heading to the other room.

Dane dragged all the cards, stalling until Marigold got back. He hadn't come with her, but God knew he wanted to leave with her. As people started grabbing their purses and dishes, several of them hugged him and he told them how nice it was to meet them. Dane wasn't sure he'd ever been around a kinder group of people. It made him realize how isolated he'd become, sharing his world with basically just Ethan. His cousin Celia came into town somewhat frequently, and he always made an effort to see her, and he was always sure to have lunch at Jesse's bar a couple of times a week. But other than that, he'd made no efforts to surround himself with a group like this one.

Finally, Marigold made her way to Dane with a smile. "It was a nice surprise, getting to see you tonight. You have no idea how glad I was to get your text. I was in the process of being sabotaged by my family. You were like a beacon of light in the train tunnel."

He lifted his eyebrows. "Wow. That sounds intense."

"Yeah, well, I weathered it, thanks to you."

"Man, and all I had to do was send a text."

She giggled and then gave him a closed-mouth smile. "Mmm hmm."

He couldn't take how much he wanted her. "So, where are you headed now?"

"Home, I suppose...unless there's a sock on the door handle, then I guess I'll go sleep on the beach."

He nodded, his heart rate rising already. "Ah. Beach bum. I should have known."

"I know. I'm a menace. I'm an embarrassment to the South Walton beaches."

He smiled, looking away from her so she couldn't see just how much he wanted her. "We still have those movies to watch," he said, hoping like hell he was reading her signs correctly.

Bo showed up holding his hand out to Marigold. "Give me your keys. You're blocking us in. I'll bring 'em right back."

"No, it's fine. I'm coming." She turned to Dane. "I'll see you later."

He nodded, not knowing what that meant. Later tonight? Later, as in sometime in the future when they happened to see each other again? He watched her walk out the front door, turning back to him with a smile and a wave just before she shut the door.

Chase put his big hand on Dane's shoulder. "You're an absolute moron if you don't go for her."

Shayla rolled her eyes with a smile as she moved past them and headed out to the back door. "Y'all grab a beer and join me when you're done gossiping."

Dane cut his eyes at Chase once Shayla was outside. "You were single for years and didn't go for Marigold...or did you?"

Chase let out a deep breath. "That's an involved story." He glanced out at Shayla, who was settling into a chaise lounge with her phone, and then he turned back to Dane. "I came close to going there a few times, but I wasn't in a good place, and I wasn't sure if she was either. She was a huge flirt before I met Shayla and we cut up all the time, but she never gave me a vibe that made me feel like I could open that door. And to be honest, I didn't really want to. I was sleeping around a lot back then and she was a girl I could just hang with and not have that complication screwing things up." He held up a hand. "Now, I'm only human, so I'm not going to sit here and say I didn't think about it, especially a handful of times when we were drinking and it was just the two of us. But I liked her so much as a cut-up buddy, I just wasn't ready to risk that."

Chase looked outside at Shayla lying back in the lounge chair with her eyes closed. "When Shayla came along, it was like something out of a dream. I'd never felt like that before, even with my ex-wife. I was so thankful I wasn't hooked up with anyone and neither was she. I swear, I'm not a religious man, but if I was, I'd say God or fate or something stepped in, because I can't imagine my life without Shayla now. It just seems like everything's exactly like it should be."

Dane nodded. "That's nice, man."

Chase considered him. "You know I talk a lot, right?"

"Mmm," Dane uttered, holding back a smile.

Chase waved him off. "I'll shut up, but before I do I just want to tell you that Marigold is worth whatever trouble you have to go through. If you're into her, and by the looks of the two of you tonight at dinner I'm guessing you definitely are, you need to stay the course. She's funny and she's real and honest, and one of the best friends I've ever had. To see her hooked up with a guy like you would do nothing but make me smile, man."

Dane didn't need it, but he certainly appreciated Chase's stamp of approval. "You smile most of the time anyway."

"Well, that's true. I guess I'm just full of shit. Let's go have a beer by the pool."

Dane took a look at Chase's girl out by the pool and thought about his own girl...or the one he wanted to be his...whose *later* may have meant tonight. He held out his hand to Chase. "I think I'll head out."

Chapter Twenty

After half an hour of driving around and then sitting in a parking place in front of Dane's condo, Marigold found herself standing in front of his door. Her fist was poised to knock, her whole body pinging around like a pinball machine. She could totally just walk away and continue her years-long celibacy run. She was comfortable in her celibacy. There were no risks involved. Safety, stability. These were things Marigold needed in her life. Having sex and opening herself up to all kinds of liability didn't provide safety and stability. Yet here she stood.

The door opened with her fist still ready to knock. He must have heard the elevator ding. There he stood wearing a UK T-shirt and a pair of black athletic shorts, giving her a little glimpse at his yummy thighs that she hadn't yet seen, not helping her need to stay safe and stable.

She adjusted the spaghetti string of her purse. "I was just in the neighborhood."

Taking her hand, he pulled her inside and closed the door behind her. Without further ado, he reached down and kissed her, slow and soft, his hand gripping her hip. She let out a groan of pleasure to rival one of a porn star. It'd been so long since she'd been kissed with this much intention that she supposed her inner porn star needed a release.

He backed her against the door, kissing her like the zombie apocalypse had come and was getting ready to end them both, and then pulled away, staring at her lips like he wanted them for supper.

He stepped back from her, running his hand through his hair, seeming to get ahold of himself. "I don't want to be your goddamned friend. I want to take you into that bedroom and lick every inch of your body. Then I want to make love to you for eight hours straight, and not stop until we both pass out. If you want that, too, then I'll race you to the bed. But if you don't, then I'll walk you to your car, and we'll forget this whole thing ever happened."

She stared at him, wanting desperately to know more about this licking thing.

He tossed up his hands. "Or, I guess, there's option number three, where we take it slow and—"

She jumped him, like literally, wrapping her legs around his torso. To his credit, he caught her, not missing a beat. They kissed as he walked them into the bedroom where he lay her down, his hands roaming over her body, and then he pulled away, tugging at the bottom of her shirt. "Can I take this thing off?"

"Oh, sure," she said, sitting up, freaking forgetting

how sex worked. Clothes didn't melt off, apparently, though her body was hot enough to do that.

She lifted her arms as he pulled the shirt off, and then reached around to her back and unhooked her bra. He threaded his fingers into the straps and pulled it off slowly like he was unveiling a piece of art.

"There's not much there to look at," she said.

His answer was to cover one with his hand and the other with his mouth. He certainly didn't seem disappointed.

She relaxed back and let him do his thing, switching from breast to breast like he couldn't get enough of either. God, why had she wanted to rush through this before? Finally, lifting off of her, he pulled his own shirt off, giving her the first real look at his chest. Running her hands over his shoulders and down his biceps, she realized how much she'd missed the feel of a man's skin.

"There's not much there to look at," he said, mimicking her.

She met his gaze. "Oh, yes there is."

As he moved back down on top of her, her core lit up as his hardness pressed against her. She let out a heavy breath, her body needing some sort of release.

He lifted off of her. "Am I crushing you?"

"No," she said, pulling him back down on top of her. His body on hers was like the best weighted blanket on the planet. She ran her hands through his hair, pulling back from his kiss just to look at him and make sure this was all real.

"What?" he asked.

She shook her head. "Nothing."

He smiled at her, so cute, all tousled and red-faced. "Thanks for coming over."

"Thanks for having me," she said.

He moved against her, and she wrapped her legs around him, her skirt having conveniently ridden all the way up. He tugged at the sides. "Can I take this off?"

"Please," she breathed.

He pulled himself back from her and hooked his fingers into the waistband. "Does it just slide off?" he asked.

"Oh yeah, baby," she said with a grin.

He grinned back and worked his fingers inside of her underwear's waistband. "Do these just slide off, too?"

She nodded. "Mmm hmm."

He pulled her skirt and underwear off, his eyes trained on her naked body as he went. "Now that's something to look at."

She tugged at his waistband. "No fair."

He stood up off the bed and pulled his shorts down to the floor, stepping out of them. She almost gasped at his naked penis right there in front of her, practically having forgotten what they looked like.

"You okay?" he asked, one knee on the bed, poised to climb back on top of her.

"Oh, for sure. Totally okay." She motioned with her fingers. "Come here."

As he climbed onto her, she wanted desperately to grip it, but after she'd come on so strong last time, she wanted to play chill and let him do all those things he'd promised when she'd walked in the door.

He started a trail of kisses down her neck and her

arms, staying true to his word of kissing her whole body. By the time he got to her torso, her body was so hot she was afraid she would scald him.

He ran his hand over her hip and then to the inside of her thigh, scooting down further and then nudging her thighs apart. She slid her hands under either side of the pillow behind her head and then covered her face with both sides of it as he licked and sucked on her inner thigh. "Fuck," she said into the pillow as her body went into electrical overload, buzzers and flashing lights going off all over the place.

He cupped her sex with his hand, and just the idea of him getting ready to touch her was practically enough to make her abandoned vagina sing an opera.

"You're going to smother yourself," he said, rounding both hands over her hips and then squeezing her ass.

She pulled the pillow off her face. "Sorry, I'm just doing what I've got to do to stay still."

He slid his hand around to her front and his thumb made its way to her clit. She inhaled a sharp breath, gripping the sides of the pillow.

"Don't stay still on my account. You can squirm all you want."

She'd had all the teasing she could take. She gripped his shoulders. "Just, continue, please."

On cue, his tongue made sweet contact, leaving her breathless for a moment as she settled in. It'd been so long since she'd done this. She'd way underestimated her need for it.

Moving with him, she cupped the back of his head. He had her all over the place, lifting up off the bed and wriggling for release. No surprise that it didn't take long at all. A girl who had not had an orgasm outside of her own touch in years could only take so much. She let out a huge breath of air as the crescendo hit its peak and her body filled with sweet, heated release.

He kissed his way back up her body, his cock brushing her thighs. "Mmm," she said, her body mushy.

He collapsed beside her, and she opened her eyes, meeting his gaze. "Where are you going?"

He chuckled. "Right here. I thought you might need a minute."

"No, I need more."

"You want me to go back in?" he asked.

She gripped his cock. "I'm ready when you are."

He smiled. "That works, too." He reached over her for the nightstand, his cock teasing her thigh as he pulled out a condom.

"Can I put it on you?" she asked. "I've never gotten to do that."

"Sure," he said, ripping open the package and handing it to her.

She smiled as she pulled it out, fascinated with this whole process for the first time. "I just roll it on?" she asked, already doing it.

"Squeeze the tip so there's no air bubble."

"Wow, you're an expert at this, aren't you?"

"Damn straight," he said with a grin.

"All right, soldier," she said, looking at his penis. "You're ready for battle."

His smile was so wide, dimples she'd never noticed before were dimpling. He hovered above her looking like he wanted to say something, his smile fading into another expression she tried to pinpoint.

"What?" she asked.

He bit his lip. "Nothing. You ready?"

"Mmm hmm," she said, refraining from further joking, though it was difficult.

She held onto his back as he slid inside of her, the pain of intercourse after a long sabbatical biting through her core up to her chest.

"Should I stop?" he asked.

"No, keep going," she said, gripping his shoulders.

He moved inside of her, filling her up, reminding her of what an amazing thing sex was, but especially outstanding when the man doing it with her was someone she trusted. That had been the missing piece with all of the others. They seduced her, just like his friend Jesse had tried, but when they'd made it this far she'd felt the disconnect from them before it even began. With Dane, the connection felt real and like it wasn't going anywhere.

She could have it all wrong. He could be using her and planning to pull the plug on this thing they had going as soon as the hotel bidding was done, or even as soon as they were finished tonight. But for now, she had to go with her gut and trust that he was on this ride with her.

He dropped down closer to her so their bodies were melded together, the energy they were putting off so hot they could warm Alaska. He slowed and kissed her, smoothing her hair back. "Are you good?"

"Yeah," she said, and then kissed him back.

He kept going, his face contorting in a way that made

her feel ridiculously proud. "Let yourself go, gorgeous," she whispered, making sure he knew not to wait for her. She'd already gone once, and she'd never had an orgasm through intercourse, so she wasn't holding her breath for round two.

He collapsed onto her, burying his face into her neck. She smiled up at the ceiling as she ran her fingers through his hair, so happy she had come.

DANE LAY on top of Marigold, his whole body relaxed in a way he hadn't felt in years. He kissed her neck, damp with sweat from their workout. He pulled back and met her gaze. "Did I screw it up?"

"How?"

"I'm sorry," he said, pulling a damp hair off her cheek. "I couldn't wait any longer."

"You shouldn't have. I don't usually...not through intercourse."

"Oh," he said.

"Don't look so worried," she said with a giggle. "As you can see, I have no problem with it in other ways."

"Is that a challenge?"

"Hey, you're welcome to knock yourself out next time." She winced. "I mean, later or whatever."

"I definitely want there to be a next time if you do."

She nodded, and he kissed her on her sweet, perfect lips. The last thing in the world he wanted was to remove his body from hers, but the condom had to be taken care of. Goddamn condoms.

As he rolled off of her and walked to the bathroom,

she whistled at him, making him smile. Everything about her made him smile. When he got back to the bed, she had the sheet pulled up to her neck, covering up her beautiful body, which was such a shame. But he was more than happy to snuggle up with her underneath it.

After he settled in beside her, she took his hand and held it between their chests. "Do you know that I've never had condom-less sex?"

Being the caveman he was, his first reaction was pure satisfaction. Maybe he could be the first. "Are you serious?"

"Mmm hmm. I'm paranoid about getting pregnant."

"Have you ever been on birth control?"

"I'm on it now. I've got an implant. The thing lasts for years."

He really needed to contain his excitement. There was a good reason she hadn't stopped him from using that condom. "I thought you said you hadn't been with anyone in a while."

"Oh, I haven't." She let go of his hand and played with the patch of hair on his chest. "But it doesn't mean I wasn't hopeful. I thought if I ever got off birth control that I'd be throwing in the towel, and I just never wanted to do that."

He put his hand on her hip, letting it roam over her ass and then back into place, in disbelief that he finally had free rein to touch her body at will. "You know, you could have had sex any time you wanted over the years."

"I know." She met his gaze, smiling at him. "Your friend Jesse was willing."

He practically growled. "You're not allowed to go back there without me."

She lifted an eyebrow, and he realized she didn't know him well enough to know he wasn't serious about that.

"I'm kidding, of course. Sort of."

"If I would have wanted to have sex with him, I would have done it that night or any subsequent night after that."

"But you didn't trust yourself to," he said, repeating the words she'd told him when they ate at Jesse's bar.

"I just didn't want to have it with some guy who I didn't trust."

His chest warmed. "Does that mean you trust me?"

"I'm letting you play with my ass right now, aren't I?"

He realized his hand had automatically gravitated back to her ass cheek, his finger lightly outlining the curves. "I can't help myself. Your ass is perfection."

She did a slow blink ending in lazy eyes. "Dane, please."

He stilled. "What?"

"Come on, man."

"Seriously, what?"

She sat up, tucking the sheet around her chest, covering her body. "I saw Erin."

He winced at the sound of Erin's name in this warm, wonderful space. "So?"

"So, she's nothing like me. You know it."

"Thank God."

"No, I mean her body. She's got one of those trendy,

voluptuous bodies that all the girls are rocking these days."

He couldn't help a smile. "Her body is trendy?"

"Yes, it absolutely is. All the girls want big boobs and beautiful round asses." She motioned at her body. "Look at me. I'm like if a twelve-year-old boy turned thirty and started getting saggy."

He reached for her leg, hiding his face in the pillow so he could laugh.

"I'm serious."

"You're nuts," he said, coming up for air.

She pointed at him. "I've been totally robbed, you know. There was a time when skinny was sheik. The Kate Moss era. Why couldn't I have been around back then?"

"Come here," he said, pulling her over on top of him. She sat straddling him, holding the sheet to her chest. He peeled it off of her, letting it puddle on his stomach. "Your body is perfect in every single way imaginable." He ran his hands over her bare breasts and then up to her shoulders and down her arms. He wanted to say more, but he didn't know her well enough. He couldn't confuse sex—especially sex after a year of abstinence—with something more serious. Not yet.

"You know I totally set you up for that, right?" she asked.

He smiled at her. "That's okay. You deserve to be told how beautiful you are."

She collapsed on top of him, and then rolled off. "You are really spoiling me here, Dane Knight. You better watch doing that. I can be a handful."

"I'm aware."

She pouted at him, her lips so kissable it was all he could do to restrain himself. "I guess I deserve that."

He leaned in and kissed her, his hand roaming again of its own volition.

She pulled away. "What about you? Have you ever had condom-less sex?"

He deflated and rolled over onto his back. "Yeah."

"With Erin?" she asked.

He covered his eyes with the back of his hand. He supposed these were fair enough questions. "Mmm hmm."

"Okay," she said. "So have you been tested since then?"

He moved his hand off his eyes. "Yes," he said, with a little more gusto than he'd meant to. He'd forgotten about that.

"Did you think you needed a reason to be tested?"

He let out an irritated breath. "Actually, yes. I suspected she was cheating on me."

She sat up again, this time without the sheet, which he appreciated. "Are you freaking kidding me?"

While he liked her outrage, he wasn't sure he understood it. "No, I mean, I never got any proof, but I didn't look that hard. At that point, we had stopped having sex and I was pretty much just her unpaid driver and babysitter. I probably shouldn't admit how long that went on, but..." He trailed off, unable to get into it again.

"I know. The boys."

He just nodded. That was all he could do.

"I don't get it," she said.

"I know. I'm a total sucker."

"No, not you, her. I just can't imagine having you and throwing it away for sex with some other guy. I mean, you're good at sex."

His whole body heated up. "Thanks."

She covered her eyes. "Oh, God. I've done that thing where I don't filter the words before they come out."

He pulled her over on top of him again, but this time, there was no sheet between them. "I like your unfiltered words."

She ran her hands over his chest, squeezing both of his nipples between her fingers with a grin. "So, how did that test work out for you?"

"Negative."

She scooted back a little and reached between his legs, pulling out his cock, which was already halfway there. "I don't know if I'm brave enough tonight, but if there's a next time..."

"I'm definitely up for a next time," he said, and then closed his eyes as she worked her hand up and down his cock, bringing it right back to attention.

She scooted down further. "Until next time..." He gripped the sheets as she made his whole body quake.

Chapter Twenty-One

Dane woke up in the warmest, most stellar way, his body plastered to Marigold's backside. If he didn't have to piss, he could have lain like that for the entire day.

She stirred, and he kissed her shoulders. "Mmm," she said. "Morning."

"Morning," he said, pulling her hair aside to kiss the back of her neck. His phone, which was on her side of the bed, rang and she passed it to him.

He took it and winced. Erin.

"I wasn't trying to look, I promise," she said, getting up.

"Don't get up," he said.

She waved him off. "I've got to pee, anyway."

He tossed the phone onto the nightstand next to him. As she left his bed, he stared at the ceiling for a moment, the contentment he'd felt at the start of the morning temporarily squashed by Erin. He couldn't let her do that to him. This was too much of a perfect moment to be trashed.

He went to the hallway bathroom, and when he got back, Marigold was grabbing her clothes off the floor.

He went to her. "No, no, no. Please don't do that."

"I need to go. I've got to open the shop at ten."

He glanced at his alarm clock. "It's only eight. You've got a little while, don't you?"

She let out a sigh, staring at him. "I don't have a good history of this."

"History of what?"

"I don't want to overstay."

He sat down on the bed, pulling her on top of him so she was straddling his lap. "Look, in case you can't tell, I'm interested here. I just want one more hour with you before you have to head off to work."

She smiled at him. "Okay."

He grinned. "All right. I gotta get another taste of you." He flipped her over on the bed and started heading south.

She shoved him away. "Are you insane? I'm so totally gross down there right now."

"Oh sweetheart, trust me when I say that you're anything but gross." He went back in.

"I'm serious, Dane. We had sex last night with a condom. I'd be mortified to have you down there. Let me take a shower first."

"Oh hell, yeah. I'm coming with you."

She glanced at the bathroom. "Actually, I saw you had a big garden tub with jets in there."

"You want to take a bath?"

"Do you have any bubble bath?"

"I'm sure I don't, but let me go check Ethan's bathroom. I'd bet my left nut he has some."

"Don't say that. I like your left nut."

Dane grabbed his keys off the bar and headed next door, easily finding some bubble bath. He started to head out of the bathroom when he saw Ethan's toothpaste sitting there on the counter. He swished some around in his mouth and then rinsed.

When he got back to the apartment, he found her lying in the bathtub, her arms stretched out beside her. She had her toes held up to the faucet in the middle of the tub, water running down over her feet. "You are such a lucky dog," she said.

He could not get the bubble bath poured and himself into the tub fast enough. Dropping the towel to the floor, he stepped inside, and then sat down across from her, their legs tangled up in the small space.

She rubbed her leg against his. "I'm glad I shaved."

He ran his fingers along the stubble on his jawline. "I probably need to."

"Are you kidding? Stubble on a girl's thighs is the best part of oral sex."

He rubbed his hands up her calves and over the outside of her thighs. "Woman, don't tempt me."

She waggled her eyebrows. "Is it jet time yet?"

He pressed the button. "Get ready for the bubbles to go nuts."

On cue, the bubbles grew, swallowing them up. The smile on Marigold's face as she gathered them and let them roll down her arms and shoulders made him think things he really didn't need to be thinking. He couldn't believe some asshole hadn't snatched her up by now. She was picky, that was clear. His buddy Jesse could have just about any woman he wanted, and she'd turned him down, plus, no doubt, countless others.

Why him, he wondered. What had Dane done so right that she opened herself up to him above any others? He had to quit thinking these thoughts before his ego grew so big it had to get its own apartment.

"I'm going under," she said, her body scooting down toward him as she submerged herself in the water. She came up, like a goddess, the water dripping off her beautiful, blond hair, suds running down her chest. "I know my makeup's running all over the place."

"It's not, actually," he said. "Well, just a little, but it looks kind of hot."

"All rock star, huh? Joan Jett circa The Runaways?"

He grinned. "Wasn't there a movie of them? Bella was in it, right?"

She squeezed his calves. "Oh my God, Dane. Do you know much I love the fact that you refer to Kristen Stewart as Bella?"

He relaxed against the back of the tub and she joined him on that end, straddling him. She kissed him and then smiled. "I used some of your toothpaste."

"That's good because I used some of Ethan's when I was over there."

She grinned and then kissed him some more. She ran her hand over his chest. "Do you know what I love? This patch of hair on your chest."

He huffed a laugh. "Ethan has his waxed."

"Ethan has this same patch?"

"Mmm hmm."

She sat back on her side of the tub, nuzzling her feet on either side of his ass. "What's it like looking exactly like someone else?"

"I don't think we look that alike."

"Well, true. You two can be told apart. But what's it like looking that similar?"

"I don't know. I guess I just don't think about it that much. You have a sister. Do you two look alike?"

"I guess we do. She has less pizazz. On purpose, that is. She dresses very business-like, even when she doesn't have to, and she would never color her hair."

"Do you color your hair?"

She scrunched up her face. "Is that a deal-breaker?"

He chuckled. "Yeah. I'm mortified."

"She wears her hair shoulder-length and just so. I on the other hand..." She held up her long, wet hair in explanation.

"I love your hair," he said. "I loved how you wore it the night of our first date."

"With the braid?" she asked.

"Oh yeah. And the time you had it in those big, soft curls when you had on your cat costume."

"Dane, you are sleeping with a woman who dresses up in cat costumes not on Halloween. Are you sure you've thought this through?"

His phone went off again in the other room, sending a black cloud over their tub of perfection. She lifted her eyebrows. He shook his head and then scooted them together in the middle of the tub. "I've thought about little other than you since the day I met you."

She smiled, letting her head fall backward. "Oh, when you say this stuff it's really scary."

"I'm not trying to be scary."

She rested her arms on his shoulders. "You're utterly frightening, my friend."

Marigold's ringtone sounded from the other room—a continuous one that signaled a call rather than a text. Her expression dropped.

"Are you expecting a call?"

"No, but I may know who it is."

"Do you need to get it?"

She rubbed her face and then smoothed back her hair. "I suppose I need to speak to him at some point."

"Him?"

She shook her head like she was shaking off a bad thought. "Malcolm. He's this guy who works for my family's business. I've known him since college. I'm actually the reason he's in the family business. I brought him in."

"Is this an ex of yours?" Dane asked, treading lightly.

She scrunched up her face. "I guess. It's a weird situation."

She was quiet then, which was unusual for her. He knew he shouldn't push, but his curiosity got the better of him. He took her hand. "You wanna tell me about it?"

She squeezed his hand and then let go. She looked away, and then back at him. "I've been...I should say instead I've *felt* indebted to him after something he did for me back in college."

He narrowed his gaze, focusing in on her. "What did he do?"

She squeezed her eyes shut and shook her head. "It's not really something I like talking about."

He put his hands on her thighs near her knees. "Okay. You don't have to."

She put her hands on top of his and stared into his eyes. "You're okay if I don't tell you?"

"Of course I am. But I hope over time I'll earn your trust so you feel like you can."

She smiled and then leaned in and kissed him. She pulled away and considered him, then looked down at the suds on her knee. "I was at this frat party, and these two guys were messing with me, blowing up my ego. Like a fool, I followed them to their room where I suppose I thought we were going to bake apple pie and play chess."

She looked at him for a reaction to her joke, but he couldn't do anything but focus on her story.

She went on. "As you can imagine, things moved very fast, and before I knew it, one was undoing my jeans while the other was grabbing my boob with his tongue down my throat."

Dane took in a sharp breath, feeling his blood pressure rising.

She waved him off. "It was all very Kavanaugh/Blasey Ford, except I went into the room willingly."

"Were you able to get them off of you?" Dane asked, trying to rein in his anger.

"That's where Malcolm comes in. He stumbled into the room and broke up the whole thing."

"Just by being there, or did he step in?"

"No, he stepped in. I yelled for help, and he came over all valiant and was all, 'What the fuck?' and like literally pulled me out from between them. Then they told him to fuck off and started punching him."

Dane imagined the situation, picturing himself there turning into some kind of Jackie Chan character on these assholes.

"I started screaming like a banshee then a few other people came in and some guys pulled them off, but by that time, it was bad." She motioned at her nose as she stared off at the wall behind him. "I just remember his nose sitting on his face in an unnatural position, and his weakened body lying all limp-like against the side of the bed, blood all over his face and neck. Someone called an ambulance and it came and they took him to the hospital. It was all totally surreal. I went with him in the ambulance."

"What happened to the guys?"

"Malcolm wouldn't press charges. I guess he was embarrassed about getting his ass kicked or something."

"What about you?"

"Did I press charges? No," she said, without waiting for him to answer the question.

"How come?"

"I wanted to...I would have, but I had no proof of anything other than what Malcolm had seen, and I knew if he didn't want to press charges for himself he certainly wouldn't have wanted to help me do it, so I dropped it."

"And they got away with it?" Dane asked.

She nodded. "Unfortunately, but I just had to come to terms with it."

The whole situation made Dane's stomach turn...the injustice of it all.

"Wow," she said. "You look seriously pissed."

He met her gaze. "Sorry. I know this is in your past. It's just so...enraging."

"That's a really good word for it."

He nodded and took her hands. "I'm so sorry that happened to you."

She shrugged. "I'm over it," she said, but she bit her lip, and he could tell she wasn't being totally truthful.

"So, you and this guy started dating?"

"Oh, yeah...well, yeah. We tried. I tried. I guess we hung out for a few months, but being around him gave me a sense of ick. I thought it was probably because I associated him with what happened, and that wasn't fair, so I kept trying. Finally I just couldn't try anymore. He was graduating and I knew he was looking for a job in the hotel business, so I introduced him to Dad."

Dane's radar went up. "So, hang on. He wanted to be in your dad's business?"

"Yeah, that's actually how I knew him. We were both in the hotel management program. He was a couple of years ahead, but I'd seen him around."

"Was he a member of that frat?"

"No, actually, he wasn't."

"Did he know somebody there?"

She looked at him curiously.

"I mean, typically guys can't just walk into a frat party. You have to know someone."

"I'm sure he did. What's with all these questions?"

He shook his head, realizing he was overstepping. "Sorry, I'm just inquisitive sometimes. I didn't mean to pry."

She ran her hands over his knees. "No, you're fine. I'm like that, too...lots of times." She gave him a smile that eased his upended nerves.

"So, that was him calling, you think?"

She ran her hands over her wet hair. "Yeah, I think it's him. He and my parents came into town together yesterday. They went back early but he stayed to look into the hotel stuff. I need to get together with him at some point and go over the plans."

"Do you need to do that today?"

She let her head fall back. "Yeah. We can do it at the shop though."

"Won't that be distracting with customers coming in and out?"

She shrugged. "It's not like I have much of a choice."

"Will you let me watch your shop while you work with him?"

She stilled. "Are you serious?"

"Of course I'm serious."

"You would work my shop so I could consort with the enemy about the hotel we're trying to take from you."

"Well, when you put it like that...yes, I'd love to."

She gave him a curious look. "Seriously?"

"Seriously. I may need you to train me on the register."

"I don't have one."

"Really?"

"Yeah, I figure it all on the calculator then I do hand-written receipts. It feels more mom and pop that way."

"Then I guess I'm already trained. Is everything priced?"

"Oh, yeah. I can't stand to go into a store and pick up stuff that's not priced."

"Then we're all set," he said, sliding his legs to either side of her. "But can we play a little first?"

She straddled him, lowering herself down onto his lap. "Absolutely." She kissed him. "What do you want to play?" She pressed herself against his cock and it came right to attention.

He ran his hands up her torso and around to her back. "Anything you like."

"Anything?"

He lifted an eyebrow, and then conceded. "Actually, I probably would do anything you wanted."

"Ooh, that sounds like a challenge."

"Consider the gauntlet dropped."

She grinned and kissed him, making every inch of his body melt right into her.

Chapter Twenty-Two

"You think you've got it down?" Marigold asked. Dane glanced around the store. "I'm golden. So are you meeting him somewhere?"

"He's coming here. I want to show him a few things for reference. But we're having coffee at Fiona's place next door to work things through."

"Is she open?"

She pulled a set of keys out of her pocket and jingled them. "Got the place all to myself."

"Pays to have friends in high places."

"For sure. Thank you for doing this for me," she said.

"No problem. But you'll have to make it up to me later." He pulled her to him.

She grinned at him. "I knew there'd be a catch. There's always a catch." She kissed him lightly on the nose. "Which is why I better get my money's worth. Do you mind if I run to Amavida to grab a couple of drinks? I want to mess with as little as possible at Fiona's place."

"Of course not. Go."

"Can I get you something?"

"Nah, I'm good."

She smiled. "All right." She grabbed her purse from behind the counter. "He's not supposed to be here till eleven, but if he happens to show up early, just tell him to wait on the bench right outside. It's a pretty day. He'll be fine."

"Got it."

He glanced around her shop which was as unique as she was with its sparkling lights, its colorful fish hanging on ropes, stuffed giraffes whose necks stretched toward the ceiling, Rastafarian jellyfish dangling down, and hot pink chairs with sayings painted in the seats like *Sit your butt down* and *The princess's throne, eff off*. He loved how the shop radiated her own personality.

After fifteen minutes of Dane walking the aisles of Marigold's store and not greeting any customers, the door opened. A guy about his own height and weight with dark hair walked in, glancing around like he was on a mission.

"Malcolm?" Dane asked.

The guy stilled, staring at him. "Yeah. Who are you?"

Dane walked over to him and held out his hand. "I'm Dane, Marigold's friend." *Boyfriend* seemed presumptuous, but he wished he'd had the balls to say it. "I'm just watching the shop so the two of you can work."

The guy shook his hand. "Work?"

"Yeah. Aren't you here to talk to her about her shop?"

Malcolm narrowed his gaze. "Who are you, again?"

Dane let go of his hand, standing up a little taller. "Dane. She's out grabbing drinks for the two of you.

She'll be back soon. You can wait outside on the bench for her if you like."

Malcolm eyed him, and then strolled down an aisle. "You're not her gay friend are you?"

Dane was starting to think the *ick* Marigold felt when she was dating this guy had nothing to do with him reminding her of those two assholes. He radiated plenty of his own bad vibes.

"I believe she has more than one gay friend, but no, I don't fall into that category."

"What category do you fall into?" he asked, picking up a statue and inspecting it.

Dane stared him down until he met his gaze. "I'm a good friend."

The guy smirked. "She keeping you in the friend zone? Don't sweat it. It's what she does."

Dane rested against the counter, crossing his arms over his chest. "You're welcome to wait on the bench outside."

Malcolm met his gaze. "I'm good right here. You can go out there if you're uncomfortable though."

Dane would not let this asshole rattle him. He walked around to the other side of the counter and picked up his phone, looking for a distraction.

"What's your line of work?" Malcolm asked.

"Property development," Dane said.

"Oh yeah? I'm getting ready to build a hotel down the street."

"Maybe," Dane said, unable to resist. Malcolm looked at him like he'd just announced an alien invasion. "You've got to win the bid first."

Malcolm pointed at Dane. "You've got an interest in that land?"

"Same as you."

Malcolm huffed a laugh. "You think you know about building hotels?"

"I think I do, actually."

"Does Marigold know you're trying to bid this land out from under us?"

"Last I checked that land wasn't under you or anyone else at the moment. It's fair game. And yes, she knows."

Malcolm shook his head wearing a sardonic smile. "She always was way too trusting."

"That something you know from experience?" Dane asked, knowing he had to get out of the muck with this guy, but unable to resist.

Malcolm stared at him for a moment with a look in his eye that made Dane's skin crawl. "The land isn't what I really hoped it'd be. We'd have to modify our plans fairly severely. We may end up withdrawing our bid... focus on a bigger plot in a better location."

Dane wondered what this guy was up to. He didn't seem the type to drop a dare.

Malcolm glanced around the shop. "You know she hasn't renewed this lease. I may just have to take her home with me and put her to work in our Savannah location. I'd hate to steal her from you, though."

Dane glared at the guy, knowing he'd love nothing more. "I think she's capable of making her own decisions."

Malcolm narrowed his gaze at him. "I'm not sure how well you think you know her, but if you think Marigold's a girl who would sit on your couch eating bon-bons and mooching off your money, you've got the wrong girl. She's gonna make her own way come hell or high water. And if you think she can afford to live in this town at these inflated prices you're nuts."

Dane guessed he hadn't really thought all of this through. He hadn't gotten into her personal business— what she was paying for rent, how much money she needed to make to live, that kind of thing. That was her business, not his. But if she was getting ready to be out of a job, and if that meant she was considering a move back to Savannah, that was definitely his business.

The bell on the door dinged, and Marigold came in looking flushed. "I'm so sorry. That took a little longer than I thought it would. Did the two of you meet?" she asked, looking between them.

"Yeah," Dane said.

Marigold eyed the both of them. "Great," she said, and then held a cup up to Malcolm. "One cream no sugar still?"

He smiled at her. "You know me so well." He met Dane's glare. "Nice to meet you, man. Good luck on the bid."

"Same to you," Dane said through gritted teeth.

Malcolm held the door open for her, giving Dane a final triumphant smile as she passed through the doorway. Dane hated the idea that this guy was some kind of knight in shining armor for her. There was something squirrelly about him that Dane didn't care for. He seemed way too possessive of Marigold. *Put her to work in our Savannah location.* He'd said it like he owned the place. For all Dane knew he did, partially at least. He'd traveled there with her family. He seemed to be an integral part of the organization. Dane pulled out his phone to see just how integral.

A Google search including the word "Malcolm" and "Appleton Hotels" provided more results than Dane was comfortable with. Apparently this guy was fairly high up on the food chain there and had recently been promoted to Senior VP of New Development. He was Dane's direct competition.

Dane tried searching just his first and last name in quotations along with Savannah, Georgia, and then just Georgia. He seemed fairly clean. The door opened and Dane set the phone down like he'd been caught. He let out a hard breath at the sight of a stranger. "Hi, welcome. Can I help you find anything?" He hoped the answer was no, because he didn't really know too much about her store other than what he'd observed in the past little while.

"Just looking," the woman said, meandering.

He shook his head at himself and then sat on the stool at the counter, glancing around, wondering exactly what he thought he might find on Malcolm. But then he realized he was focused on the wrong thing. The real worry was whether Marigold wanted to go back to Savannah or not.

Chapter Twenty-Three

Marigold took another sip of her tea while Malcolm droned on about his new promotion and all the opportunities he was going after on behalf of Appleton. She checked her phone for the time, knowing they'd already been gone from the shop close to an hour. Yet they still hadn't broached the subject of her shop.

"That's really cool," she said. "I think we better wrap things up over here so I don't keep Dane at my shop all day. I'm sure he's got better things to do with his day off."

Malcolm stared at her. "So, that's the guy, huh?"

"What guy?"

"Come on, Goldie. He's your new beau, isn't he?"

She despised it when he called her Goldie. She'd made it clear on many occasions, but Malcolm didn't seem interested.

"I don't know if I'd call him that...yet."

He picked up his cup and then let it slide down between his fingers. "I just don't see it, you and him."

This was typical Malcolm. He was engaged to be married but still couldn't handle her being with someone. "There's nothing to see."

"You don't think about us, what could have been?"

She rubbed her forehead. "Malcolm."

He squeezed her knee. "I think about that last time a lot. You ran off. I thought we were starting something."

"That was my mistake," she said, shaking his hand off her knee. "I was in a bad state. I'm sorry if I led you on."

He sat back, considering her. "You were just scared. You'll do the same thing to this guy."

She met his gaze, her heartbeat picking up speed. "What are you talking about?"

"You haven't been in a relationship in a long time."

"How do you know?"

"I follow you on Facebook, for one thing. There's not been anyone steady since before you and I were together last."

"That was like five years ago, Malcolm."

"Four and a half, actually."

"All right, we're getting off track. Let's talk about the shop."

"I'd really rather talk about us."

"I'm serious, Malcolm. What about the shop? What about my plans?"

He let out a sigh. "We really want you back in Savannah."

Her blood started to boil. "Who's *we*?"

"Your family and me."

"And your fiancée?"

"You say the word and she's gone."

She stood. "Malcolm, stop all this. This isn't right." She walked to the other side of the room just needing to get away from him for a second.

He stood. "It's how I feel. Your family loves you. They all miss you. They want you home. I want you home. Did you know your sister has been trying for a baby?"

She jerked her head around. "What?"

He smiled. "Yeah. You're gonna have a niece or nephew soon. Come home to Savannah. You can have your pick of jobs at the hotel."

"I don't want a job at the hotel. I want this shop here."

He looked down at his hands and lifted an eyebrow. Meeting her gaze, he said, "Well, that's not going to happen, even if we get the bid."

Her heart sank to the ground, an avalanche of disappointment threatening to buckle her.

She nodded, holding back the tears. She wouldn't let him see her cry. "Is that why you're here? To let me down in person?"

"I'm here because we all want you home, Marigold. We want you back in the family business. Look, come home and train with me. That way when we get the new hotel built, you can come back here and work it."

She rubbed her palm against her forehead. "Just... come on. Let's leave. I've got to figure some stuff out."

He walked over to her and took her by the shoulders. "Please, Marigold. Think about it. Okay? Will you think about coming home?"

She met his gaze, her stomach like a vat of acid. "Go back to Savannah, Malcolm."

Staring her down, he finally turned and walked out the door. She pulled herself together and then made her way back to the shop where Dane was standing behind the counter flipping through his phone. He looked up at her. "You okay?"

She forced a smile. "Oh, yeah. I'm fine. Just...it's nothing. Thanks so much for watching the store. Did we have any sales?"

"No, I'm sorry. We had a customer earlier but she left without buying anything."

"That's certainly nothing new. You can head out now. Thanks so much for helping."

"I can stay." He took her by the hips and shook her a little. "We can play around between customers."

She kissed him on the lips. "I would love to, but I have some work to do here."

"Can I see you tonight?"

"Mmm hmm. Oh, wait." She looked at her phone. "Fiona texted me a while ago. She asked if we could have dinner together just the two of us at the house. I'm guessing there's trouble in la-la land with Bobbie. Can we hang tomorrow? Are you doing anything?"

"Tomorrow's perfect." He slid his hands behind her back. "If I can wait that long. I'm seriously not sure I can. Come over later tonight if you can. I'll come down and get you."

She gave him another peck and then pulled away, feeling the connection between them waning alongside her dream of staying in the place she loved. "I'll see how it goes. It may need to be a girl night thing."

He nodded. "Completely cool. I'll just plan on seeing you in the morning."

She squeezed his hand. "Have a good day."

"You, too." He kissed her, and then headed out the door, taking a piece of her heart with him.

Chapter Twenty-Four

The sun had set over WaterColor when Marigold arrived home from the shop. She'd made signs that she'd posted all over the store. STORE CLOSING. ALL SALES FINAL. She'd created flyers that she'd hang all around town tomorrow morning.

She opened the door with her key to find Fiona cooking solo in the kitchen. "Where's Bobbie?" Marigold asked.

"She's at home. I made us dinner, that sweet and sour chicken you like."

Marigold stilled, Fiona being too kind for there not to be something wrong. "Everything okay with you and Bobbie?"

Fiona smiled a half-smile. "Everything's really good."

Marigold dropped her purse. "She's moving in, isn't she?"

Fiona held up a hand with a serving spoon in it. "We're not kicking you out. You can take as long as you need to find a place. If you want to stay till the end of

December like we originally planned, that is no problem whatsoever. But her roommate's this horrible, misogynistic guy who she can't stand to be around, and I don't want her to have to live like that anymore."

"Of course not," Marigold said. "It's totally fine, Fiona. Don't feel bad. Tell her to come on tonight if she needs to."

Fiona smiled. "Thank you. But I told her I needed one last night just the two of us."

Marigold wrapped her arms around her friend. "Thank you, for everything. You've saved my life these past couple of months."

"You're the perfect roommate. We're never home at the same time."

Marigold chuckled. "That's the only kind of roommate who would call me a good one."

"Not true," Fiona said, squeezing her arm.

"I'll get out of your hair. Just let me figure something out, okay?"

"There's no rush. Please hear me when I say that."

Marigold smiled at her. "Okay." But Marigold knew when romance was involved, three was a crowd. Boy, this day had shaken up to be a doozy. It was almost too stressful to even be upset about.

"Are you hungry?" Fiona asked.

Marigold decided the biggest need she had at the moment was to eat her sorrows away. "I'm about to bite into this countertop I'm so hungry."

"Grab the wine glasses and the bottle on the bottom shelf in the door."

Marigold did as told, looking at the bottle. She whistled. "You sure? This is a good one. And it's unopened."

"I know," she said with a smile.

The last supper, Marigold thought, and then got out the corkscrew. She turned on Flora Cash, one of Fiona's favorites, watching her light up. Being kicked out of this apartment was like a neon sign flashing at her. Nowhere to live, no shop, no prospects of a job, despite the now fifty-eight resumes she'd submitted. The stars were aligning, and they were directing her home. Marigold just had to decide if she had any fight left in her or if she was ready to throw in the towel.

Chapter Twenty-Five

When Dane heard the elevator ding, he jumped up and met Marigold at the door. She'd insisted on meeting him at his place, which was fine with him because he was hoping they'd never leave it all day long.

He opened the door to find her standing there looking somehow more beautiful and desirable to him than when he'd left her yesterday, which seemed damn near impossible. "Hey," he said, sweeping her into his arms.

She smiled, but it didn't go all the way to her eyes. "Hey there, handsome."

He pulled away. "Are you okay?"

"Yeah," she said, brushing him off and walking into his place sort of aimlessly.

"How's Fiona? Are she and Bobbie through?"

"Oh, far from it. She's actually moving in."

"Oh," Dane said, swallowing what that must mean for Marigold.

"Fiona's not rushing me out, but I'm not sure what kind of shelf-life my charm will have with Bobbie. She has no problem adoring Fiona right there in front of me. Looking back, I think she may have been marking her territory a few times she made no effort to quell some major PDA in front of me. She probably wants my bedroom for all her stuff."

"Do you need a place to stay?" he asked, treading lightly.

She waved him off. "I'll be fine. I can hop around from place to place until I figure things out."

Dane's phone buzzed, and he picked it up and winced. Erin. She'd called several times now, and he'd chosen not to answer. As much as he would love to see the boys, things were going well with Marigold. This wasn't the time.

"Do you need to get that?" Marigold asked.

"No." He motioned for her to sit down on the couch with him. "So how did it go with Malcolm yesterday?"

She made an irritated noise. "You know, I really don't want to talk about it."

"Okay," he said, trying to be cool, but really starting to worry. He shifted in his seat. "Anything particular you want to do today?"

She scooted over next to him and laid her head on his shoulder. "Can we just sit here a while."

He pulled her in closer letting her snuggle up into him. He sniffed her hair, drinking her in, wishing he could put an end to all of the shit she was going through.

His phone buzzed again and he silenced it without even looking at the caller ID.

She pulled away from him. "Get that."

"No, I really don't need to."

"She's called twice already since I've been here. How many times did she call yesterday? I know about the once yesterday morning."

"I...I don't know."

She let out a huge sigh and then stood. "You know, this just isn't working today. I've got a bunch of stuff to do at the shop. Can we do a raincheck?"

He stood and took her by the shoulders. "Please don't go. I'm sorry she's calling. It's like she's got goddamned radar or something. She knows I'm dying to be with you and she's ruining it."

"That or she really needs you to take the kids."

"They aren't my responsibility."

She scratched her cheek. "No, they're not. But I'm still gonna go. This just isn't working. Not today...maybe not...I've just got to go."

"Marigold," he said, following her to the door, but there wasn't much else he could say. If she wanted to go, he had to let her go.

She stopped at the door and turned to face him, taking his shirt into her hands by the collar. "I had an amazing time last night. Like freaking off the charts. I loved it. And I think you're probably the best guy on the planet."

He blinked, not sure what to say to that. It was so at odds with what she'd just said a minute ago.

She planted a long kiss on his lips, and then walked away without looking at him again, pushing through the door to the stairwell and disappearing behind it.

His phone rang again, and this time he stormed over to the coffee table and snatched it up, ready to hurl it against the wall, but he stopped as he saw the caller ID. Panama City Beach United Methodist Church. While his first instinct was to ignore it, he had a gut feeling this was a call he should take.

"Hello?"

"Oh, thank goodness. I was hoping calling from the church phone would help. Hi, this is Brittany McLaughlin. I've got two boys here ready for pickup. Did you get held up?" When he hesitated, processing what was happening, she said, "That was me calling a second ago from my cell phone, but I figured you weren't picking up since you didn't know who I was. But we have you down as today's pickup. Erin left us your number. Class was over a half hour ago and the sermon has already started. Did you get the time mixed up?"

He sat on the couch, unable to speak for the moment.

"Dane?" the woman asked?

"Yeah. Just a minute." This was it. It was time to make his choice. He could tell this woman that he never agreed to pick up those boys and that he and Erin hadn't been together in over a year. He could say that while he loved and cared for them more than he ever could have thought possible, he had to cut this codependent cord and quit caving. He'd explain that the more he caved, the more she would keep throwing a bomb into his life whenever she wanted.

He would say he was sorry, but he couldn't be involved, and for her to do whatever she needed to do. Call the police. Call the Department of Human Services.

Call Erin. But he was sure Erin would not pick up, assuming Dane would handle this for her.

Dane let his hand drop to his leg, staring at the phone, knowing whatever he did now would set the tone for years to come. He thought of Jaden and Noah, pawns in a game Erin controlled, two little boys who never asked for this mother or for no consistent father or father figure. He thought about all the times he or Ethan were desperate for a father or any male role model—how they both were always so starved for that missing piece in their life, not having any sort of grandfather or uncle to help them through. Jaden and Noah were in that same boat. They had no one except whoever Erin brought temporarily into their life.

He thought of Noah's breakdown when she took them away the other night. He remembered the look of hope on Jaden's face, and then the subsequent letdown when he realized life would continue as it had.

"Hello?" Brittany said from her spot there on his knee.

He closed his eyes and raised the phone to his ear.

Chapter Twenty-Six

Dane sat at his friend's bar with a half-eaten plate of food in front of him, watching Jesse flirt with two women a couple of barstools down.

"Ah, so you're a Gemini. That makes you...," he said, squinting at her, "excellent in bed, right?"

She grinned back at him. "You have no idea."

Dane rolled his eyes, unable to believe the crap that guy got away with because women thought he was *hot*. Dane supposed the fact that he had a certain non-threatening charm about him probably helped, but still.

Jesse looked over at him. "Dane, you're a Gemini, too, aren't you?" Dane glared at him, and Jesse lifted his eyebrows. "Lisa here is a Gemini."

Lisa, who had huge boobs spilling out of a tank top, faced him with a smile. "The twins."

The whole scene was almost too ridiculous to address. Dane pulled a bill out of his wallet and set it on the bar. "I've got to get back to work," he said to Jesse.

Jesse followed him to the door. "Hey, man. I'm sorry. I just couldn't resist. Don't go."

"I've got a meeting in a little while," he lied.

"What's going on with you today?" Jesse asked. "You're definitely not yourself."

Dane ran his hand through his hair. "I'm fine. Just a little stressed."

Jesse put his arm around Dane. "Come here. Step into my office." He guided Dane toward the back. "Kelly," he said to one of his servers who was standing with another one watching a game. "Can you work the bar?" She nodded and headed that way.

They sat in a booth in the corner. "What's going on, man?" Jesse asked.

Dane pressed his hands against his face hard, and then wiped them away, trying to relieve some pressure. "Erin left the boys at a church in Panama City on Sunday morning with my name and number for pickup."

"I'm assuming that wasn't pre-arranged?"

Dane shook his head.

"Do you still have them?"

Dane stared at his friend. "Yep."

"Any word from her?"

Dane shook his head, so furious he could barely speak.

Jesse closed his eyes, inhaling a deep breath. As superficial as he could be sometimes, Jesse always came to the plate when he needed to with true compassion. "Man, I'm so sorry."

"I am, too."

"How are they?" Jesse asked.

Dane shrugged. "They're fine. She told them she was just going on a little trip and that they were staying with me. Other than me continuing to come up with excuses as to why we can't call her, they're doing okay. Jaden's suspicious."

"He's the older one?"

Dane nodded. "He got a little adamant last night about checking in with her, so we left her a voice mail message. I'm gonna tell him she called back today to check in on them."

Jesse stared at Dane hard. "How are you doing?"

Dane huffed a laugh. "It's crazy. I'm so pissed at her for doing this that I want to put my fist through a wall, but then..." He wasn't sure he wanted to say the next words aloud. He met Jesse's gaze, gauging him.

"You don't want her to come back," Jesse said, reading his mind.

Dane nodded, staring down at the table carved with people's names and initials.

"How does Marigold feel about all this?" Jesse asked.

Dane gave a humorless smile. "She has no clue. She was there when my phone was ringing with Erin's caller ID coming across it, before I talked to the lady at the church. She said she couldn't do this anymore and then gave me a really nice compliment about how I was the best guy on the planet before she kissed me and then left without even looking at me."

"That sounds like the kiss of death."

Dane gave him a look.

"Do you love her?" Jesse asked.

Dane swallowed hard, thinking about how she made

him feel when they were together, how her smile and her goofy jokes made his heart light up. He thought about her cuddled up next to him on the couch and how he'd never felt so safe and complete as he did with her beside him. He thought about them in his bed, their bodies moving together and how if he knew for sure they could never do that again, he wasn't sure how he could continue breathing.

He nodded wordlessly.

"And you love those boys, too."

"No doubt about that."

Jesse smiled at him and shrugged. "Then you need to go for what you want, in both respects."

Dane considered him. "What do you mean?"

"You love those boys, and they're important to you. Ask for shared custody or visitation. Get a lawyer. Put that shit in writing. Agree to take them, but only if it's on a regular schedule."

Dane shook his head. "I don't know. I'd be entangling myself with Erin permanently."

"How old are they?"

"Six and eight."

"The eight-year-old will be a teenager in five years. They'll be in their own world by then."

A tug-o-war started with Dane's heart—dealing with Erin versus being a permanent part of the boys' lives.

"How's that supposed to work? I don't get married till they graduate high school?" Dane asked.

"Who says that's a rule?"

"What woman in her right mind would get mixed up

with a guy who is committed to keeping his ex-girlfriend's kids?"

Jesse smiled. "One who's already in love with you?"

Dane shook his head, his neck seeping with heat. "She's not in love with me."

"You sure about that?"

Dane wanted it to be true more than he'd ever wanted anything in his life.

"Work this shit out, man. Text Erin. Tell her what you want. My money says it'll draw her back from wherever she is."

"And then what about Marigold?" Dane asked, letting Jesse guide him right where he needed to go.

Jesse held both arms up in the air like the answer was obvious. "Go for it, man."

Chapter Twenty-Seven

Marigold had spent the past week selling her store's items for below cost, wondering how she was going to pay her final invoices. The good news was that the word of her store closing had spread, and the people had come out en masse to pilfer her things. Her store was starting to look dismal, but that was part of the process, she knew. An empty store equaled less to have to toss out or store somewhere, like she could afford a storage unit right now.

The hardest part of the past week had been that she hadn't heard a word from Dane. She hadn't expected to. She had been the one to leave him Sunday, but she still held out hope.

She hadn't texted him either. If she had, she would have needed to explain that she had pulled out of the hotel bidding altogether and was a huge-ass failure. Those were not words she was ready to utter to anyone yet, especially a guy she was trying to impress.

Her body had been physically aching for him. All she

could do while she was slashing prices and watching customers walk out the door for the last time was dream about his body on top of hers. She loved his body. He wasn't super buff like Bo, but she had never gone for big muscles. They'd always intimidated her. He was just perfect for her, every inch of his boy skin, the indentions in his muscles, the light spread of hair on his arms and his chest and that little patch just below his belly button. She'd been living in a perpetual state of heat for a week.

She picked up her phone, unlocking the screen, tapping her fingernails against the counter. She didn't want to text him. She just wanted to see him. It was Saturday night though. The guy had a life, unlike her.

She grabbed her purse from the back and headed home, knowing Bobbie and Fiona were both out. When she got there, she changed into her workout clothes, but the night was cooler than it was the last time she did this, so she slid Dane's hoodie over her head. She'd say she was returning it to him. That was a legit enough farce of an excuse.

She locked up and headed down the beach in the direction of Dane's place. This time, she made no pretense of being out on a walk. She just stood below his balcony, staring upward. When he didn't magically appear, she texted him.

You home?

She knew that he was because the television was on. Good. He hadn't moved on to the next notch on his bedpost just yet. She hadn't thought he would have, but the reassurance was nice. Her text alert dinged.

I am. Are you?

She smiled as she typed.

Not exactly. Take a peek out your balcony door.

When he appeared at the balcony, an almost resigned smile came across his lips. Dang. She had completely misread all of this. He seemed so crazy about her just last Sunday, but here he was, the crazy all gone from his disposition.

He shut the door behind him, really softly, like he had someone in there. A cold chill that had nothing to do with the cool fall night covered her.

"Hey," he said, leaning against the balcony railing. "You out for a walk?"

"Yep."

He glanced down the beach to their left. "You been far?"

"No, actually, just from there to here." She pointed in the direction of Fiona's place.

"Ah," he said, nodding.

Her heartbeat raced, realizing the full extent of his rejection and her humiliation. "Well, I just wanted to say hi."

He nodded, staring at her hard. He glanced toward his place and then back at her. God, did he have someone in there? This was worse than she could have ever imagined.

"Can you come up a minute?" he asked.

Temporary relief flooded her, only at the idea that he didn't have another woman in there. But the look on his face didn't have her feeling great about his motives. She shrugged. "Sure. Only because I wanted to return your sweatshirt."

He nodded, seriously. God, she'd been teasing, it being obvious she was making a full-on effort to see him. She entered through the lobby's back door and headed up the stairs, winding herself from the effort. God, she needed to exercise.

She went to knock on the door, but he opened it at the same time. She smiled. "Hi."

He ran his hand through his hair, looking at his guest bedroom door, and then back at her. "Hi," he said in a voice much softer than hers had been.

"Are we hunting wabbits?" she whispered.

He waved her in, and then led her to his guest room. He opened the door to reveal a king-sized bed swallowing two blond-headed little boys whole. Her heart sank to the ground.

He closed the door, meeting her gaze with an apologetic expression. "Let's go outside," he said, and headed to the balcony. After closing the door behind her, leaving it cracked, he ran his hand through his hair, smiling at her, and then tossed up his hands. "I wanted to text you this week. It's all I've thought about. But I just didn't know what to say. I didn't know how to explain."

She narrowed her gaze. "How long have they been here?"

He closed his eyes, letting out a deep breath, and then set his gaze on her. "All week. My ringing phone last Sunday morning wasn't Erin. I mean, it was the first time or two, obviously. But after that, it was a lady who taught Sunday school at a church in PCB. Erin dropped off the boys and gave her my name as a contact for pickup."

Marigold's stomach curdled. "Have you heard from her?"

"Just the voicemail she left when I didn't pick up. She said she was sorry, and that it was just something she needed to do."

Marigold felt like someone knocked the wind out of her with her hands tied behind her back. "So you've had them all week?"

He nodded, glancing in the direction of the bedroom. "I've taken them to school every day and picked them up. I've been fixing dinners and school lunches. It's been insane."

"I'll bet." Her mind raced with the semantics of it all. "What about their school stuff?"

"They both had a backpack when I picked them up with some school stuff and a few clothes. I had to go to Target and get them more clothes and stuff."

"Dane, this is nuts."

"You're telling me?"

She turned toward the railing, gaping out at the dark ocean night like it held answers to this mess. She turned back toward him. "Does anyone at the school say anything about it?"

"They know me from when I used to pick them up when she and I were together, and beyond." He looked down at the Adirondack chair on his balcony, shaking his head.

Marigold held her hands out to the sides. "So, this is it? You're their caregiver?"

"For now."

"And you're okay with it?" she asked. He ran a hand

through his hair, looking everywhere but at her, and she was regretful she'd said that. "Don't answer that."

"No, it's a fair question." He tossed a hand in the direction of the bedroom. "I love them. I've loved them from the moment I met them. I grew up with no father. I know what that's like. And I'm not making any excuses for Erin, believe me, but being a single mom isn't easy. What she did was wrong. But knowing the struggles my mother went through raising us alone, part of me can't hate her for this."

Marigold rested against the balcony railing, letting it all process through. She knew nothing of single parents and abandoned kids. Any opinion she would have would be based on a lifetime of a tight-knit family who was so close they all worked in a business together, other than her of course. She was a square peg in a round hole with them, so she'd fled. These boys wanted what she'd tossed away.

"Hey," he said, moving toward her. "I didn't mean to upset you."

She glanced up at him. "What?" And then she felt a tear fall down her cheek. She didn't even realize it was happening. She wiped it away. "No, I'm not upset. Not about this." She closed her eyes, shaking her head as if that could clear out the cobwebs that were occupying her brain. She opened her eyes and met his gaze. "I'm so sorry you're going through this, Dane."

He smiled. "You know what's weird? I'm not."

Her stomach navigated a wave of unease. "Have you notified anyone?" she asked.

"I haven't."

"What are you going to do if she comes back for them, or when, I guess?"

"I don't know. I'm thinking about a lot of options. I'm thinking of asking her if I can see them more, maybe set up a weekly visitation. Maybe if she has some help, she won't need to do this again."

So many things were going through Marigold's head, mainly the fact that he needed to know that these boys weren't his responsibility. But he knew that. It didn't need to be said aloud.

"Look, I wanted to have more information before I talked to you about this, which is the main reason I haven't contacted you this week. I don't meet with the lawyer until Monday."

She tried to mask her shock. "You're meeting with a lawyer? Like an...adoption lawyer?"

He moved toward her and took her hand. "Listen, Marigold, these past few weeks with you have brought me out of a funk I never knew I could break free of. You've been like a light in a dark tunnel. You're this precious gift that I never dreamed I could possibly receive. I love the way you make me laugh with every other thing you say. I imagine a life with you, and that life is filled with joy and love and infinite satisfaction." He dropped her hand and held both of her arms, bearing his gaze into hers. "I'm fucking crazy about you, Marigold. I'm trying to be careful here because I know this is a lot to put on you right now, but no matter what happens between us, I need you to know, unequivocally, that my feelings for you are the realest and most genuine thing I've ever known in my entire life."

Marigold's whole body quivered like the aftershock of an earthquake. She put a hand over her mouth, not having a clue what to say next, and afraid of what unintelligible sound would come out if she tried.

He took a step back from her. "I know this is all so unfair to you. I can't ask you to be with me right now because I have no answers about the future and what it will hold with those two boys in my life. I'm at Erin's mercy. I can't even imagine what you think of me or the way I'm handling this, but I just know, as much as I love you, I can't abandon those boys right now."

Marigold's hand shook as she lifted it to pull a strand of hair out of her eyes. "Wow," she said, her voice shaky, too. "And to think I was on a mission for a booty call."

Her joke fell flat on its ass, but it wasn't like she understood how to deal with things other than with humor.

"I don't know what I'm trying to ask of you here," he said. "I'm just giving you the information I think you need."

To make a decision were his unspoken words.

A little blond head appeared at the door. "Dane, can I stay up with you? I can't sleep." It was the older boy, Jaden.

"Hi, Jaden," Marigold said, trying her best to force a genuine smile, but probably looking like something out of a creepy fun house between her tears and what had to be her running eye makeup.

"Hi, Miss Marigold." He turned back to Dane. "Can I get some water?"

"Of course. You don't have to ask. You know where

the cups are." The boy walked away and Dane turned back to her.

She shook her head. "Man, those two are lucky to have you."

"I don't know about that. What does a single guy living in a condo on the beach know about parenting?"

She smiled at him, her heart melting with love for this man. "A whole lot more than you give yourself credit for, I'm sure." She embraced him, holding him tight to her chest. As his arms wrapped around her back, her heart ached with love and loss so badly it almost made her sick at her stomach. She pulled away glancing into the living room where Jaden was sitting on the couch watching television. "I'm gonna get outta here."

Dane nodded slowly. "Okay. Will you let me get Ethan to walk you home?"

"No," she said, "Seriously, it's like five steps down the beach and it's WaterColor. I'm good."

He nodded, and a hard realization set in that if she decided to be with him, she would not be the top priority in his life.

She reached in for a kiss, threading her fingers through his hair, letting the feel of his lips on hers sink down deep into her soul like nourishment. She pulled away and smiled. "Bye, Dane."

She walked into the living room, finger-waving to Jaden. "Goodnight, Jaden."

The little boy gave her a shy smile that tugged hard on her heart.

Chapter Twenty-Eight

By the end of the second week of Marigold's store closing, she was pretty much wiped out of stock. She kept pulling the merchandise toward the front of the store and had already sold off a few of her fixtures. Several of the shoppers had been other local storeowners, gathering merchandise for their own stores at rock bottom prices. She was thankful to get the sales, but it'd be weird to see her stuff in other people's stores—if she stuck around 30A long enough to see it.

She'd been running on autopilot the whole week at her store, unable to process what was going on with Dane. He loved her. He said it to her a week ago, not in those exact words but in a roundabout way. *As much as I love you* had been his phrasing. Had it slipped out? Had he truly meant it in the real sense?

She knew at this point the ball was in her court to make the next move. He'd laid it all out for her, and she needed to respond. She just didn't know how. Scenarios kept running through her brain, the worst being what if

Erin never came back? If Marigold and Dane were together, and Dane was the fill-in father for those boys, what did that make her?

Marigold had taken great lengths over the years to ensure she never got pregnant. She'd been on birth control since she entered college, way before she ever had sex. She wanted to be prepared for any scenario, including the one that happened to her that horrible day at the frat house. She'd never told any of the guys she was with that she was on birth control so they'd always be sure to wear condoms. But she'd told Dane. Why had she done that? Heat spread to her neck as she told herself why. She was close to letting him in...all the way.

The events of her life were culminating into a ball of fire. The closing of her shop. Booted from her apartment. Her need to find a new career and steady income. She was barely functioning in her own life, much less was she ready to jump into someone else's, especially when the stakes were so high.

She rested against her countertop, staring at the phone in her hand. Her father was one call away. She didn't have to manage one of the hotels. She could pretty much pick her position, or at least her department. Maybe she'd work in catering for the Savannah location. She could work at one of the gift shops. She didn't have to go to Savannah. She could go to Tampa or Maryland. All she had to do was call her dad and ask him one question. *When can I start?*

She was so close to making that call. She just had to get to a place where the words didn't make her want to throw up.

The bell on the door dinged, and her heart leapt into her throat as Dane appeared in the doorway. "Hey," she said, her smile wider than her face would allow.

He glanced around, brow furrowed. "I just heard you were closing. I can't believe you didn't tell me. I can't believe I didn't know."

"Oh yeah," she said, waving him off like it was nothing. "We had bigger fish to fry last weekend."

He stared at her, his face beet red. "So, what about your shop? The hotel?"

"I pulled out of the bid, my part of it, at least. It was time to close."

He frowned. "When did you..."

"A couple of weeks ago. I was actually coming over to tell you about it last weekend when..."

He huffed, running his hand through his hair, glancing around like he'd seen a ghost. "I'm so sorry. I should have been here."

"No," she said. "It's a one-woman job."

He shook his head, glancing around in disbelief. "I'm so sorry I haven't been here." She couldn't be sure, but was he on the verge of tears?

She went to him, studying his bloodshot eyes. "Are you okay?" she asked.

"Yeah," he said, but he clearly wasn't.

She put her hands on his shoulders and rubbed down his biceps. "What's up, Dane?"

He shook his head, but his eyes told a different story. She stared at him, waiting, willing him to open up.

He looked down, scratching his head. "Um, Erin came and got the boys today. She's actually the one who told me about you closing. I've been so caught up in them I haven't even..." He shook his head, his body quivering.

"Oh, Dane," she said, pulling him to her, holding his numb body against hers, the life feeling like it had drained out of him. He'd clearly resigned himself to being the boys' father—taken steps to solidify it. She pulled away and studied his face, his vulnerability sending a need coursing through her like a wildfire. She kissed the corner of his left eye, and then his right, wanting desperately to make him better with her touch, but he was hurting in a way she couldn't heal.

Their mouths met, his soft lips like a drug for her soul. Her hands went to his hair, her fingers threading through as their kiss intensified, the need inside of her growing faster and more urgent by the second.

She pulled away and went to the door, flipping the sign and locking up. She took his hand and dragged him toward the storeroom, closing the door behind them.

In a move pulled straight from a bad movie, she used one arm to swipe everything from her desk and then pushed him down on it, climbing on top of him, and then pulling off his T-shirt. Wrapping her arms around his back, she drank in his skin, the contours of his body between her fingers sending heat through her core. The idea that this man and his body was hers to do with as she pleased was a concept too unbelievable for her to digest.

He tugged at her shirt, and she lifted her arms for him to pull it off. Cupping his jawline, she kissed him over and over like she could never physically get enough of his taste while he undid her bra in the back. She let him discard it and watched his hands move to her bare breasts like magnets. She smiled at him, shaking her head. "You're such a guy. All about the boobs."

"Oh, yeah," he said, going in for one of them with his mouth as she leaned back to give him full access, his tongue working tricks that made her body sizzle from deep within. When he'd had his fill, she got down off of him and went for the button on his shorts. He hopped up, helping her out, unzipping and letting his shorts and underwear fall to the floor. Dropping to her knees, she took him into her mouth, gripping his sweet ass as she moved up and down on his hard length.

"Fuck," he uttered, and she glanced up at him to catch him watching her.

Letting her hands slide down, she gripped his inner thighs, causing his body to heat like a sauna. Pulling off of him, she let her finger trail between his cheeks with a tease as he met her gaze with a hunger she hadn't sensed in her lifetime.

She slid her skirt and thong down her legs and off over her boots, which had zippers and required way too much distraction and effort to remove at the moment. Pushing him down on the desk again, she climbed back onto his lap and found his cock, positioning it at her point of entry.

"You okay with this?" she asked him. Consent for unprotected sex was no joke for her.

"Fuck yes," he said, gripping her arms.

She slid down onto him, gasping at his length filling her up. As she moved up and down on him, waves of sweet decadence filled her from head to toe, his bare skin against hers more indulgent than a warm, fudgy brownie with a mound of ice cream on top.

His hands cupped her ass as she rode him, and she leaned in close to him, their bodies melting together in a frenzy of heat. She didn't mean to, but in a pure moment of carnal hedonism, she bit his neck.

"Fuck," he yelled.

"Sorry," she said, hesitating.

"No, it's fucking awesome."

She grinned as she moved on him, faster and faster like she was a cowgirl at a rodeo going for the county record.

Oh, God, what was that building inside of her? A pleasure coming from deep within...or was her clit rubbing against something? Whatever it was, she didn't want it to stop.

She clung onto him. "Hold on, Dane."

He leaned back, gripping the edges of the desk. "Okay," he said, like he was ready for battle, but struggling hard.

The buildup came from within this time. She wasn't sure if she would even know the difference between an orgasm with her clit and one from her G-spot, but now that it was happening, there was no mistaking it.

As she let herself go, sweet release filled her. Dane's groan signaled his own release, and so she squeezed him to her, their hearts pounding against one another's.

She pulled back from him to look at his face but could only find herself going back in for another kiss. She smiled at him. "Thank you."

"For what?" he asked, his breathing still labored. She

lifted an eyebrow, and the hint of pride in his expression came through. "I didn't do anything. You did all the work."

"You provided an excellent workplace."

His body shook with silent laughter.

She wrapped herself around him, their bodies too warm for her to break away just yet. He kissed the crook of her neck, and then squeezed her so tightly she lost her breath for a moment, but she didn't even mind. It could be even tighter as far as she was concerned.

A FEINT KNOCK SOUNDED from outside the storeroom, like it was coming from the front door. Dane had been hoping he would never have to leave. Marigold, on his lap where she belonged, stilled, and then closed her eyes. "Crap."

"Do you need to get that?" he asked, praying the answer would be no.

"What time is it?" she asked, glancing around. "I've got a guy coming to buy a fixture at four."

"I think it's about that time," Dane said, hating this guy, whoever he was.

She ran her fingers through his hair and kissed him. "I'm so sorry. I'll be back."

She pulled off of him, leaving him feeling like he'd just parted with a vital organ. He'd always thought he knew the difference between love and sex, but he'd not had a clue until now. The term making love had always been a cheesy, romantic cliché. He understood that term at this moment with full clarity, like he'd been in the dark his whole life and was just now waking up to the light.

As she stood there glancing around for her clothes, buck naked with nothing on but those boots, her hair cascading over her bare shoulders almost reaching her breasts, he thought he might be the luckiest man on the planet. "God, you're beautiful," he said, without even realizing the words were coming before they were already out.

She gave him a wry look. "I'm a naked chick. Of course you think I'm hot."

He hopped down off the desk, his mouth open to say so much more, but that goddamned knock came again.

"Coming!" Marigold shouted, grabbing her shirt and sliding it over her head. "Where is my underwear?" she asked, glancing around. "Oh, screw it."

She pulled her skirt up over her naked ass, and then opened the door. The idea of her walking around with no panties on made his cock start to come to life again.

He dressed and then ran cold water over his hot face. He was in deeper than he'd ever been in his life, so deep that he had no clue how to come back. God knew he never wanted to go back to life before he knew her. Life with her was everything he never knew could be possible and couldn't have dreamed of wanting if he'd tried.

He opened the storeroom door to find her talking to a guy about their age who was handing her his credit card. The guy smiled at her in a way that signaled way more than a customer/retailer interaction.

The guy looked up at Dane, his smile melting away. *That's right, asshole. Keep moving.*

The guy cleared his throat and took his credit card from her. "Yeah, Fort Walton," he said in answer to a polite question she'd asked him.

"Need any help getting that to your truck?" Dane asked.

"I've got a dolly, but thanks." The guy's smile turned into a serious nod. Good.

As the guy went to a display and wrapped it with a bungee cord to his dolly, Dane put a hand on the small of Marigold's back protectively. She looked up at him with a knowing smile that said she had his number. That was okay. He was pretty much past any pretenses at this point. His heart was so exposed he might as well shed his skin.

"Let me get the door," Marigold said, heading that way and letting the guy through. "Come back if you decide you can use the matching one."

"I will," he said and then nodded at Dane, a concession.

She closed the door and gave him a look. "You're a jealous guy, aren't you?"

He shrugged. "Can you blame me? That guy was hitting on you."

She waved him off. "I wasn't going to let it go anywhere. I'm just trying to get these fixtures out of here. If a smile and a wink does the trick, then so be it."

He wrapped his arms around her. "How much for the rest of them?"

She smiled. "You're really cute sometimes, you know?"

His heart pricked for her and what she was going through. "I'm so sorry you're losing your shop."

She pulled away from him. "It's fine. I had a good run. To be honest, there's a real freedom that comes with it. I mean, there's a crippling fear of the unknown, but I'm taking things one step at a time. Today, sell off merchandise and fixtures. Tomorrow, figure out the future."

He had a future in mind with her. It was so easy, too. Come back to his condo and let him take care of her for the rest of their lives. But that wasn't how this was going to go down, as much as he wanted it more than anything he'd ever wanted in his life.

She met his gaze, her expression worried. "I'm so sorry about the boys. What did she say when she picked them up?"

He shrugged. "She said she needed a break, and she knew I'd say no if she asked upfront."

"Would you have?"

He let out a hard breath, the turmoil of Erin bearing down on his shoulders. "I don't know."

She gave him a smile with a nod, like she'd already known the answer. She glanced around like she was looking for something and then met his gaze. "Actually, I think I'm moving back home."

His heart froze. "To Savannah?"

She nodded. "Or possibly West Palm Beach, or maybe even Tampa. I've got a lot of options. There's an opening for a gift shop manager at our Naples location. Of course, I'd have to live in my car at their real estate prices, so it'd be a whole lot more practical for me to pick, say, our Myrtle Beach location. It's on the Pawley's Island side. I think I could actually afford to rent an efficiency apartment there, if one exists. I've been doing cost-of-living analyses of these places, and, to be honest, I have no idea how people can live these days." She stopped, rubbing her forehead. "You know you can shut me up at any time."

He just stood there, processing the fact that she was seriously considering leaving. *Don't go.* The words were on the tip of his tongue. But he couldn't ask that of her. He couldn't promise her anything.

She met his gaze, searching it. "Dane, I'm in love with you, too. I mean, you didn't actually say those words to me, but I think you might have indicated them, and you said a lot of sweet things the other day, and so I think I'm not completely out of line here, but anyways, that's neither here nor there." She took a huge breath and then let it flow out of her like it was helping to heal her in some way. She clasped her hands together and held them in front of her. "I love you. I think you are an amazing man with the biggest heart on the planet, and I feel a hundred percent confident that I will never ever find anyone as perfect as you. But as much of a complete idiot that this makes me, the fact remains that you are tied to a situation that I'm not prepared to be a part of." She motioned around her store. "Look at me, Dane. I'm losing my shop. I have no job. I have no place to live. I have a stack of unpaid invoices and debtors wanting their money. I'm a complete mess. You have two kids who need you. They're counting on you. And if I become a serious part of your life, they'll start counting on me, too. But I've got to get my own life in order before I can become anyone else's caregiver. Can you understand that?"

His heart crumbled under the weight of her words. While everything she said made perfect, logical sense, he didn't care. It wasn't what his heart wanted. His heart needed her. And there was no substitute. Nothing but a life of what ifs and dreaming of the one that got away lay in front of him if she left, but he was powerless to stop her.

He nodded, the pressure in his sinuses bearing down on him. He needed to leave before he showed her just how weak he really was. He went to her, putting his shaky hands on her shoulders, it taking everything in him to stay temporarily strong. "I love you, too," he said, and then pressed his lips against hers, feeling the tremble of her whole body.

He pulled away, unable to meet her gaze one last time, his heart twisting in pain.

Chapter Twenty-Nine

Chase loaded the last box into the truck Marigold rented and then peered around to her car, hooked up to the trailer behind it. "Are you absolutely sure you can navigate this thing?"

She held up both hands. "I've got it all mapped out. It's ready to pull straight out of here, and I don't plan on stopping until I get home. If I'm desperate to pee, I'm going to park it in a big grocery store lot or something, somewhere I can just pull straight forward. Trust me. I got this."

Chase stared at her, his brow still furrowed, and then he finally nodded. "I know you do."

She pulled him to her, resting her cheek on his massive chest. Chase wasn't a bulky guy, but he was about six and a half feet tall, so he might as well be a giant compared to her. He wrapped his arms around her, settling in for a long hug. "I wish you'd consider staying with Shayla and me."

She huffed a laugh against his chest. "I may have a

hard time catching a clue sometimes, but I know better than to move in with a couple in love on the verge of walking down the aisle."

"We've got the pool house. Shayla lived there."

Marigold pulled away eyeing him. "Yeah, and she was so out of your way there that you just happened to fall in love with her."

"Come on. Just think about it."

"You're forgetting the pesky little fact that I have no job."

He waved her off. "You don't need any money. I've got money."

She smiled at him, knowing he was partially serious and loving him for it. "If I ever decide I need sugar parents, I'll head your way."

He kissed the top of her head like a loving brother. "Be safe, okay? If you have any trouble with anything, call me, anytime."

She nodded, her heart crumbling with the thought of leaving this place and the people she adored so much here. She held the tears off as he got in his car and backed out of the space, holding up a hand in a wave.

She headed back inside her empty shop where Desiree was sweeping the floors. She emptied the dustpan into the trash. "I was thinking you weren't getting out of here until the end of November."

"That was the plan, but my landlord said he would forgive November's rent if I'd get out early. He has a tenant ready to move in now. She's putting up one of those drop-in child care centers."

"Sounds like a goldmine to me—all these tourists who want a break from their kids."

"I hope they can find her back here," Marigold said.

Desiree set the broom in the corner. "I really wish you'd consider staying. I think Cassidy's looking for help for Thanksgiving. She always gets a lot of pie orders."

"I know. She already mentioned that to me. But it would just be temporary. Besides, I kind of need to go now." She gave Desiree a look, hoping she would read between the lines.

Desiree, always intuitive, just nodded. "Well, I certainly do understand that. Oh, before you go," Desiree picked up her purse, "I need to give you this." She handed Marigold a check, the word *commission* in the notes section.

Marigold eyed her. "Uh, did I sell something of yours in my sleep?"

"The lady you sold my last painting to bought two others that I had just gotten back from a restaurant that had them on the wall for years."

She handed Desiree the check back. "You're high if you think I'm taking your money. I didn't lift a finger."

"You made the initial sale. I'd never have sold the other two without you."

Marigold stared at the check. "God, what if we could do this for real?"

"You think I haven't thought about it? Me painting, you selling. We'd make a damn good team."

Marigold nodded. "We've both got to work on that lottery win."

Desiree smiled. "I bought a ticket yesterday." She

pulled Marigold in for a hug. "I'll miss my girl. You swear you're coming back when that hotel gets built?"

Marigold swallowed hard. That had been the promise Malcolm had made to her. Come home and train with him and then work at the hotel on 30A once it was built, but Marigold knew her family wanted her home. For all she knew, they never even submitted a proposal to build this hotel. "Yep, I promise," Marigold said, her heart falling apart already.

Chapter Thirty

"So, that's the new reservation system," Malcolm said with a proud smile. "It's way more user-friendly than the old system. The staff loves it. Well, they will love it. Some are resistant to change, but we've all got to evolve, right?"

"Hmm? Oh, yes. Of course." She smiled and nodded, her body physically in Appleton's flagship hotel in Savannah, but her mind back on 30A.

"Come on. I'll take you to lunch."

"Malcolm," she said as a warning. When she'd made the decision to come back to Savannah and give the hotel business a try, Malcolm had been overjoyed, slathering himself to her side from the second she'd arrived. She'd warned him that he was going to have to back off. He was engaged after all. So, he'd promptly broken up with Heather. As shitty of a thing to do as that was, Marigold figured it was better Heather know the truth about her potential husband now rather than continue to get strung along by him.

Marigold didn't have the ego to think he'd broken off his engagement because he loved her. He'd wanted nothing more than to be a part of the Appleton family since they were in college. A marriage to her sealed his fate and his inheritance.

"A working lunch," he said. "We've got a lot to cover still."

"I need a break, Malcolm," she said, truer words never having been spoken.

He raised his eyebrows. "Are you sure? We can do Cotton & Rye?"

"I'm sure. I brought some vegetables."

An employee grabbed Malcolm's attention, and Marigold took the opportunity to find her way to the kitchen where she'd stored her lunch. Her sister sat at a round table reading from a tablet while Marigold took her lunch out of the employee refrigerator. "How's your day?"

"Busy," she said without looking up. "How's training?" she asked, blatant irritation in her voice. It'd been that way since Marigold returned.

Marigold plopped down next to her. "Should I be bold enough to think your irritation is aimed at me, or are you just having a rough day?"

She gave a sardonic shake of her head. "Leave it up to Marigold to get right to the point. You always did."

"Should we dance around the fact that you've welcomed me home with the warmth of a snowman this past week, or do you want to get this out in the open?"

Camellia put down her tablet. "Okay, why did you let Malcom end things with Heather?"

"Let him? I'm his mommy?" Marigold asked.

"I liked her and I was looking forward to having a sister-in-law of sorts. But now that's done. He'll be back to square one. You know he's not the most charming guy on the planet. Heather put up with a lot of crap, including Mom."

"What did Mom do to her?"

"Oh, please, Marigold. Don't be so naïve. It was Mom's idea for Malcolm to propose to Heather. She thought you'd go insane with jealousy and come running back."

Marigold narrowed her gaze, not believing her mother. "Are you serious?"

"Don't act so shocked."

Marigold rubbed her forehead. "I just can't understand. Why now, after all these years, do they want me back so bad?"

"They've wanted you back all these years, but you've had the shop. When you talked to Dad about moving the shop to a new hotel on 30A, they saw their opportunity."

Marigold tossed up her hands. "Why?"

Camellia let her head fall to one side. "I really have to spell this out for you?"

"Apparently so."

"It's baby-making time," Camellia said with such venom Marigold was afraid she was going to strike at any moment.

Marigold remembered Malcolm saying Camellia and Pete were trying to get pregnant. "You don't want to have a baby?"

She picked up her fork and dropped it. "I don't want to do a lot of things."

"Like what?"

She started packing up her lunch. "Nothing."

Marigold put her hand on Camellia's forearm. "Please, tell me."

Camellia considered Marigold and then let out a sigh. "Maybe if my whole life wasn't determined for me before I had a chance to make my own decisions, I wouldn't resent some of these things."

"What things?"

She tossed up her hands, glancing around. "Working at this stupid hotel. Agreeing to marry Pete, which we all know was pretty much an arranged marriage. And having babies, which most women my age are doing, but when it's expected of you it really takes the joy out of it."

Marigold sat there, taking all of this in for the first time. "Camellia, I had no idea you felt this way about your life."

"Of course you didn't. You've been living your own life down in Florida. I've had to stay here and take the brunt of all this. Do you know how hard Mom is on my ass about taking prenatal vitamins and eating right? No fish for me, not until after I've had all the children they require."

"You don't have to do any of this. You can live your own life."

Camellia eyed her. "I'm not you. I can't detach from our family."

A wave of guilt engulfed Marigold. "I didn't detach. I just needed some space."

"I need space," Camellia said, pointing at her own chest.

"Then take it."

"It's not that simple, not for me."

"Why, because you don't want to disappoint Dad? Trust me, it's simple. I do it all the time."

"Oh, please. You know you've always been his favorite," Camellia said.

Marigold about fell out of her chair. "Me? We've always mixed like oil and water. You've always been his favorite."

"Only since about college, and only because I've worked my ass off for it. Do you have any idea how hard it is being your sister? Do you have any idea of the way people look at you and then the way they look at me? How is it fair? We have the same parents, but you turned out beautiful, and I turned out like this."

"Camellia, we look alike."

"We resemble one another, but you're like a buffed and shined version of me. Dad always looked at you with pride and me with sympathy." She huffed a laugh. "God, listen to me. I'm a grown woman acting like a child. Just forget it. I've got to get back to work."

"Don't you see?" Marigold asked, pleading with her sister. "This is what family does to us. This is why people move across the country to get away from their families. They make us crazy. They reduce us back to children. Look at me. I'm still driving this ridiculous car Dad gave me when I was sixteen because I'm trying to hold on to a piece of him, or of me, or of our relationship, or God knows what." She shifted in her seat. "Look at the two of us, fighting over who our father adores more, and all he wants is for us to make babies, apparently. Why is that, by the way? They just want to be grandparents?"

"They're consumed with Appleton being a family business. It's all about branding, Marigold," she said with lazy, sarcastic eyes.

Marigold let out a sigh, resting her elbows on the table. "So I guess I'm supposed to be pumping out kids with Malcolm?"

"That's the plan."

Marigold tossed up her hands. "And I'm not even a part of it."

"That's the Appleton way," Camellia said, arms spread out wide. She focused in on Marigold. "Why did you come home?"

"I ran out of options. My business failed. I put out umpteen resumes for real jobs and it was nothing but crickets. I even tried applying for waitressing jobs, but nobody's hiring this time of the year. We're going into the slow season."

Camellia gave her a look. "You didn't want to apply to work at a hotel?"

Marigold dropped her head to the side, giving her lazy eyes as a response. Camellia of all people knew working at any hotel other than an Appleton would be a betrayal beyond any either of them could possibly inflict on this family.

Camellia pursed her lips in concession.

Marigold went on. "I can't afford to live on 30A on a retail salary or even in PCB or Destin. Those places aren't cheap either. I'd have to find roommates, and at that point what am I doing all of it for? All my friends are on 30A."

Camellia narrowed her gaze. "Is money really the only reason you came back here?"

Marigold let out a sigh. "Maybe not completely. I may have been running away from...a boy."

"Ah, so now we're getting to the heart of the matter. Tell me about the boy."

Marigold told Camellia all about Dane and how he was the most incredible man she'd ever known. She told about Erin and the boys and the impossible situation.

Camellia let out a huge huff of air. "Well, I know the sisterly thing for me to do is to tell you to steer clear of this complicated situation. And Mom and Dad would definitely want to steer you right away from this guy and toward Malcom." She held up a hand. "And I definitely think you do need to work on getting your life back together before jumping into anything with him." She eyed Marigold. "Maybe this is just me wanting to rebel against Mom and Dad, but I'm telling you now that if you stay here, you're just going to keep getting distance from him. Go back to 30A. Start the process of rebuilding your life, and then when you're ready, check in with him."

Marigold let out an exhausted sigh. "I hear you, and I'd like to have that option, but—"

"How much do you need?" Camellia asked.

"Money?"

"Yep. How much? Money's something I've got tons of. Dad pays Pete and me a fortune."

"I can't take your money," Marigold said, wanting desperately to take the money.

"Ten grand? Twenty? What do you need? One of us needs to get out of this place."

Marigold felt her eyes widening. "Camellia, I can't take your money."

Camellia grabbed her purse from the chair beside her. "Seriously, get out from under Mom and Dad before you get sucked in and can't get out."

Marigold giggled and then covered her mouth, feeling guilty. "This is nuts."

Camellia met her gaze. "Do you love this guy? I mean seriously like head over heels, want to rip his clothes off all the time, miss turning down your own street because you can't get him off your mind love him?"

Marigold squeezed her hand. "Yes, like a million times all that."

"Then you're going. And I'm banking it."

Marigold's heartbeat raced. She couldn't believe she was considering this. "Come with me," Marigold said, still not even sure she was going.

"To 30A?"

"Yeah. Why not?"

"Because I'm married, for one."

"Do you love Pete?"

"Since when did that have anything to do with marriage?"

Marigold's shoulders sagged. "You don't have to live like this."

"I know. I'm just complaining. It's okay a lot of the time. But it wouldn't be for you. You've never cared what Mom or Dad thought. You've always been an independent thinker. I need their approval. It's a sickness." She smiled at Marigold. "Go back to 30A. I'm going to write a check for you." She pulled a pen out of her purse and clicked the bottom of it. "It's a gift, not a loan. I've got more money than I know what to do with. Consider it an investment in your store or whatever. What do you want to do, open another one in a better location? We drove by your store when we were there. Your location is pitiful."

Marigold thought about Desiree's comment about winning the lottery and opening their own gallery. "Actually, I won't take your money, but I will let you consider an investment. How do you feel about art?"

Chapter Thirty-One

Marigold dangled the key to her treasured convertible over the palm of the guy who'd given her his card that night of the hotel announcement. She wasn't ready to hand it over, but if she was going to get her life together, ridding herself of this ridiculous car from her childhood was a good first step.

"You haven't changed your mind, have you?" the guy asked.

She let out a sigh and met his gaze. "You promise you'll take good care of it?"

"Honey, this car is for my granddaughter. I'm going to have this thing so spiffed up by her sixteenth birthday you won't even recognize it."

She huffed a laugh. "I hope it gets her into as much trouble as it got me into back in the day."

"When it does, her granddaddy will be right there to bail her out," he said with a wink. She dropped the key into his hand and watched him settle in behind the wheel.

When she got back inside Seaside Sweets, Cassidy was coming through the swinging half-doors. "Last of the pies. We still have the order of cupcakes that needs to be picked up."

"The Captain America ones?"

"Yep."

"Poor kid. Having a Thanksgiving birthday can't be fun."

"Would be better than a Christmas birthday."

Marigold made her way behind the counter. "This is true."

Cassidy, being the amazing person she was, had welcomed Marigold back with open arms. She needed her through to Christmas and had floated the possibility of Marigold keeping the store open in January and February while she traveled. But Marigold knew she was just trying to help. Marigold would test it out, and if she found she wasn't hitting a certain weekly goal, she wouldn't continue to take Cassidy's money.

"So, you've been back a week now. Have you spoken to anyone yet?" Cassidy asked.

She didn't need to clarify who *anyone* was. "I haven't been brave enough just yet. I'm trying to get myself in order before I even think about going there. I mean, it sounded like he was looking at trying to get more involved in those boys' lives, not less. I want to be with him, but I'm not sure I can handle all of that."

Cassidy nodded as if she understood perfectly. "The boys are too much," she said definitively.

"Well, no, they've actually been fine the couple of

times I've been around them. It's just living this life where you never know if your day is going to include kids or not. I can't live like that. And besides, look at me. How am I supposed to provide emotional support for two boys with a mom who keeps dumping them off? They need stability. I'm about the furthest thing from stable that there is."

"Out of curiosity, how is your relationship when the boys aren't there?"

Marigold leaned against the counter. "Oh, my God. Cassidy. I'm freaking nuts over him." She glanced around to make sure they were alone, and then set her gaze on Cassidy. "I told him I loved him before I left for home."

Cassidy lifted her eyebrow. "And?"

"And he told me he loved me, too." Hearing the words said aloud gave them life, making her whole body tingle at the thought.

"Love, wow. That's rare, you know?"

"You're telling me? I'm thirty, and that's the first time I've heard those words or said them. You know, Malcolm, who has been trying to marry me for a decade, has never even said that to me."

Cassidy gave her that look that told Marigold she was in for a battle.

"What?" Marigold asked, lifting off the counter and crossing her arms.

Cassidy backed away. "Nothing. I'm just listening."

"You have opinions. I see it in your eyes."

"I've not said a word."

"But you're thinking words."

Cassidy chuckled and Marigold waited her out,

staring at her hard. Finally, Cassidy tossed up both hands. "I'm just saying finding a guy like Dane and having him fall in love with you, and you him...that's rare. I'm not saying you won't find a different guy. You're as beautiful on the inside as you are on the out. But the kind of guy who would put up with that woman's bullshit because he cares about those boys who aren't even his... that's a man."

Chills ran up Marigold's spine, a blanket of warmth covering her body.

"I know we all have this thought of an ideal relationship that's clean and baggage-free, but it's just not reality," Cassidy said. "Life is messy and complicated, and we have to take the bad with the good. And those boys getting to experience a healthy relationship with you and Dane is good. I know this isn't what you would have chosen, but maybe it's an opportunity to do some good yourself."

The bell on the door dinged and they looked up to find a haggard woman with two little blond boys in tow. "I told you I don't like the chocolate ones except for if they have the white icing on top," one of the boys said.

The other one tugged at her shirtsleeve. "You said whoever shut up would get two and I did but he didn't. You couldn't hear him but he whispered at me. It's not fair if he gets two."

The woman put her hand to her forehead, eyes closed in desperation. "Please, just get whatever the f..." She stopped herself, inhaling the breath of the century.

Marigold stilled as she realized exactly who this was. "Fuck," she said under her breath.

Erin opened her eyes. "Both of you be quiet or you're getting nothing, do you hear me?"

"But Mom, you said—"

Erin held up both hands. "I know what I said, but I need two seconds without either of you speaking a word. Can I have two seconds?"

"Marigold!" Jaden ran toward the counter, and Marigold tried to figure out what to do. It was too late to run.

Erin blinked. "Oh," she said, her eyes hyper-focused on Marigold like she was seeing a three-headed gorilla.

"Welcome to Seaside Sweets," Marigold said, forcing a smile.

Erin jerked a thumb at the door. "Um, boys, we're gonna go."

Noah's face contorted. "No! You said I could get two."

Jaden made his way behind the counter and wrapped his arms around Marigold's legs, wordlessly. She hugged him back, her heart filling to the brim.

Erin rubbed her forehead. "Boys, I said—"

"Please, come on in," Cassidy said, waving them over. "Hello, I'm Cassidy Anderson. Are you a friend of Marigold's?"

Cassidy was such a quick study. Marigold could tell that she'd caught on to exactly who this was. The fact that Marigold had spent the past week filling her in on the whole drawn-out situation complete with full descriptions of all the players didn't hurt.

"N-no," Erin said, looking somewhat contrite and really caught off-guard.

Marigold held her hand out over the counter, Jaden having unlatched from her but still close by. "I'm Marigold Appleton. You're Erin, right?"

Erin reluctantly took Marigold's hand. "Yes, Dane's ex," she said, glancing at Cassidy as she said it. She wasn't being bitchy though, just informational. Erin looked Marigold up and down. "I heard your shop was closing." She pursed her lips in concession. "Sorry to hear that."

"Yeah, well," Marigold said, not sure how else to respond.

They all just sort of stood there in awkward silence while the boys put their hands on every single thing in sight.

"Hey," Cassidy said. "I've got a batch of cupcakes that got a little too brown to sell. Would either of you like to help me ice them for practice?"

They both got really excited, Noah turning to Erin. "Can we?"

Erin eyed Marigold and then Cassidy, her shoulders sagging. "Yeah, that'd be great. Thanks." Cassidy disappeared into the back with two chatty boys in tow.

Marigold leaned on the counter. "You want a brownie?"

Erin looked her up and down. "Something tells me you don't eat them."

"Oh, I do. But I also starve myself the rest of the day. It's super unhealthy and dysfunctional." The slightest hint of a smile crossed Erin's lips. Marigold plated two brownies and handed her one along with a water bottle. "Let's go sit."

Erin walked toward a table, slowly, still feeling

Marigold out. Marigold sat down and handed her a fork, no idea why she was doing this, but just knowing it felt right to be this woman's friend and not her sworn enemy.

Marigold took a bite of the brownie and shut her eyes. "Oh, God. The first bite's always the best. The chocolate, the salty caramel. Better than..." She stopped herself before she finished that sentence.

"Better than sex?" Erin asked.

Marigold shrugged. "Well, better than some sex, for sure."

Erin did smile then and took a bite. After she chewed a minute, she met Marigold's gaze. "Damn. You weren't kidding."

Marigold eyed her. "Did you just leave Dane's house, or were you on your way there?"

She furrowed her brow. "Dane's in St. Louis. You didn't know that?"

Marigold gave her a small smile. "Nope. We're not together."

Erin blinked. "Seriously?"

Marigold nodded, taking another bite of brownie that she didn't even want anymore.

"What happened? I thought you two were probably serious. You're the first girl he's ever had around the boys."

"I don't know. It's just...the timing isn't right." She didn't mean to, but she glanced in the direction of the kitchen.

Erin frowned, and then rolled her eyes dropping her fork. "Fuck." She pulled a napkin from the dispenser and dabbed at her mouth. "You'd think I'd be thrilled, but I just feel like shit." Erin eyed her. "He chose my kids over you?"

Marigold bit her lip. "Essentially, yeah, I guess he did. But I'm not bitter about that. Really, I'm not. I totally get it. He adores them. And they're fabulous kids."

"So fabulous that you want nothing to do with them," Erin said.

Marigold closed her eyes, wincing. "That's not what I—"

"I know. That wasn't fair. I get it. I'm probably not that much older than you. Do you think I meant to be a thirty-two-year-old single mom of two?"

Marigold knew she needed to watch herself, but she couldn't squander this opportunity. "What happened between you and Dane, if you don't mind me asking?" Erin gave her a warning look, so Marigold held up a hand in surrender. "I know I have no right to ask that, but I just can't imagine why things fell apart. I mean, he loves your kids so much, and he wants to be a part of their lives. Why would you not want that?"

Erin scratched her head, moisture pooling in the corner of her eye. "It's not him. It's me." Marigold waited while Erin collected herself, resisting the urge to fill the uncomfortable silence with babble. Erin looked up at her with a sardonic smile. "Apparently, I'm not happy unless I'm screwing things up. And even then, I'm not happy. Dane was this amazing guy who was perfect in every way including with my kids, which should be the only way that really matters. So, of course, I had to go and make sure that he never would want me again."

"Was there someone else?" Marigold asked, too curious to refrain.

Erin inhaled a deep breath and shrugged. "Not anyone who mattered." Marigold tried hard to keep her expression impassive. Erin glared at her. "I didn't sleep with Dane after I slept with the other guy, if that's what you're wondering. I'm not a monster."

"I'm not judging," Marigold lied.

"Yes you are. You've been judging me since the moment you came off that elevator, probably before that."

"Okay, yes I am. But only because I think you're nuts for giving up the best guy in the world."

Erin's eyebrows went up. "Like you're doing?"

Marigold drew back, heat running up her neck.

"Look, do you think I enjoy screwing up Dane's life? He hates me. I see the resentment in his eyes every time he looks at me. If you think I like experiencing that every time I see him, you're crazy."

"Then why do you do it?" Marigold asked, her voice coming out more desperate than she wished it would have.

Erin held out a hand toward the double swinging doors. "Why do you think?"

Marigold felt like a hammer knocked her upside the head. "I...I just assumed you needed a break or something."

She huffed a humorless laugh. "What do you think I do when they're with him? Go get a massage and relax like a sane person? I spend the entire time stressing out about what I've done to Dane and how I'm dragging him farther down into this pit with me. And then I spend weeks telling the boys that we can't see him again because he's got his own life. And then Noah will cry, my God how Noah cries. And Jaden will just mope or worse, tell me it's okay and then shut himself off with his earbuds and his stupid game. So I cave. I cave every time. And I screw Dane over and we start the cycle again."

Marigold just sat there, taking in Erin's burden, the enormity of what her life must feel like. She eased her hand toward Erin's, which was holding the fork, messing with the brownie. Erin cut her eyes down to Marigold's hand, stilling, but letting Marigold take it. She squeezed it and held on, wordlessly, because there were no words to make this situation better.

A tear fell out of Erin's eye and she grabbed for a napkin with her free hand. "Why couldn't you have been a bitch?"

Marigold smiled. "I'm sure there are plenty who would say that I am, or have been at some point, at least."

Erin looked up at her with bloodshot eyes. "If my boys had to be around you once in a while, that wouldn't be the end of the world."

Marigold squinted. "Was there a compliment in there somewhere?"

Erin rolled her eyes. "I don't know you, but if Dane has chosen you after what I put him through, you can't be all bad. Besides, the boys freaking love you."

"Really?" Marigold asked, both surprised and elated.

Erin pointed in the direction of the counter. "Do you think Jaden hugs people like that normally? I'll just tell you, he doesn't."

Marigold grinned. "Wow. Well, they're not so bad either. Sorry, I don't know much about kids."

"That's probably why they like you. You don't make them feel like kids."

"I'm sure it's because I act like a kid myself. I'm a complete hot mess. That's the main reason I ended things with Dane. I feel like I've got growing up of my own to do before I could even consider taking care of someone else's kid." Erin's eyebrows went up, so Marigold held up both hands. "Not that I'd be taking care of your kids. But I'd be there when they were, eventually at least, and I'm sure situations would come up, and—"

It was Erin's turn to take Marigold's hand. "Relax. Of course you'd be taking care of my kids when they were there. You're an adult. I'd expect you to discipline them and deny them stuff." She grinned. "All that fun stuff us moms get to do."

Marigold about lost her stomach at the word *mom*.

"Oh, now don't look so terrified," Erin said. "It's not all miserable."

Noah busted through the double swinging doors. "Mom! Look at my cupcake."

Erin viewed the atrocity. "It's perfect. Can I have it?"

He pulled it in toward his chest, smiling. "No. I get two. You said I got two."

"One for now and one for later, okay?"

"Okay," he uttered as he bit into his cupcake, icing up his nose.

Jaden came out inspecting his cupcake like a pastry chef, and then biting into it.

Erin stood. "What do I owe you for this?" she asked,

indicating the boys and the cupcakes. Marigold waved her off, and Erin narrowed her gaze. "You know, oddly, I think you're just the type of woman I'd choose to be around my kids, if I was forced to choose one, that is."

Marigold smiled. "That means a lot. Thanks."

Erin gave her a tempered smile in return, and then gathered her boys, who, wrapped up in their cupcakes, followed their mom out of the store like little ducklings.

Cassidy sidled up beside Marigold. "Well, how did that go?"

Marigold sighed. "I think she might have helped me understand her a little."

"Wow. That's big stuff."

Marigold eyed Cassidy, pursing her lips at her. "You sure you don't think I'd screw up these kids worse than they already have it if I was in Dane's life right now?"

Cassidy smiled at her. "I'm fairly certain they'll be just fine. Now, all you've got to do is go get your man."

"If he'll have me," Marigold said, her stomach already in knots at the idea of approaching him after all they'd been through.

Cassidy wrapped her arm around her. "Something tells me this is all going to work out just like it should."

Chapter Thirty-Two

Dane unloaded groceries, putting the ice cream bars in the freezer. The boys would be back on Saturday for a sleepover, so he wanted to be prepared.

He pulled the champagne out of the brown bag and held it up, waiting for the flush of pride for winning the hotel bid to hit, but he was just too damned depressed to celebrate. He'd have to put on a brave face for Ethan.

Maybe the real celebration was the deal he'd struck with Erin for visitation—every other weekend. They'd even had it written up by a lawyer and notarized, and the agreement included wording to prevent her pulling the same crap she'd been doing lately. He knew it was just a piece of paper in the end, and that she could still do whatever she wanted, but it made him feel more stable and less like he was covering for a bomb to drop at any time.

Three weeks had gone by since Marigold had told

Dane she was leaving. He'd stupidly driven by her shop a handful of times, hoping to see her convertible. But from what he could tell, she was out of there and someone else was already moving in.

He'd even driven by Fiona's condo late at night, but still nothing. She was gone. That was all there was to it. And as much as his hand burned to type a text to her, he couldn't. She had moved on. She was living in a different city, seeing old friends or meeting new people, starting a new job. The last thing she needed was him throwing a wrench in her plans.

When she'd told him she loved him, he wasn't sure he'd known a warmth so real, even though it was said with a huge *but*. He'd taken those words and held them in his heart, wishing like hell he could somehow make all of this work. Erin, the boys, Marigold—it was a puzzle that he couldn't solve, no matter how hard he tried.

A knock sounded at the door, and Dane opened it to find Ethan standing there arms wide open. "Who's ready to celebrate?"

Dane plastered on a smile, needing to keep his spirits up for Ethan's sake. This was a big deal they'd won and would be a great resume builder for their company. Ethan hated it when Dane *moped* as he put it, and tonight was a time for celebration, not sadness.

Dane held up the bottle of champagne. "Bottoms up."

Ethan gave him that resigned smile that said he knew him all too well to fall for any bullshit. "Are you sure you don't mind if Ashe comes?"

"Of course not. You're in a relationship with him. He's important to you, so he's important to me."

"Thank you, brother."

The elevator dinged and Ashe walked off of it with their assistant Ginger and her boyfriend Mark. "Look who I picked up downstairs."

"I hate to crash your party, but I don't ever turn down an expensive meal on the Knight brothers," Ginger said.

Ethan put his arm around her. "You probably did more to get this deal done than any of us."

"Well, I won't argue that."

Dane held up the bottle. "Are we ready for a toast now?"

Ashe rubbed his hands together. "Ooh, you got the good stuff. Yes, please."

Dane took the bottle into the kitchen and pulled out five wine glasses. "Sorry I don't have champagne flutes," Dane said.

"If you did, I would seriously be questioning your orientation," Ashe said.

Dane's text alert sounded, and he pulled it out of his pocket, wondering who it could be since the two people who texted him most were there with him. His heart almost jumped out of his chest when Marigold's name populated his screen.

Are you busy?

Dane set the bottle down. "Uh, Ethan, will you please take over here? I'll just be a second."

He walked out to his balcony and closed the door behind him, staring at his phone. He didn't even know what to say. He typed the word *no*, but he needed a little something more to it. His brain just wasn't working properly at the moment.

"It wasn't a trick question."

Dane's head jerked up at the sound of Marigold's voice. She stood there on the beach below, holding her shoes, wearing his hoodie over the top of one of her little flowy skirts, looking like a mirage in the desert.

He pocketed his phone with a shaky hand. "What are you doing here?"

"Well, I never did return this hoodie."

He blinked, still not able to believe his own eyes. "I thought you were in Savannah, or somewhere else?"

"I was, but it didn't stick, so I came back. Can we talk a minute?" she asked.

He glanced toward the living room where Ethan, Ashe, Ginger, and Mark were chatting, holding wine glasses but not drinking them. "Um, stay there. I'll be right down."

He went back inside, scratching his head. He wasn't sure what to do. He didn't want to ruin the celebration, but he needed to go talk to Marigold. He picked up the glass they'd poured for him and held it up. "Ethan, do you want to do the honors?"

Ethan held up his glass. "To our biggest contract yet, and to not fucking it up."

"Here, here!" Ashe said, holding up his glass. They all clinked glasses and drank up.

Dane set his glass down. "Um, Marigold is outside, on the beach."

"What?" Ethan asked, his voice rising.

"Would you all mind finishing this drink without me? I won't be long. If I haven't finished by the time you all are done with your champagne, go on and I'll meet you there."

"Invite her," Ashe said. "I haven't seen her in forever."

"I'll be back," he said. When he stepped out the rear doors of the lobby and down the stairs to the beach, the closer he got to her, the harder his heart pounded.

She held a pair of short boots in front of her with both of her hands, fidgeting with them like a crutch. "Hey," she said, her smile uncertain.

"Hey." He pocketed his hands, not sure what this vibe was. As much as he wanted to throw his arms around her, he had no idea why she was there. He didn't want to assume anything, and he couldn't help but want to protect his injured heart.

"Congratulations. I heard you won the hotel bid."

"Well, once your family pulled out, it certainly made it easier."

"You totally deserve it."

Despite the cool night breeze, warmth crept into his cheeks.

"How are the boys?" she asked.

"Good," he said.

"Good. That's really good. Are they here?" she asked, glancing up at his balcony.

"No, actually, they're not. But they will be this weekend. Erin and I have an agreement in place. I have them every other weekend now."

As her eyes went wide, his stomach sank. He'd had to put it on the line. If she was here to reconcile things between them, she had to know where he stood. If that was a deal-breaker, then he'd have to live with that.

"Wow, that's...wow," she said.

He nodded, confirming his position. He knew people on the outside thought he was nuts for taking on the responsibility of someone else's children, but this is what he needed to do, not only for them, but for himself. Walking away or calling the police or some stranger to come pick them up when Erin dumped them off wasn't an option for him no matter how tough he thought he could be.

She let out a huge breath, puffing it through her lips like she was blowing out a candle. She lifted the back of her hand to her forehead like she was wiping off sweat, but it was too cool of a night for that. "I'm working at Seaside Sweets now, with Cassidy."

It was his turn for wide eyes. "Oh. Wow. That's great." He couldn't believe he'd driven by her place of work a thousand times these past few weeks and never even knew it.

"She's doing some traveling, and I'm going to run her shop for January and February."

"Nice. That's great that you can keep it going for her," he said, still wondering what her long-term plans were. "Will she still need you in March?"

"I'm not sure, but I may have another gig then anyway. Desiree and I are looking to start a business together."

"Oh yeah?" he asked.

"An art gallery, eventually. It may be messier than that at first. We may use Seaside Sweets for a few shows. We'd transform it, of course, but Cassidy's totally fine with it all. We're still in the early planning stages, but we definitely want to work together. She wants to paint more, and I love selling her art. She has some artist friends who want in as well."

"That's great," he said, his heart warming at the idea of her doing what she loved.

She waved him off. "Anyway, I'm living with Cassidy for now. She's asked me to stay at least through February so someone can watch her house while she's gone. I told her she was nuts for not renting it out during that time, but she doesn't want to deal with renters...or she's just being extremely kind and providing a homeless friend with a home."

He nodded, his heartbeat increasing as he wondered exactly what she was doing here, what she was trying to say.

She stared down at the ground, running her foot back and forth through the sand. She met his gaze, causing his stomach to flip. He swallowed hard, and she tossed her boots into the sand. Clenching both fists, she held them to her chest tightly. "I miss you like mad, Dane. I know I said I needed to get my life together but I'm doing that." She shook her hands slightly as she stared at him, seeming to be summoning courage for something. She bit her lip, and then let it go. "You are the guy that I never knew could exist for me. No man has been able to crack my code the way you have both when we're on a hayride screaming at vampires and zombies, or when we're in bed, or on a desk for that matter." She waggled her eyebrows, and it was all he could do to keep from shutting her up with a kiss right then.

She grasped his shoulders, sliding her hands down to his biceps. "To get to my point, you're my person, Dane. You're the guy I've been waiting for all these years. You're kind, thoughtful, considerate, and more of a man than any man I've ever known. For all those reasons and so many more, I love you with all of my heart." She stared at him with those big, beautiful eyes, just about making his knees buckle. "I want to be with you. I want to do this with you."

As much as he wanted to cave, they had more to discuss. "The agreement I have with Erin, it's legit. It was drawn up by a lawyer and all that good stuff. I'm going to have the boys every other weekend."

"I know. I heard you. I think that's great." She took his hands. "Dane, the fact that you are the kind of man that would agree to, or probably initiate something like that..." She trailed off, looking at him for confirmation. He shrugged and nodded concession. She let the tension drop from her posture, and then squeezed his hands. "That is one of the reasons why I've fallen for you."

His throat threatened to close from the hope of her words. "I don't know what the next few years are going to look like. We've got this agreement, but it's just paper, and she knows I'll never sue her or do anything to upset the boys. She could take them anywhere at any time. I have no legal claim to them, not really."

She nodded, wiping her eye with the back of her hand. He didn't realize she'd been welling up. That made him want to bring her in for a hug, but they had to work through this.

"I know. I've thought about all this kind of thing. I mean, I didn't know about this official agreement, but I've already been thinking about her dropping them off with you and if we were together, how I'd fall in love with them and then they'd get snatched away, or how I'd be all excited that we were planning a trip to New Orleans for the weekend, and she'd drop in and ruin it all, and a million other scenarios. But in not one of those scenarios was I sorry to have hung onto the best man I've ever known."

He shook his head, because she seemed so sincere, and it was just ludicrous.

She stepped away from him, her hopeful expression dropping. "What?"

"No, I just think that's crazy. You're making me out to be some kind of saint and God knows, Marigold. I'm far from that."

She stood there, head dropped to the side, sizing him up. "I don't think you're a saint, but I do think you make really good boyfriend material."

He couldn't help a smile. "God, woman. You have no idea how fucking in love with you I am." The grin that spread across her face was enough to make him hand over his life savings, the deed to his condo, and every ounce of his heart.

She made a motion with her hand. "See, would a saint drop the F-bomb when professing his love?"

He brought her in close to him. "You're sure you want to do this with me?"

"You have no idea how fucking sure I am."

He slid his arms around the small of her back, knowing that he'd do everything in his power to make her way too happy to ever want to leave him.

"You do know I'm never returning this hoodie, right?" she asked.

"It's all yours, babe. And so am I."

She grinned again, and he slid his hands over ass, lifting her up onto him. Hiking herself up, she wrapped her legs around him in response and went in for a kiss, causing his whole body to light up. He'd never let her go again.

Applause erupted from above, and they broke away to look up and find Ethan, Ashe, Ginger, and Mark clapping and whooping from his balcony. Marigold hopped down. "Uh, how long have they been standing there?"

Ashe cupped his hands over his mouth. "Just enjoying the show. Don't worry, we didn't hear you."

Marigold gave a skeptical nod.

"Fuck off, all of you," Dane shouted.

Ginger waved. "Hi, Marigold. I'm Dane and Ethan's assistant. This is my boyfriend Mark. It's nice to meet you."

Marigold waved back with a smile. "Nice to meet you, too. Congratulations on the bid win."

Ginger did a circular hand motion with a bow.

"Come to dinner with us," Ethan shouted.

"No, I couldn't intrude," Marigold said, looking a little guilty.

"I already changed the reservation to six earlier today," Ginger said.

Dane frowned, looking between Ginger and Ethan, and then back to Marigold. "Did they have something to do with you being here tonight?"

Marigold exchanged a look with someone on the balcony. "I have my spies."

Dane met Ashe's gaze. "I thought you said you hadn't seen her in forever."

"Oh, yeah," Ashe said, waving him off. "I lied."

"Come on," Ethan said. "They're gonna give away our table."

"Do you want to come to dinner with us?" Dane asked.

"Well," Marigold said, lifting up his hoodie to reveal a nice, black blouse with ruffles and stuff. "I was hoping that's how this night would end."

"Man," Dane said, glancing at his people on the balcony and then putting his gaze back on her. "Am I that predictable?"

"Yes," they all said in unison.

He took her hand and pulled her close to him, snaking his arm around her back. "You all go on. We'll meet you there in a bit. We've got to..."

Ethan waved him off. "Yeah, yeah. We know what you've got to do. Come on when you're done."

"Or we can bring you dinner in a couple of hours," Ashe said.

Ethan turned to him with a finger pointed. "No, they're coming out to celebrate. This is too important of a night for us."

"We'll be ten minutes behind you," Marigold said, grabbing his ass.

"Make that twenty," Dane said.

The Next Chapter...

Cassidy couldn't believe how fast January and February went by. As much as she enjoyed her time with her friends in Jamaica, she was so glad to be home, and the people inside that bar were the reason why.

She closed the door to her car and hopped out, making her way across the street to the Bohemian Guppy where her friends had gathered to welcome her home. But honestly, they used any old excuse they could find to get together.

"Cassidy!" Her niece Seanna jumped up from a table full of their friends and ran over to the door, throwing her arms open to pull her in for a hug. Cassidy inhaled the scent of Seanna's hair, having missed the fire out of her. Not having had children of her own, Seanna was the closest thing to a daughter Cassidy would ever know. She didn't think it would be possible to love a person more than she loved Seanna, so the pang to have her own child rarely reared its head.

"I missed you," Cassidy said, holding on a hair longer than she should have.

Seanna pulled away, studying her. "That's not a tear I see forming there, is it?"

Cassidy waved her off, shaking her head.

Seanna gave her a wide smile. "I didn't think so."

Cassidy held up a hand in greeting to their table full of friends who were yelling for her and waving her over. Marigold jumped up and headed their way. "Hey, before you come sit, I want to make an introduction."

Marigold steered her in the direction of the bar, pointing at a young guy behind it with shaggy, brown, or maybe sort of auburn-ish hair. "This is Jesse," Marigold said. "This is his place. He's the one I told you about who's looking to add a cookie to his menu."

Jesse set two beer bottles on a server's tray and then met Cassidy's gaze. She'd seen this guy around. Too handsome for his own good. She held out her hand. "It's nice to meet you."

Someone at the bar got Marigold's attention and she drifted away.

"Seaside Sweets, right?" Jesse asked.

"That's my place," Cassidy said.

"You make cookies?"

"Among many other things, sure."

His eyebrow went up. "Wanna talk business sometime?"

"Anytime you like."

"Marigold says you've been off refurbishing schools in Jamaica."

Cassidy didn't like to spread the word about exactly

what she did when she traveled, but she supposed she hadn't told Marigold not to say anything about it. She gave an indifferent shrug.

"Pretty impressive," he said.

"It's really not. I do it with friends and we get into plenty of trouble."

He bit his lip with a hint of a smile. "I'll bet you do."

Jesus Christ, was that an actual flutter in her stomach? How ridiculous. The last time she fell for a handsome bartender's flirtation the *American Pie* movies were still popular.

She pulled her wallet out of her bag. "Do you care if I grab a drink from you here? Looks like they got started without me."

"Sure if you'll put your wallet away."

She slid it back into her purse. There was a time in her life when she'd insisted on paying for her own drinks so she wouldn't feel obligated to anyone for anything. But she'd lived enough life to know a drink never obligated a woman to do anything but enjoy it. "Thanks. I'll take a draft beer. I'm not picky."

"No preference?"

"Not really."

He pulled a cup from a stack and poured her a beer. He stuck an extra cup underneath it before he handed it to her. "So your hand doesn't get too cold."

She couldn't help a smile. "A gentleman in a bar. You're a rare breed."

"A cookie baker with a body like yours...even a rarer breed."

She glanced around the bar at all the girls about half her age. "Do these lines ever work on these young women?"

He leaned on the bar, his tattooed forearms on display. "You tell me."

It'd been a hot minute since Cassidy had fallen for the charms of a handsome guy...and certainly never one his age. She usually dated older men. The idea of her in bed with a tattooed twenty-something bartender was laughable. He was flattering her—his duty as a bartender and a business owner. For a second, she thought about taking him up on his offer just to watch him fumble for a retraction.

She spotted two young women a couple of tables away, both of whom were glancing at him. In their defense, he was something to glance at. She nodded at them. "Stick to women your own age."

"I'd really rather stick to you."

She took her cup and held it up. "Thanks for the beer."

"Anytime. Can I get you anything else?"

Oh, how tempting this guy's smile was. For the briefest of moments, a scene of the two of them rolling around on a blanket on the beach, legs and bodies entwined, flashed through her imagination, heating her body through to the core. She blinked herself awake. "I think I'm all set."

He flexed his muscled arm as he gripped the lip of the bar. "If you change your mind, you know where to find me." He held her gaze, suggesting a world of satisfaction she hadn't experienced in decades. Damn, the idea of taking him up on that offer was becoming more tempting by the moment.

It's finally time for Cassidy's happily ever after!

Grayton Beach Dreams is available now!

Being with him would be too reckless. But maybe just this once...

Having spent his college years and early twenties faithful to his sweetheart who ultimately dumped him for his brother, Jesse Kirby will never again be anyone's fool. He's been making up for lost time by sampling every woman he missed out on. But as thirty approaches, the revolving door to his bedroom isn't doing it for him anymore. When he meets the altruistic Cassidy Anderson, he realizes it's time to make some meaning out of his life. Sure, she may only be interested in him for his body and his literary tattoos, but he will make her see him for the man he now knows he can be.

Cassidy Anderson has always lived her life to serve others and dated stable men her own age or older with the same goals in mind. As she considers an offer from one of those stable men, twenty-nine-year-old bartender Jesse Kirby sets his sights on her, giving her options she doesn't need to consider. It's been so long since Cassidy has experienced a body and a libido like his that she isn't sure if she can pass him up. But just for a taste, because a relationship like theirs could only be headed for heartbreak.

Acknowledgments

Many thanks to Kristen Kovach for beta reading for me and helping me enhance the story in so many ways. And thank you for always making me feel like a rock star writer! You have no idea how much I value your continued encouragement!

Thank you so much to Sandy Kovach for your beta read. You really helped me see this story from a different perspective, and your feedback was extremely important in helping me with characterization and description. I hope I can call on you again soon!

Thanks to Greg Howard who helped direct me to the right storyline and for your blurb expertise. And thank you for dreaming big with me on a daily basis. I can't imagine anyone I'd rather be on this long, strange journey with!

Thanks, as always, to my editor Trish Milburn who has been with me through this whole series and is so good at seeing the forest through the trees.

Thank you to my Saturday morning writing group! And to Kat O'Nell who keeps us together and who is one of the most supportive and motivating people I know.

Thank you to Jessica Calla for always wanting to read my books and for helping me get my head on straight when it's time to release one. You are my Obi-Wan.

Thank you to Beth Pattillo and Cate Hart for being the best retreat roomies on the planet. The WaterColor Wishes-themed vision board I made with the two of you on this year's retreat was one of the highlights of my writing year! Love you two for your love of history and for educating me over wine and as much book and industry talk as we can stand!

And finally, to my guys. I'm the luckiest wife & mom on the planet. I love you both more than you can possibly imagine. Coming home to our goofy, sweet family is always the most wonderful part of my day.

About the Author

Melissa Chambers writes contemporary novels for young, new, and actual adults. A Nashville native, she spends her days working in the music industry and her nights getting lost in her characters. While she's slightly obsessed with alt rock, she leaves the guitar playing to her husband and kid. She never misses a chance to play a tennis match, listen to an audiobook, or eat a bowl of ice cream. (Rocky road, please!) She's a member of several online and local writers groups, all of which she treasures and is unendingly grateful for, and has served as president for the Music City Romance Writers.

CPSIA information can be obtained
at www.ICGtesting.com
Printed in the USA
LVHW042043070623
749155LV00002B/321

9 781732 415638